Misadventure

Kevin H. Hilton

To Simon

1

The lime on the forgotten glass was fresh but not at all appetising. It had recently been placed there, not by an attentive bar tender, but by the natural action of an electric blue and orange fish-digester.

The crows, the pigeons and the occasional heron seemed to share a common goal with the kingfisher. Together they provided the woodwork, windows and brass fittings of the forgotten barge under the trees the same natural treatment. Nature's long term plan was clearly to disguise this barge as a guano heap.

The *Obsession*, was birthed on the bend of a river behind Adam Underwood's property in Northumberland. The path to it, like the riverbank, had now become overgrown, a clear indication that she had not been visited for a substantial period of time. In fact, she was now looking not too dissimilar to the condition she was in when Adam first transported her there from the Ouseburn in Byker.

Adam had repaired her and christened her *Obsession*, and for some time lived on her. Now though, she had seen the four seasons through alone, almost twice. She tilted drunkenly in her shameful state of neglect, as if the disappearance of her owner had eventually brought on a stroke. Considering the challenge it had once taken to place her in a non-tidal section of river, any trespasser happening across her might be expected to think 'WTF?'

Her ungainly poise was not just down to the shear weight of bird lime and decaying leaves however. Her bilges had taken on enough water to drown more than a dozen geese. That is of course, if the water was forcibly administered to each by way of a funnel. Such blatant violation of RSPCA recommendations might nevertheless be an action considered justifiable by any folk assaulted by a particularly violent gaggle.

The previous owner of the property and the barge, Adam's father, had once had such a gaggle. Due to the dangers involved in them free-ranging out onto the lane, they all *bought the farm* long before he did.

This day was to have been a special day for Adam Underwood, and his girlfriend Toyah Pembroke. This was their second year's anniversary.

Adam was preparing dinner for them at his place and he was not going to let anything distract him, or otherwise ruin the evening. Not even one of those Flintstones, specifically the one he had left on the bed of the milling machine in the garage. It had been hurled through the garage window by person's unknown. This time the stone was wrapped in newspaper and string, obscuring its disturbing rhyming message. He had been receiving such Flintstones by different means since he was a young lad.

He wasn't about to read too much into the odd tone of Toyah's voice on the phone either. She had rung him a short while ago to say she had something mind-blowing to show him when she arrived.

Instead he was determined to maintain his focus. He wanted this to be a night to be remembered. Sadly, that was certainly to be the case.

Adam was in the kitchen when he heard Toyah's Mercedes arrive on the drive. She had a key to let herself in so there was no need to abandon the cooking. Nevertheless Adam couldn't resist a quick peek through the hallway window before returning to finish his preparations.

Sitting behind the wheel, Toyah lifted a cylinder from inside her jacket and then passed it around her head a few times. Adam dismissed this with a shrug and returned to the cooking. He had probably spoiled the big reveal now by peeking too soon. He guessed Toyah had splashed out on a new hairstyle and was just applying some additional spray to her auburn locks to hold the masterpiece. She had certainly been known to spend inordinate amounts of time and money at her favourite hairdressers.

However, some minutes later, when Toyah had not come in, Adam's curiosity piqued. What was keeping her? Dinner would be ready soon. She must be on the phone. Adam went to check.

Toyah appeared to be just sitting there staring out over the bonnet. She was not on the phone, not even hands free. It was almost as if she was in a state of shock. Had she just received some bad news? Adam rushed out to check.

'Toyah?'

The first thing he noticed was the shine to her face. Was that sweat or was she wearing a mask?

No.

Adam had difficulty comprehending what he was seeing. Not only was it so unexpected, it just didn't make sense to be seeing Toyah in this way.

Toyah's head was completely wrapped in polythene. The remains of a roll of cling-film was on the passenger seat beside her.

Snapping out of his daze, his heart racing, he tried to open the car door. It was locked. He called out to Toyah but she was unresponsive. Yelling, he tried to put his fist through the window, just like he had seen on the movies. This only bloodied his knuckles.

Quickly he stopped himself and ran to the side of the drive and picked up a large rock and smashed the window. Thrusting his arm inside, flinging the door open, he tried to find an edge to the cling-film. He couldn't. He tried to poke a finger through the plastic over his lover's lips, but there were too many layers.

Why had she done this? This couldn't be happening. Was he hallucinating? Had he gone mad?

Pulling himself together he had an idea. He removed the key from the ignition and pierced the polythene. There was no rush of air, in or out.

Quickly, he dragged Toyah's limp form from the car onto the gravel and attempted mouth to mouth. As he leaned in he noticed her beautiful brown eyes were all bloodshot, and there was blood under her nose below the plastic. Had she had a blow to the head?

He tore open her blouse to listen for a heartbeat, but was shocked to find more cling-film wrapping her chest. He pulled up a sleeve to feel for a pulse, to find more cling-film from the wrist up. Then he noticed her legs protruding from the leather skirt and vanishing into the calf length boots, similarly shiny.

Only then did he notice the blood, over the plastic and her clothes. Where was that coming from?

'Shit, no!'

Adam had badly cut his wrist on the broken window. Then he realised he was feeling very faint. He thought he heard someone nearby, possibly on the lane. He called out for help but there was no response.

The last things he remembered was trying to keep his right arm raised while using his left hand to phone for an ambulance for the both of them. However, the call centre woman launched into what sounded like a long and pointless questionnaire. She seemed more concerned with her paperwork than Toyah and Adam's plight. Was this the end of a beautiful romance?

9

Every fibre of Adam Underwood's being seemed to be assaulted by a distorted version of recent events as he hammered a plastic bag upon the glass that separated him from the marble statue in the driver's seat.

He woke crying out but barely acknowledged the cell he lay in. However, the acrid aroma of public toilet soon brought him to the ugliness of his reality.

Trying to calm his racing heart and forget the false but rather metaphoric images of the nightmare, he noticed the sting of his wrist and knuckles. His injuries had at least been attended to by someone. But why was he locked up?

No one had come when he had called out here either. So there was little for him to do but continue lying there on his bunk, letting the real version of events play like a horror movie. How was this ever going to make sense?

Had there been any warning signs that he just hadn't paid attention to? He would never have suspected suicide in a month of Sundays. Toyah had been quirky for sure, and maybe other people in his shoes would have become cautious of her, way before this roller-coaster had derailed.

Adam's attitude was probably a product of his unnatural good luck, which had dulled his sense of risk. This made it all the more shocking when it had finally struck like a dirty bomb, with all the fallout he had yet to face.

Toyah had been such a joy to be with, though they had certainly had their share of difficult moments, as any normal couple. There had always been something fantastic about the whole making-up scenario however. It almost always gave the impression of bringing them closer each time. There certainly seemed to be a chemistry that bonded them. Nevertheless, it had come at a price. Toyah had gradually changed Adam's ways, and now it seemed even his luck.

Two years ago they had met in the Hotspur in Newcastle. The police had been involved then as now. Adam's final Admissions prank had gone wrong in a way that had far over shadowed his Old Man and the Dog prank of younger years. However, what he now found himself involved with would pale *that* into insignificance.

Back then, Toyah had taken an almost instant dislike to Adam's barge. This was put down to her claustrophobia, but with her encouragement, and willing labour, Adam's inherited house was finally made habitable. This took many months, with most of the upstairs needing to be ripped out, rebuilt and then decorated.

Toyah helped with the interior design and furnishings, yet not with any intent of living with him. She was quite old fashioned in many ways making it quite clear that she would not live with Adam unless he married her.

Unfortunately for Toyah, this situation was fine by Adam, as he liked to have his own space, and certainly didn't see himself as the marrying type. This attitude was possibly influenced by his parents failed marriage, which on reflection might easily have been saved, considering his father's leanings.

A bit of honesty might have led to an agreement for his father to live as a threesome with Adam's mother and her lesbian lover.

Nevertheless, Adam's reluctance to commit to a rather less complicated twosome, created something of a stand-off in the development of Adam's own relationship.

This decision did not interfere with Adam and Toyah's frequent expressions of passion though, especially once the bedroom had been finished. The car, the sofa and the kitchen table beyond their fantasy appeal had proven so much more awkward than a good double bed.

Another conflict that Toyah brought to the relationship was her rather OCD need for tidiness and cleanliness. She succeeded in having Adam put away, or throw away, all the *junk* that had once belonged to his father, plus that which had accumulated since.

The house looked like a different place without all the clutter. It was so much safer too, Toyah had argued.

Ben McGregor might have sided with her on that point, had he fully regained his memory of the dreadful accident which befell him there one evening, also two years ago.

A section of bannister had collapsed under Ben during a prank break-in, which was intended to turn Adam's perfume collection into a set of specimen jars. Ben had received an unfortunate couple of inches of seat-less bike frame into his grey matter.

Over the last few months Toyah had also become a changed person. She had become more relaxed about things in general, much to Adam's relief, though there had been a trade-off for this gain. She had also become somewhat secretive.

She avoided explaining what she did on her nights out, outings where Adam was not invited. He hoped that she was not two-timing him, but could not confront her with his niggling insecurity without admitting some level of distrust.

He had been very open with her from their first meeting, telling her about the continuing Flintstone enigma. She became his confidante. However, she had used this opportunity for openness to admit to her own obsession with UFO's. She claimed that since early childhood she had been abducted a number of times. Of course, Adam humoured her storytelling, having to bite back his cynicism and keep a straight face, a difficult task considering what she believed to be true.

2

Adam remembered Toyah sitting there, legs crossed hands clasped, looking all dainty but at the same time struggling with her demons.

'My earliest memory of the Nuzinamam and the Poolormanock was of the bright light burning through my bedroom curtains, then the nose of their craft silently penetrating the wall. It was all transparent, like a ghost-ship. It didn't even move the curtains as it came on in. I seem to recollect it was a large craft. The top of the nose must have extended into the attic.

'Anyway, one of the Poolormanock floated out and towards my bed. Thinking back on it now, their large almond eyes looked quite traumatised, some evidence of their persistent violation, I guess. Looking into those soulless orbs I prayed for the bed to swallow me up and protect me.

'Cynics of reports of these almond-eyed ufonauts say that the described proportions of eyes to head size are not feasible, because such eyeballs would be too large for their skull. They say that they would have insufficient space left for a sentient brain. Well, I can't say why the other close-encountees haven't reported this in their thousands of other sightings but when you look real close their eyes are actually made up of lots of little lenses, like flies eyes.

'The Poolormanock took an orange stone that glowed, from a pocket in what looked like a nappy, leaned over my prone form and dropped it into the hollow of my throat. It seemed to stick there and made my body go transparent too. I was then drawn naked out of my clothing and bedding. We floated across to and through the hull of the craft. I remember looking down at my house as we lifted up into the sky at great speed, but there was no more than a visual sense of motion.

'I was taken to a mothership on the other side of the moon in a matter of seconds, though I had little idea of what was happening until I was much older.

'Anyway, this is where I met my first Nuzinamam, a creature that looked like a cross between a Doberman and a Gorilla. It too wore the nappy style pants. I found the Nuzinamams and Poolormanocks audibly unintelligible. All communication seemed to take place by imagery conjured up in the mind, shared memories, imagination and intent. None of which appeared to be possible without one of these alien nappies. As I was made to wear one on my visits I found that they also made you feel secure, and stimulated.

'As the abductions continued over time I began to learn more about these beings and about our own race and future.

'The history books do not mention this but a number of key people have worn alien manufactured nappies under their clothing, Einstein and Schrodinger to name a couple.

'The nappies are impregnated with some form of nanotechnology, the intent of which is to get the human race to evolve to its next stage, which I have to admit I am still not too clear on.'

Toyah's story had sounded extremely paranoid and delusional to Adam. He had feared that it might be a sign of possible repression of childhood abuse. Nevertheless, with a smile he had played the good listener. She had had an almost soothing voice, which he had found he could listen to for hours, which turned out to be a godsend as she continued.

'Another occasion I was camping on the North of Skye with my boyfriend, Marcus. We hadn't long made camp, on top of an escarpment ridge when this row of bright lights came up over the edge without a sound and raced across the heather towards us. I hadn't mentioned anything of the abductions to Marcus, so he was pretty scared by this experience.

'We were taken, not to the mothership behind the moon this time, but to a much smaller vessel in orbit around Earth. I found this experience a bit confusing to say the least.

'The nappy they had provided me seemed a bit temperamental. It was almost like it was home-made, if you get what I mean.

'Then I distinctly remember seeing Marcus screwing one of the Poolormanocks, and *really* enjoying it. This disgusted me. How could he *do* such a thing?

'We had been going out for quite a while and there was no sense of him having any perverse side. However, when Marcus was brought back to me instead of having it out with him and telling him I never wanted to see him again, I found myself forgetting all that.

'I became irresistibly attracted to him, desperate to have sex. And we did. But you know how it is after you orgasm when you find you see things in a different light, well, I clearly saw I had just had sex with a Poolormanock too.

'The next thing, Marcus, complete with his own alien nappy, was being put into some rapidly tailored jump-suit with wings, a web between his legs, and sets of wheels down his chest and legs to his knees. A clear but solid mask was placed over his face, looking like he would not be able to breathe with it on, which concerned me at first, until I acknowledged that he was actually breathing rapidly but breathing nevertheless.

'Then his hood was brought up and connected to the mask. The Nuzinamams and Poolormanocks stood back and Marcus turned transparent and floated down through the floor until he was outside the ship, where he went opaque again and began to fall towards Earth.

'Because of those nappies we could see through his eyes. As the thin air began to thicken he spread his arms and legs and glided like a bird, a very fast bird.

'It was so exciting, but as the ground rush began to set in over America, there was sensed a definite need for a parachute. However, the images suggested that he should dive straight towards an area of salt flats, wings closed. He was to open his wings up at the last minute and this would bank him round for a very fast landing on his wheels.' Toyah stopped there as if stuck for words.

'So what happened next?' prompted Adam.

'He impacted the flats at around a hundred and twenty miles per hour....It was the first time that I had heard Nuzinamam laughter. After that I realised that you could not trust them at all.

'Next I had my nappy removed and was placed in a transparent but very tight flask. They ignored my screams. I couldn't move my arms or legs. I could only rock my head about at the top of the flask. My flask was taken to join thousands of others. Not in a neat line but shoved right inside an untidy heap of them. I believe this is where I developed my claustrophobia and desperate need for tidiness.

'I often wonder about others with these disorders. Have they had this experience too?

'Days seemed to pass by and then I was removed, feeling neither out of breath, thirsty or hungry. Those who removed me looked like they were wearing armour. They treated me differently, taking me aboard another vessel, and then on to another planet, the sky of which was a beautiful shade of magenta, where these beings lived inside mountains of crystal, with many other species.

'I did not stay there long though. I was returned, via another ship, to my camp on Skye at the same point in time that I had been abducted. The only difference was that Marcus was gone. I had to lie to the police the next day when I got into Portree, and simply reported him missing. His body was never found. I didn't feel I could suggest checking salt flats in America.'

Adam hadn't known what to say.

Adam still didn't know what to say as his cell door opened.

'Mr Underwood, would you follow me please?' Detective Inspector Carmichael stood there, his face expressionless.

Adam swung his legs down from the bunk, looked at his bandaged hand and the dressing that lay under his sleeve and heaved himself up.

3

Once inside the interview room, the Detective Inspector and Adam were joined by a black WPC who asked Adam whether he would like a tea or a coffee.

'Black tea, one sugar please.' Adam sat down in the seat that was indicated while the Detective set to with the digital recorder. He fiddled with it for some moments, making occasional vexed grunts of dissatisfaction.

Finally DI Carmichael said to no one in particular, 'Is it just me or does this technology randomly change its interface, so the user cannot record with it the same way twice?'

Adam offered what support he could, by shrugging.

'Okay then, our interview will be recorded as evidence for the trial, Mr Underwood.'

'Trial? What trial? I didn't do anything!'

'Hold on lad, hold on, I haven't managed to switch the buggering thing on yet!...Right then. Interview commencing at oh twenty-three hundred hours, there-abouts. Questioning suspect Adam Underwood is investigating officer DI Carmichael, with witnessing officer WPC Hanley.'

Just in time she returned to the room carrying two cups of tea, placing one in front of DI Carmichael, the other in front of Adam, with a smile.

'Cheers.' Adam took the paper cup of scolding liquid from the Hanley.

'She's new here,' DI Carmichael offered as if explaining some irregularity.

Adam nodded and began sipping his tea.

'Is there anything you would like to say before I begin with my questions?'

'Yes actually.' Adam had an anxious look in his eyes. 'I need to go to the toilet.'

Adam suddenly realised, with everything that had happened, he couldn't remember the last time he had taken a dump. However, he certainly needed one now that he had tasted tea. He was experiencing that post-breakfast-evacuation three-minute-warning. His colon felt like it contained the channel tunnel train waiting at a red light against exit.

'The toilet?! Why didn't you go before we started? You're just like my son. As soon as he's in the bath, or as soon as he starts eating at meal times....'

'Sorry, but it *really* can't wait.'

Carmichael nodded at Hanley, suggesting she escort Adam to the gents.

'But Sir shouldn't *you* take him to the *gents*?'

'Oh don't be squeamish. He'll only want a leak. Besides, I need to drink my tea and keep an eye on this recorder…in case it changes.'

Adam's guts were as upset as the rest of him by this whole incident. 'It doesn't matter to me who shows me the way, *please*!' he begged standing up.

A minute later, with Hanley only the other side of the cubicle door, Adam barely got buttocks to seat before he was extruding what might be mistaken for a prospector's core sample.

Not knowing the full story behind the bandaged wrist, Hanley became concerned by Adam's squeals of pain that he might be harming himself. 'What *are* you doing to yourself in there Mr Underwood?'

'If…you really…want to know…I think…I may be…giving birth.'

Then there came the relief of final release but no splash, as the gigantic turd thunked into the pan like a dead salmon.

Adam felt a cold sweat come over him but that was in part because he still had to face the previous evening's incident in the interview room. Immediately his stomach began to gripe again, forcing tears down his cheeks.

'Toyah had phoned to say that she had something to show me, and that she would be straight over. I was busy in the kitchen when I heard her Mercedes pull onto the gravel drive. I went to peek at her through the window by the door.

'In the evening light I saw what looked like a long thin can of hairspray. She quickly passed this round her head a few times, looking in the rear-view mirror.

'I returned to the kitchen but when Toyah did not come inside I went to check. She was just sitting there. I called out but she didn't turn. I went over to the car, parked on the far side of the drive.

'That's when I noticed the shine on Toyah's head and the distorted appearance of her face.' Adam took a deep breath before continuing.

'I tried to open the door but it was locked. She was smothered in cling-film. Why had she done that? Why?!'

'That's what we intend to find out Mr Underwood. Do you remember any more details?'

'I punched at the side window again and again, but could not break the glass. Then I ran to the side of the drive and got a rock. I smashed the window and pulled her out.'

'Didn't you try taking the polythene off her first?'

'Oh yes. Yes. I couldn't do it with my fingers, so used her car key.'

'Go on.' There was almost the glimmer of a smile on Carmichael's lips.

Was the DI enjoying this? Adam wondered crossly. He shook his head and continued, 'I tried to breathe air into her and check for a heartbeat but discovered her whole body was wrapped in cling-film. She, she...must have driven to mine like that.

'I'd heard somewhere that as long as a person could be resuscitated within three minutes they could be saved from brain damage. But I knew it would take an ambulance a good thirty minutes, speeding all the way just to get to my place, *if* the woman with the questionnaire sent one at all.

'Then I passed out. I was bleeding from my wrist which I must have slashed on the car window.'

'Do you remember anything else? Anything at all?'

Adam paused in thought then seemed to remember something for the first time. His eyes lit up. Maybe it was murder, somehow. 'Actually, I think I heard someone in the lane or the bushes, just before I lost consciousness.'

4

DI Carmichael appeared, to Adam, to have been practicing the marital-art of *listening without listening.*

'How long have you and Miss Pembroke been practising *autoerotica*?'

'*Auto* erotica?....Well, I suppose we've done it a few times.'

'I see....Were you never aware of how dangerous it was?'

'Dangerous?....Uncomfortable I'd say.'

'That too, I don't doubt. Now you say you were both party to this?'

'Yes but I don't see what any of this has to do with Toyah's death?'

'You *don't*?'

'No. Look, is this turning into a murder investigation or some sort of intimate chat?'

'I'm glad we both agree we are looking at murder now not suicide.'

'Good. We need to use logic to rule out accidental death.'

'You *think*?...So, you bound one another up, only this time it went wrong?'

'No!'

'I think you'll find it did.'

'I mean we never bound one another up.'

'Right....So you bound *yourselves* up?'

'No! What is it with you and binding? Is it some police restraint issue you have there? Toyah wasn't into anything like that!'

'And you know this for a fact because you asked her and got knocked back?'

'I really don't like your attitude Inspector. She was very honest and open, and never suggest anything even slightly....*experimental*. That's why I'm now convinced that she was murdered. Especially since remembering that sound in the bushes.'

'But you said that *you* had done it, I quote *a few times.*'

'I was under the impression you were enquiring as to whether we had ever had sex in a car.'

'Mr Underwood! Autoerotica is self-stimulation in the sexual sense. It has nothing to do with cars!'

'What?! This investigation is a farce! Why aren't you finding the murderer instead of asking me about wanking? Do you get some sort of kick out of this?'

'No Mr Underwood. I'm just establishing the facts.'

'The facts are that my girlfriend Toyah turned up to my house and while I got on with the cooking for our anniversary dinner, someone smothered her in cling-film. And by the time I went to see what was keeping her, she was dead!'

'So she came to the house?'

'No. She stayed in the car.'

'But you just said she came to the house.'

'Do pay attention. She was on the drive. If you are going to play word games, Detective, I want my Solicitor.'

'This is only a preliminary enquiry.'

'Well you're making it feel like Crown Court.'

'Did Miss Pembroke have a lot of money?'

'She was comfortable I guess…Had a good job.'

'What did she do?'

'She's….Was….An accountant.'

'Did she have any enemies?'

'Not that I'm aware of.'

'Well I guess that about wraps things up for now. No pun intended.'

'Tsk!'

'Hanley will see you back to your cell.'

'What do you mean? I thought I was going home now.'

'We have a forensic team working on the scene of crime presently.'

'Oh. Well I hope they are more focused than you have been.'

5

Life at the McGregor household had had a number of setbacks since Ben's accident. They no longer had a car. The insurance refused to pay up because Ben had owned up to having 'lost' the vehicle *somewhere*.

His acquired object recognition difficulties as a result of a head injury meant he had to retire from his postal job. It soon became clear that he would have great difficulty getting full time employment anywhere.

This meant that they could not get a loan or mortgage extension as a means of buying another car, since they were still paying off the loan on the missing one.

It was such a surprise that Adam had offered Ben work, after what Ben had attempted to do on Adam's property.

During Ben's convalescence following the accident, he and his wife Meg had become good friends with Adam and Toyah.

Meg often commented upon the good that had come out of the accident, possibly as her way of coping with the bad.

The brain lesions were a constant frustration to them all with his cognition disabilities. On the up-side Ben's whole temperament had improved remarkably.

They had been warned by the specialists that in many cases head injuries resulted in frequent expressions of anger. However, in

Ben's case it seemed quite the reverse. He appeared to have turned into Meg's big softie. He was much better with the children now. Meg began to joke that she should have had him lobotomised years ago.

Ben's daily routine now involved Meg taking Beth to nursery at the University, while Ben took Robbie to school in North Shields, before going on to work.

'I don't want to go to school dad.'

'Sorry son but you have to.'

'But I can't read anymore.'

'Is that so?

'Yeah the teacher said I might be brain damaged like you.'

'Did she now?'

'Yeah….Why don't I come to work with you and Uncle Adam?'

'Well it's very heavy work, and sometimes it can be dangerous.'

'Do you get in trouble with the police?'

'No.'

'Well why don't you come to school with me and we can learn to read together?'

'I wish I could, but you know I can't learn symbols anymore.'

'Well why don't you practice another musical instrument, like the triangle?'

Ben frowned. Robbie had lost him, again. But at least they had found the school, and with the promise of meeting in the afternoon they parted.

Ben headed for Newcastle centre, where Adam had arranged to pick him up. But Adam did not show.

Ben took out his mobile and looked at it. The symbols seemed to change every time he saw them. Text messages were a complete waste of time. He did have work-arounds though, that the occupational therapist had him practice. He was able to learn certain things by using different methods of memorising. He learned the keys on personal phones and remotes by position and touch. He also learned Braille, and placed greater importance in colour, though that was not fool proof.

There were no voicemails from Adam. By rehearsed button routine Ben speed-dialled Adam, but there was still no response from Adam. Adam's mobile appeared to be switched off. Ben then tried the house and got that answer machine.

'Underwood Home Renovations. I'm unable to answer my phone right now. I'm sure you know what to do next.'

'Hi. It's Ben man. Hope all's alright. Call me when you can. I'll make my way over to Mrs Chesney's and get on with the extension the best I can.'

With the stations looking pretty much the same, Ben had to count and recite the stops, processing the metro lines by direction and order. On long trips he would tie knots in a piece of string to guard against losing count. He could no longer read maps effectively, and the meaninglessness of road signage and controls had meant he had had to surrender his driver's licence. Truth be told, he *had* driven Adam's van once, a short distance, in a familiar area, and managed fine. After all, driving was a skill that relied heavily on feel and spatial awareness, which had been unaffected.

Getting off the Metro at Gateshead, Ben walked the rest of the way to Mrs Chesney's, arriving late but at least arriving. Although there were still a few tasks to take care of on the exterior of the extension, all those tools were in Adam's van, so he would have to progress with the interior work using what he had at hand.

Entry into the house always took a few minutes as Mrs Chesney used a stair-lift and two wheelchairs to get around upstairs and down. In addition to which she was a rather security conscious person, though not particularly technologically minded. This made the check-in procedure frustratingly longer than her efforts to reach the door.

Adam and Ben's access often involved them having to remind her of what she needed to do in order to release the lock on the door. This was because she insisted that it must be done electronically rather than manually.

'You're late!' she snapped in greeting. She sounded somewhat nasal this morning.

'Yes, sorry.'

'And alone?'

'Yeah, I couldn't raise Adam. I think he must be off colour.'

'That makes two of us,' she back-wheeled to let him by.

Closing the door and stepping past, Ben moved straight upstairs, preparing himself to attempt working without Adam's support.

'Would you like a coffee?' she called after him.

'If that's no trouble Mrs Chesney.'

'I'm in a wheelchair Mr McGregor, not a straight-jacket.'

'Right...' he made it sound as if he was making a mental note of that point.

Soon he was looking at the tools and procrastinating. He knew he could be looking at a tape measure, spirit level, pencil, or Stanley knife, but couldn't be sure which was which without feeling them. Even then he sometimes became confused if he wasn't concentrating.

The only tool he could identify with any certainty without touch was the electric drill because of its Black and Decker corporate colours. He often had to fight the temptation to work just with what he recognised, still finding it difficult to ask for help.

He heard the grunting and groaning of Mrs Chesney as she made her way up stairs with the mug of coffee on the juddering stair-lift, but Ben had learned not to interfere.

Nevertheless, beyond Mrs Chesney's will power and independence there was a definite sense of melodramatic performance; fishing for sympathy. This presented something of a paradox. If nothing was said she put more effort into the show, and if anything *was* said she turned it into a remark to be defensive about. In truth, Ben McGregor had to admit that all things considered, could no longer be *arsed*.

She had only just handed over the mug when the doorbell rang, giving her the opportunity for a reverse performance. With an exasperated sigh she spun her chair around and headed for the stairs. The lift was only halfway down when the bell rang again.

'I'm coming. I'm coming!'

She turned this into an extended performance, not pulling the downstairs chair close enough in to the seat of the lift so that she crumpled to the floor, her grumbling only answered by more ringing of the bell.

'Be patient man!' She said as she pulled the wheelchair over on to her. A level of effort she normally reserved for observing audiences.

Then, as if she had decided she was tiring she righted the chair, clambered into it and went to the door's security panel, just as the bell rang yet again.

'What is it?!' She shouted at the head on the small screen.

'Special delivery.' The postman attempted to show the security camera an extremely large package, sending the screen into darkness. Another challenge for Mrs Chesney to struggle with.

'Are you sure it's for me?'

'Well it's got number twelve, just like your house, and if you're Mrs Chesney then that's good enough for me.'

She opened the door. 'Put it down there,' she said, pointing at the hallway carpet.

The postman followed this action by poking a pen into the still pointing hand then slapped paperwork impatiently on top of the box. 'Sign here, please.'

Managing another sigh and a groan she leaned over, bringing the chair up onto two wheels, but strangely managing to stop it tipping the whole way with support from one foot. Then, with the paperwork signed and separated, providing a copy for her, the man was gone.

'What a thoroughly unpleasant young man,' she paused for Ben to comment. 'I *said*, what a thoroughly unpleasant young man!"

'What's that Mrs C?'

'Oh *heavens* don't call me *that*! Mrs Chesney will do just fine. Mrs C makes me think of cancer.'

'No that's the Big C.' Ben corrected, walking over to the top of the stairs.

'Mrs Cunningham was a neighbour,' she explained. 'Lived across the road at number seven, died a very slow and painful death leaving her only son to fend for himself.'

'How old was he?' Ben started down the stairs, feeling awkward talking from the landing.

'Oh, young Cunningham would be about, let's see, mmm, mid-thirties.'

'Mid-thirties? I should hope he *could* fend for himself.'

'Yes, yes. Most of the time he is fine, just as long as he remembers to take his medication. Otherwise, you see, he reverts to his paranoid schizophrenia. I sometimes thought he'd be the first to kill Oscar.'

'Oscar?'

'Yes. A long story. For another day. I have a job for you, when you have a moment,' she headed into the kitchen.

Ben finished his coffee and followed her, now curious about this *Oscar,* and how many times *he* or *it* could be killed.

She rummaged through a draw and pulled out an envelope marked with a '12'. However, this could just as easily have been an 'R' or a footpath post blocking the way for a large swan, for all Ben could make out.

'Take *this* and *that* box in the hallway, up to the spare room and set it up for me would you. There's a dear.'

Ben would have had a bad feeling about this task had he not been distracted, questioning the concept of a spare room. He had thought the reason for the extension out the back was because Mrs Chesney didn't have *any* rooms spare.

Each door had a flowery name plaque, which Ben didn't even consider referring to. Instead, applying logic he decided that the spare room was commonly the smallest room, the box room, above the stairs and front door.

Opening the door he found a pink single bed with frilly pink pillows, which fought for sickliness with the pink kitten wallpaper and matching curtains.

The one thing that Ben's eyes were drawn to in the room, whether to avoid pink blindness, or fear of a greater evil, was the empty black dressing table. Empty but for the *Hello Kitty* stickers positioned randomly over it, which for a moment had him convinced that it was only a well-travelled suit case.

Placing the parcel next to the table Ben returned to the extension, laid his hands on the Stanley knife. He was soon back to open the package.

'What on earth?'

Inside was a large device, cloaked in bubble-wrap. It definitely didn't feel like a portable television or anything else which Ben might have expected an old woman to take delivery of.

Lifting it out and onto the table, where he removed the bubble-wrap, he discovered a grey metal box with what felt like a timer set into it, and a miniature radar dish standing on top, which he guessed was either a parabolic microphone or some sort of transmitter. Last but not least was the power cable and plug. The apparent lack of an on switch suggested that the timer was the only control.

Knowing it would be a waste of time opening the envelope but doing so anyway, Ben revealed simple hand written instructions. Unknown to him the instructions described how to adjust the pre-set daily activation time. In addition there was a note on directing the transmission dish so as to avoid any collateral interference.

What the instructions did not mention was the purpose of this device as a radio frequency interference generator.

With a grunt of disinterest, Ben simply plugged it in and switched it on at the wall. There was a slight buzz from the timer but nothing of real concern, so he removed the packaging from the room, closed the door and returned to his work.

6

Adam had not been informed that unless he was being charged he was free to go. He was merely prompted about his right to a phone call before returning to his cell. So he had called Ben. But he thought it best to ring the home number to leave a message, and avoid the chance that Ben might accidentally lose a mobile call for help. At the McGregor residence there was at least a chance that Meg would pick up the message and be able to respond effectively.

Adam was finding that if he didn't keep his mind focused on some form of action, the trauma returned to the forefront. Now that he had left his phone message and was back on his stinking bunk, the anxiety began to gnaw again, causing him to sink further into the clutches of depression. It was obvious to Adam that the police had him down as a murderer.

He didn't know how long he had lain there, but eventually a DI Jenkins, a colleague of DI Carmichael's, came for him. The questions were about to begin again. This time Adam went to the loo before the interrogation, with the intention of drawing it out and clearing his head but the smell in the gents being worse than his cell, he thought better of that.

WPC Hanley was present for DI Jenkins' interview of Adam, but she clearly wasn't happy to be there this time, for some reason. Adam was soon to discover why.

DI Jenkins identified those present for the sake of the recording then launched straight into his questions.

'So, your lady, was she a bit of a huffer?'

'A what?'

'A huffer. You know, 'I'll huff and I'll puff.' A bit of a gasper?'

Adam was appalled by this man's technique, half expecting his next comment to be *Nudge, nudge, wink, wink, say no more*. It was quite clear from the opening lines he was actually going to be worse than DI Carmichael, if that were possible.

'Would you people please speak plain English? I've told your colleague all I know.'

'Well I'm going to tell you something you don't know, Mr Underwood. We have had the report from forensics and it appears that you didn't cover your tracks as well as you might have thought.'

'What do you mean?'

Jenkins loved to play the *We know exactly how you did what you did* trick, to sweat the truth out of interviewees. 'You'd be amazed how clever forensic science is these days. They can tell from the crack angle on a single piece of broken glass and its temperature, the time of day the glass was smashed.'

'Seriously?...Well that must be good then. So I can go home now.'

'No. I put it to you that you and Miss Pembroke were having problems in the sexual activity department. Let's face it, it cannot have been easy for her to climax if your groans of pleasure carry any hint of that dreadful accent of yours. Devon is it, or Somerset? It makes *scouse* sound upper crust.'

'I can't believe this is proper procedure.' Adam looked across to WPC Hanley, who was shaking her head with a frown.

DI Jenkins however, was making no attempt to suppress his amusement. Then to further wind Adam up, in the hope of initiating a slip, he attempted a farmer impression for the benefit of the digital recorder 'I *can't* believe it's not better...than Scouse.'

'My girlfriend has died damn it!'

'Yes. As well *you* know.' He stared at Adam with a glint in his eye, the only indication of what was to follow. 'You thought you'd....win Miss Pembroke round....with sex aids, vibrators and the like. After a while you got caught up in plastic fetishism and bondage and that brought you to good old cling-film. Cheap and readily available, that sensuously thin material that heightens the sensitivity of the skin.'

'No!'

'Winding it round your partner, turning her into your little mermaid, only sometimes you got carried away and forgot to give her flippers, binding her arms to her sides, before going on to seal off her head.'

'Ridiculous!'

WPC Hanley was growing equally outraged by the second.

DI Jenkin's continued oblivious. 'That turns out to be a key point in your relationship

39

because she experiences the intense pleasure that suffocation can bring, as panic races her heart towards multiple orgasms. Then after that folly, all future foreplay and intercourse sees her demanding more. Sometimes you'd leave it on too long and she'd get prickly heat from the sweat.'

'Fucking *Hell* stop! Stop!!' Adam put his hands to his ears. He couldn't believe what he was hearing. '*You* sound like a man with experience!'

DI Jenkins turned a funny colour. Loosening his collar a little he recovered himself. 'I also know a great deal about killing, but that doesn't make *me* a murderer.'

Adam exhaled some of his tension, and confided with WPC Hanley. 'I'm not convinced.'

'Do you know it is possible to kill someone with a coat hanger, without leaving a mark on them?' Jenkins said with enthusiasm rather than threat.

'I don't doubt it, but I just don't want to know.'

'It gets inserted up the anus and dragged up and down the colon, causing fatal blood loss. Villains know all the tricks. But then so do our *forensics*!'

Adam held his head in his hands. This was a nightmare. That was it. He would wake up screaming on that bunk again any second. But he didn't. He tried to steer his own questions back in line with maintaining his sanity. 'So what did the forensics say about the person on the lane?'

'There was *no* person on the lane.' Jenkins paused for effect. 'Some weeks ago, you overstepped the mark and took Miss Pembroke beyond her personal limit and it scared her so badly that she didn't want to do another *Filming* session ever again. But you had other ideas, having developed your own need to torture and control. Hearing her desperately pleading helped you feel like a *real* man *didn't it*.'

Adam was speechless.

'So on the evening in question she tried to get away. Locking herself into her car, fumbling with the keys in her terror, trying to get them into the ignition. But you smashed the window with a rock and hauled her out and upstairs, kicking and screaming. Living in such a secluded spot, it's perfect for your sordid activities, where no one can hear the screams. The blood, your blood, was found to be half an hour to an hour older than Miss Pembroke's determined time of death.'

'Then there's been a mistake.'

'The only mistake would be in believing your story. How would you explain the drag marks in the gravel and your carpeting, and the corresponding scuff marks on the heels of Miss Pembroke's shoes?'

Adam thought long and hard. The phrase *stitched up* came to mind but not a response for the recording.

DI Jenkin's pressed on, clearly enjoying being in control of the situation, 'Of course, accidents do happen don't they Mr Underwood. And with cases like this the court is likely to drop the murder charge, this being your first time, in favour of Miss Pembroke's death being one of…*Misadventure*.'

7

Ben was first back to the house, with Robbie in tow. Ben wasn't happy. Robbie's teacher had taken him to one side and told him that Robbie was continuing to swear like a trooper. Ben simply said that he'd rather that, than hear him swear like a God-botherer. She had told him to go home and consider what sort of example he was setting for his son, while she prayed for his soul.

Out of earshot down the corridor, Ben made it clear he was not impressed. '*I* come to collect *you* from school, and *I'm* the one who gets the *fucking homework*.'

A little later, after a silent journey home, Ben marched straight upstairs to the bathroom to wash the day off, leaving Robbie to wander into the kitchen.

Robbie stopped at the phone and pressed the *play-messages* button, like he had seen his mother do. It was Uncle Adam first, saying something about the station. Robbie wasn't really listening to the words but next he heard his grandmother's voice saying something about a Mr Morley and how someone had recently gone down on his infested member, which now needed sawing off before it killed someone.

Ignoring the rest of her news, Robbie walked away from the machine just as he had watched his mother do many times before.

Meg returned with Beth, and bags of shopping, to find Ben and Robbie equally starving, after having watched 'Home and Away', 'Neighbours' and 'Hollyoaks.'

It was a strain on Meg, coming home from one job right into another, especially when she knew Ben's eyes would have been glued to the young women on the TV.

Nevertheless, she had learned not to ask Ben to help get the dinner ready, since his accident. Give him his due, he had tried once, but opened too many cans trying to work out what was what. Even then that chicken curry and rice had turned out to be chunky steak custard with millet.

It wasn't until they sat down to dinner that Meg had time to ask, 'What sort of day have you had?'

'Bit more of a challenge than usual.'

'Oh? Why?'

'Adam didn't show, all day, so I had to get on with Mrs Chesney's extension on my own.'

'Is Adam ill?'

'Don't know. Couldn't raise him. I was thinking if I can't get hold of him after dinner I should get a taxi over to his place to check.'

'That would be expensive Ben.'

'Yeah, but he's a mate.'

'What I mean is one of us could get a lift over there.'

'One of us?'

'Okay. Well I'm thinking of Alf, Alf Tanner. He's offered me help in the past, but he, well you know, still doesn't trust you.'

'You said that was just a misunderstanding.'

'You yelled across the street at him Ben. *Effing pervy paedophile*, if memory serves me correctly. And then of course you had to cross over there and *chin* him for good measure.'

'Well what did he expect? He started to protest.'

'He'd only handed Beth a lollipop.'

'Aye, well.'

'He's unlikely to believe that you're now a changed man.'

'Arr sod him. Anyhow, you said that when you'd dragged him into his hallway you had noticed he had an old picture of the cast of Grange Hill on the wall.'

'I also told you that the picture was a group shot with his niece.'

'Yeah, right.' He popped his last fork full of food in his mouth and continued. 'So why were all the girls starkers, eh?'

'Tsk!' She got up to clear the dishes away, refusing to bite further on Ben's wind-up.

8

Alf had been dozing in his armchair before he answered the door.

'Oh it's…' That attractive wife of the thug across the way. '….Meg. Come in dear. Don't stand out there.'

'Thanks.'

'Can I get you a drink?' He remembered the bottle of sherry he had almost polished off before falling asleep.

'No thank you Mr Tanner.'

'Alf, please.'

'Oh okay. What it is…is that Adam and Toyah, friends of ours, are not answering their phones. I've just tried calling them both, and we're a bit concerned because Adam should have been at work today but wasn't.'

'Oh dear.'

'It's probably nothing, but I'd hate to think there was some sort of problem and I, I mean we, hadn't done anything about it. So I was wondering…' Meg realised he was nodding like one of those ornamental dogs in the back window of old people's cars. She started to consider that he might have Parkinson's, just never noticed it before. '….Wondering if you would mind giving me a lift to Adam's…Just to put my mind at rest.'

His nodding continued, then he realised she had finished, engaged his brain and replied. 'Certainly my dear. I'll just get my keys.'

As he began his search, Meg found her eyes drawn to the school photo. Though it did say Grange Hill at the bottom she didn't recognise any of the cast. The girls were only wearing their gym kit.

'Which one did you say was your niece?' She asked when he returned waggling the keys.

'Niece? Oh no. I never said I had a niece.'

'Oh, well it *was* some time ago, but I'm sure you said niece. Mind you, you *were* holding your chin at the time.'

'I remember that, yes. You asked about it, making polite conversation no doubt, in contrast to your husband's assault, and I must have said it was my nice picture.'

'Your *nice* one?' She frowned.

'Yes. I have some others, which are not so nice. Shall we go?' He opened the front door and she almost stumbled out sideways.

Moments after setting off, Alf stopped the car at the junction at the bottom of the road, and turned to her with raised eyebrows. It was only then that Meg realised that after Alf's last comment she hadn't thought to say where they were going.

When she told him it became clear by the look on his face that Alf had thought this was just going to be a five-minute favour. 'I'll have to go get some petrol.'

'Sure. I'll pay for that.' She hoped she had enough money in here purse. The card had been rejected again.

'No, no. I'd be needing petrol anyway.'

Alf hated the smell of petrol at the best of times, but by the time he drove onto the forecourt matters were already looking bleak. He was feeling decidedly queasy with the sherry churning in his stomach. He definitely didn't want another sherry later. He muffled a belch, tasting the packet of After Eights he had consumed as that afternoon's TV dinner, in front of Ceebeebeeies.

Standing there with nozzle in hand, he didn't notice the Irish Wolfhound at first. It had been tethered by its owner to a metal frame holding three fire extinguishers and a display of flowers, just outside the kiosk door. However, as Alf opened the petrol cap, the dog saw a cat go round the back of the petrol station. It went in hot pursuit, with incredible determination.

In an explosion of flowers, the frame twisted and crashed to the ground, shedding its load of extinguishers easily but noisily. The heavy frame went clanking after the big dog, chasing the little cat. The owner, having just settled his bill, tried to catch up, calling on deaf ears.

The pump's habitually pointless delay of dry-retching with the trigger gripped, suddenly turned to a gusher and the petrol flowed down Alf's trousers and over his shoes, breaking him instantly out of gaze mode.

He shoved the nozzle into his tank, and let out a groan of disgust. He tried to tell himself that it wasn't too bad, certainly not bad enough to return home. In truth though, if he came too near a spark he might easily be mistaken for a protesting fanatic.

Underway again, they had to drive with the windows open, and Meg began to wish she had brought a jacket against the wind-chill. Nevertheless, it was better than choking on the fumes billowing up from Alf's foot-well.

His fight against the embarrassment of potentially gagging onto the dashboard was a close run thing. All the twists and turns of the country roads to Adam's place, took him to his limit.

He kept twisting his head to the open window but never actually committing to a sherry blur. The tension was unsettling for Meg, and she began to wonder whether Alf had been drinking. She didn't ask. By the time they arrived they both looked pale.

As Alf pulled onto the drive, they could see no lights on in the house. Adam and Toyah might have been down the local, but the large white tent on the drive, with police tape sealing it off, suggested otherwise.

'Oh my God!' This was not what Meg had expected.

'Now Meg. Don't jump to assumptions.' Alf started to feel better, some of his colour coming back, as he remembered the sense of control he had once had, in his time on the force. 'I'll just take a peek.'

Meg didn't know what else to do. She just sat there in disbelief.

Alf took a torch from his boot and trudged over to the tent. Parting the Velcro on the entry-flap part way down for the torch and higher up for his head, he poked his torch then his head inside, and surveyed the scene.

The open car door had been dusted for prints and there was shattered glass everywhere, including the gravel where he spotted blood. However, Alf's mind became side-tracked with the memory of his worst day on the force.

Toyah's open car door transformed, in Alf's mind, to the open door of the up-ended chest freezer at the scrap yard, some ten years ago. It had contained the remains of a dismembered male, most of it by then gone to the dogs and fly-blown.

It had been reported to them by the yard owner who claimed he didn't know where the freezer had come from, and that it hadn't been there the last time he had taken anything up the back.

The police had insufficient body parts to identify the deceased. At the back of the freezer was an upmarket trainer with the gory remains of the foot still inside. Next to that were the remains of an upper arm baring a tattoo unhelpfully declaring *I love Pitbull*.

Alf let go of the torch, frantically scrabbling for his tartan handkerchief, which he didn't get inside the tent quite quick enough. Pursing his lips against the forceful flow of vomit, in case it marked the crime scene, it burst forth from his nostrils in two burning jets, down the inside of the tent. He snapped his head out, quickly blew his nose in the handkerchief, smelled the petrol and vomited into the handkerchief, in a mechanically controlled fashion that was strangely reminiscent of a Pez dispenser.

'What is it?' Meg called.

Alf waved a dismissive hand before his whole body quivered and he once again doubled over and vomited, this time loosing globs onto his now peeling shoes.

'Oh my God. What's in there?' Meg called through the car's open window, considering getting out for a look herself.

Alf just shook his head, picking up the torch and staggering to the car boot, He seemed to stay there for some considerable time, ignoring Meg's repeated questions.

When he finally got back in beside her, he attempted to explain himself. 'Sorry about that. I quit the force to avoid such scenes, and now just try and lead a simpler life. I better get you to a police station. I really don't think I should have looked.'

Meg began to shiver.

9

Adam was back in the interview room, but this time the recorder was left off, and there was no accompanying officer and no DI Jenkins, just a barely apologetic DI Carmichael.

'So…' Adam tried to get what he'd been told straight in his head. 'You're telling me, that *shit* Jenkins…was lying about the forensic report?'

'He was just trying to crack you. As I said, the main thing is that the report has now been issued and you are in the clear.'

'But what about the murderer?'

'There is no evidence of one, Mr Underwood. You are going to have to face the fact that for whatever reason, your girlfriend, Miss Pembroke, died through misadventure.

'There was no sign of a struggle. Strangely, she would appear to have been quite calm during the experience.'

'What do you mean? What about the blow to the head?'

'What blow to the head Mr Underwood?'

'The one that made her nose bleed.'

Carmichael read on, 'The lack of generalised stretch distortion and wrinkling of the plastic film layers suggests that the deceased had breathed out prior to sealing the cling-film. The resulting vacuum of strained inhalation on the respiratory system and exposed capillaries caused bleeding from the eyes and nose.'

'God!'

'The majority of the body looks to have been wrapped in cling-film an hour or so prior to death, indicated by the level of sweat and patches of redness found on the flesh.'

'Someone must have done that to her.'

'The plastic was dusted for prints and all prints were found to be those of the deceased.'

'She must have been drugged then!'

Carmichael shook his head. 'There were no known substance traces found in the deceased's system.'

'What does *known substance traces* mean exactly?'

'Well, forensic tests showed nothing Mr Underwood.'

Adam sighed. 'What am I going to tell her parents?'

'That's up to you. But we have already informed them of her death.'

'Shit.' From recent experience, Adam could just imagine the approach, and hoped DI Jenkins hadn't been the one to make the call.

As if DI Carmichael could read his expression he said, 'Don't worry, we had WPC Hanley tell them.'

Carmichael scraped his chair on the floor as he got up, signalling the debriefing might be over.

'Oh, yes,' this came almost as an afterthought to the DI. 'You might want to consider counselling.'

'No. I might *need* to consider counselling.'

'Do you have someone who can take you back home?' Carmichael asked as he led Adam out past the front desk.

'Would it be possible to see Toyah's body before I leave?'

'I wouldn't recommend it. She will have been all cut up.'

'Why cut her up? Someone suffocated her!'

'It's the autopsy process...Checking for other factors which might call into question initial conclusions.'

'Oh.'

'Just go home and get some sleep.'

'Adam!' A voice called from behind.

Both men turned from the front desk towards the station entrance to see Meg, with Alf hanging back looking sheepish.

'They said at the other station you were helping with enquiries here, so we came straight over. I had thought you were dead. Then we were told it was Toyah, but nobody will tell me what happened.'

'I only just heard the forensic report myself.'

'Are you okay?'

'The love of my life has been murdered on my drive and I've just been tortured for the last twenty-four hours by our boys in blue. So....What do you think?'

'I think you should come and stay over at our place tonight. See how you feel after a good night's sleep.'

Adam's sadness deepened. Meg was one of the most together women he knew, she had to be, married to Ben, but Adam couldn't bring himself to tell her what he was going through. He sighed. 'Okay. Thanks Meg.'

Her varnished nails clawed desperately at her face, her mouth wide in a reverse scream of terror that sucked and stretched polythene down towards her lungs like bubblegum. The screaming played in surround sound as Adam hammered against the driver-side window to no avail with an oven-mit.

Adam woke to find he was sitting up on a sofa, pounding the back of the seating with his sore fist. As his scream died away, along with the bad dream, he could hear the continued screams of children above. Their mother was now in attendance, their father was clumping down the stairs.

Ben had seen this sort of trauma a hundred times before, from innocent villagers to some of their own troopers. It required a calm and considered, but firm response, to bring the situation under control with a view to aiding possible future counselling. In short, family and friends of the victims of traumatic stress often experienced high demands on other people's patience.

'What the *fuck* is the matter with you, Boss?!' Ben bawled as he burst inside the lounge like he was still in the SAS. 'You've upset the bairns!'

'God, I'm sorry Ben. It was Toyah.'

'Hey man, don't go blaming the lass!' He glared. 'She's dead, remember.'

'It was awful.' Adam still hadn't explained to Ben or Meg what had happened to Toyah.

'Aye well save the details for breakfast. Now get some shut-eye, and shut your gob while you're at it. I'll be force marching you back to your place if you pull that stunt again.'

'Thanks. You're a lifesaver.' Adam decided he must have needed that reality check. After all, Ben surely knew how to handle this sort of experience.

10

Adam and the McGregor's were not alone in having a disturbed night.

The radio frequency interference generator, up river in Gateshead, activated itself at 2:00 am, when most of the neighbourhood were asleep.

It had completely missed its slot for the intended jamming of Coronation Street at number ten, just next door to Mrs Chesney.

It's efforts did not go unnoticed however, as its field of disruption poured into the Potts household at number fourteen.

At that moment Mr Potts' wildest fantasy was coming true. His son's new wife, still wearing her wedding dress was going down on him. Her pink wet-look smile made his manhood swell to bursting point. Then discomfort spread from his chest as her lips glided down his member and delivered a hummer.

Mrs Potts meanwhile was digging the road up outside, ready for the next season's potatoes. She seemed to break through to a Metro tunnel with her harpoon, and the ground just gave way. She woke up next to her husband's writhing body, as his pace-maker packed in.

His arching body suddenly locked up, and with an almighty fart it went limp. His proud erection slowly deflated as his wife turned on the light to another opportunity missed.

Across the street, in number seven, Mr Cunningham continued to dream about the beating he was taking with the rubber hose. His anger over his defencelessness built up to the point that it became his turn with the hose, to dish out the beating and beating.

Then, as he grew tired, the pain returned as he became the victim again, only to seed his anger once more.

As he began to wield the hose one more time, he understood that he was actually battering his own body bent double before him. He started to feel guilty over his self-inflicted situation, and then woke to the sound of the siren.

As the ambulance arrived at number fourteen Mr Cunningham flew out of his bed. Powered by panic, still not fully awake, just desperate not to be taken again, his legs became tangled in the sheets. It was as if someone had already attempted to constrain him, someone like Gibbsie.

Cunningham had sensed that his calls to Gibbsie were not wanted any more, especially in the early hours. He scrabbled frantically for the bedside table, clawing the top for his glasses but only succeeding in knocking his glass of water off, along with the lamp. Gathering what wits he had, he reprioritised his actions.

Freeing his legs he stumbled towards the main light switch. But then he stopped and played with his favoured lock of hair above his right ear. *Light* was what *they* wanted. What *he* wanted was his gun.

In the darkness he turned his attention to the back of his cupboard, and soon took comfort from the feel of his hidden rifle and box of ammunition. In the flashing blue light, barely filtered by his curtains, Mr Cunningham sat on the end of his bed waiting for *them*.

He imagined they would come through the front door or back, heading for the stairs, any second, any second. Stroking the trigger with his finger tip, he relaxed slowly, and eventually returned to sleep, where the hose was waiting for him.

11

Meg, hands in the sink, was in a rush to get the dishes under control before she left for work, dreaming of being able to afford a dishwasher.

'All I'm saying, Ben, is we can't have another night like last night. We have no idea what has happened, but from Mr Tanner's reaction to whatever he saw in that tent, it was something pretty gory, I'm guessing. Adam's screaming would certainly seem to bear that out. It's frightening the bairns.'

'I'm not arguing luv.' Ben said through a mouthful of toast, as the bairns messed about under the table. 'I've told him to shape up or ship out.'

'Oh, that was tactful.'

'Blow tact.' Ben turned to look over his shoulder. 'Morning, Adam. Didn't see you standing there.'

'Morning,' Adam greeted groggily.

'We were just talking about you.' Ben said with a laugh.

'Don't blame you.'

'You've been through a traumatic experience.' Meg made the effort to sound sympathetic. 'We dread to think what you must be going through.' She hoped this might bring forth some demystification, though maybe not too graphic, what with the bairns still being present and all.

'I was thinking of going home today.'

'Do you want me to carry on with the job?' Ben enquired, expecting a *no* and planning what he could do with his day off.

'Yeah, if that's okay with you. I don't want Mrs Chesney thinking we are slacking off.'

'Oh...okay then.' A hint of disappointment came through in Ben's voice, which he tried to cover by adding, 'I managed yesterday, without causing an incident.'

'Good man.' Adam sounded understandably more exhausted than the rest of them.

'Do you want anything to eat?' Asked Meg. 'A nice bacon sandwich?'

'That sounds ideal.' Adam tried to think brighter thoughts as he watched Meg dry her hands and go to the fridge. She pulled out a handful of bacon rashers, wrapped in cling-film. He turned a funny colour. 'Urh, maybe not.'

Meg stopped and frowned at him. Then, looking back at her hands, saw the bacon in terms of raw meat. 'Oh my God!'

Mrs Chesney answered the security panel for the door with a very stuffy voice, and when Ben entered he saw she was wearing a towel like a head scarf.

'Would you do me another favour this morning?' Ben followed her into the kitchen half expecting to see another strange device. 'Would you do my shopping for me, along at Tesco's? Do you know where that is?'

'Aye, but...'

'Only, I want to make myself some chicken soup to help fight off this damned cold. I'll need a few other items too, so I've written them down for you, in case you forget.' She handed him the list and a twenty-pound note.

'Right, but um…'

'Oh and would you pop this into my neighbour's, on the way.' She handed him an envelope, simply marked with the number 6.

Mrs Chesney's son Frank had arranged for Mr Tunn, at number 6, to manage a little job, for a fee. Mr Tunn's electronics experience had made him just the man for the job. He had designed and organise the construction of the device Mrs Chesney had received yesterday for disrupting her neighbour's daily injection of soap. Now he just needed paying for services rendered.

'Well I best do that right away before I get started.'

'Fine.' She pulled a strange face, hawked and spat a great wad of phlegm into the sink. Returning to the table where the bowl of steaming greenie-brown liquid waited, she pulled the towel back round, and continued with her deep breathing.

Ben had accepted the challenge, after all, how difficult could it be? He had been a postman after he had resigned from the SAS. Now he just had to come up with a solution.

Leaving the house he moved along the road into town, but did so in a zig-zag fashion, comparing the symbol on the envelope directly with what was on each gate or door.

Eleven and twelve were more obviously wrong, because he was just about able to acknowledge that they were double-digit numbers, whereas the Mr Tunn's letter bore a single digit.

Reaching number nine he stopped and looked. This looked like it, but he wanted to be sure. He wished Mrs Chesney had spoken the number, but he didn't feel he could ask when it was clearly written on the envelope. That might have enabled him to count along the street from Mrs Chesney's, which he remembered was 12.

Holding the letter right next to the figure on the gate and flicking his eyes from one to the other, then attempting to stare at them both at the same time, he felt confident enough to go to the door.

At the door he carried out the same routine having lost his previous certainty on his way up the path. Regaining his confidence he posted the letter, but found himself looking at the other numbers on the gates as he continued on along the road, now keeping to the odd side.

Though it was only a matter of seconds before he was looking across at number six he could not recognise it as the figure he'd had on the envelope.

Number nine was the house of Mr and Mrs Simms. Mr Simms had started working very long days doing all the overtime he could manage, coming home shattered.

On the one hand this seemed justified because they did need the money, what with Mrs Simms not working. However, she was going stir crazy with their colic tormented baby boy. He wailed with discomfort almost twenty-four/seven, with little relief provided by his medicines.

To make life more of a torment to Mrs Simms, she had until recently been a total crack addict.

Shortly after she had tested pregnant, she agreed to go on a detox program, but only after substantial family pressure, even though she really did want what was best for the baby, in hindsight.

It had proven an extremely difficult ordeal, but she had shown her commitment to getting clean and having a baby.

However, now that he clearly wasn't in the best of health, she found herself looking into the abyss of despair, into the welcoming, engulfing depths beyond. Her craving for a hit was an overpowering need they could not afford to support.

So it did not help matters to find an anonymous envelope with ten twenty-pound notes inside, just lying on the hallway carpet.

She stepped out of the front door, money in one hand, envelope in the other, mouth gaping. She saw no one around.

She looked back at her now trembling hands, guessing that it must actually belong to her neighbour at number 6 across the way.

Lips quivering, she urged herself to be strong, and return it. Pulling the door to, the child's wailing was cut off, and the sudden relief to her senses was so powerful she cried.

Mrs Simms shuffled slowly to the gate, sobbing. On the pavement she clicked the gate shut then headed for Dunston.

The chicken was no big problem, white meat, not with the fish, which Ben could smell. He was more concerned about what else was on the list.

There was nothing for it but to ask someone. He decided his line would have to be that he was shopping for an old woman, whose handwriting he couldn't make out.

It was pretty much the truth, but with the emphasis on *old woman* to redirect the blame. However, thinking that excuse through, he had no idea whether the writing actually *was* legible or not.

'I want toys!' A little lad yelled at his father as Ben drew near.

'You have enough toys,' explained his father.

'I want them *all*!!' the two and a half year old raged.

'Give him a braying,' encouraged a man, failing to deal with a hangover.

'Ignore him,' advised Ben.

'Which one?'

'Both of them.'

Feeling ignored and seeing that his father was now distracted by the big man with a list, the lad wandered off.

12

Mrs Chesney stared at the shopping long and hard, wondering if she was going mad. Turkey, goats milk, malted brown loaf, and more. This wasn't what she had asked for *at all*.

Either Ben was pulling a prank, though he did not seem like the sort of person to do such things, or else, he could not read, which also seemed unlikely.

She considered what other evidence there might be of this latter conclusion, and remembered the box of tricks she had asked him to set up yesterday.

When she went upstairs to check, she found the device in Frank's room, and took it to the spare room, with its instructions, muttering 'If you want something doing properly....'

Having set things up to ruin her neighbour's favourite program, day after day, she went to ask Ben why he hadn't owned up to a disability. She found him standing at the window of the extension looking at the view up the Tyne valley.

'You really do have a splendid view now from this window, Mrs Chesney.'

'I know. It used to belong to number ten.'

'Come again?' Ben turned to frown at her.

'I've had you build this extension to devalue my next door neighbour's property.'

'Well, number ten couldn't have been too fussed about it or they would have fought the planning permission.'

'Oh she'll be fussed about it alright. But after what her husband's doing time for, GBH, she mustn't have thought she had much right to complain.'

'Sorry, I don't follow.'

'I used to love my little kitchen garden. Home-grown produce always seems to taste better than shop bought. For some reason though, we don't get a lot of earth worms in this soil, to aerate the ground.

'So I would tend to my crops by turning over what soil I could with a hand fork. Unfortunately this was to be the cause of a number of run-ins with Oscar the Jack Russell, at number ten.'

'Oh.' Ben nodded, remembering a prior mention. 'Oscar.'

'The little shit would quietly wait in ambush, and when I got close to the fence, its snarling little snout would fly underneath, as far as it could go, snapping and yapping. I told Mr and Mrs Kendal on a number of occasions about their nasty little dog, and advised them to do something about it before I did.

'Of course they just laughed and said *Oscar wouldn't hurt a fly*. But one day it nipped my glove and almost tugged it off my hand. In my fury, I didn't waste a second.

'His attack would always work up into a frenzy, with him pushing his snout under again and again, gnashing and gnashing, so close to my veg. It is amazing how such a small animal can be so belligerent, and just how easily a spade chops right through a canine snout.

'A two to three-inch section of upper and lower jaw remained my side of the fence and I can tell you, that felt *good*. To be honest the pitiful squealing from the other side of the fence just made me smile. But then the commotion increased in volume with the nightmare neighbours next door.

'*He* came storming round, battered down my back gate, hurling abuse, and shoving me over onto my onions. Then just as *she* arrived, dead dog in hand, he grabbed my spade.

'*She* screamed at him as he lifted it above his head in blind rage. I tried to roll aside as he brought it down, but I wasn't quick enough.'

Ben let out the air he had unconsciously retained in his cheeks.

'The flat of that spade came down again and again and again. I've been wheelchair-bound ever since.'

'I never knew.'

'Really?'

Mrs Simms blew the full two hundred quid with the dealer, returning home on cloud-nine even before she indulged.

She split the crack into two hits and took one immediately, just to cope with the ceaseless wailing from the cot. Only then did she try and offer her baby comfort. To her mind it was just like the priorities advice given on the airlines. Sort yourself out before your child.

Even in her altered state, the child's habitual screaming ground her down. By the time she had changed his nappy, with no abating of noise, she had forgotten that she had already taken her first hit.

So it was little surprise that in her confusion, her need drove her to overdose. It was also little surprise that when Mr Simms arrived home, his distraught wife was in a heaven called 'coma'.

The ambulance turned up before eleven, and this time Mr Cunningham across at number 7 was better prepared, but sadly not in terms of his medication.

Wasting no time he opened up his bedroom window, and opened up on the ambulance, shooting out the rear tyres. The paramedics who had been about to attend to Mrs Simms dived back into the vehicle for cover and called in the attack.

Fifteen minutes later the Armed Response Unit was positioned at front and back, allowing the paramedics to enter number 9 from the rear, just in time to witness the final moment of a seizure, as Mrs Simms decided she wasn't coming back.

Negotiations with Mr Cunningham began by loud-hailer, for the whole street to hear. Mr. Cunningham's rambling replies inferred that there was a possible Mr Gibbs involved. A possible hostage situation, which put a different angle on things.

'We don't want to take you away Mr Cunningham.' Replied the officer in charge, tactfully leaving off the rest of the sentence which would have gone along the lines of '….But now we're going to have to.'

'They are poisoning me! They've already gotten to Gibbsie. Turned him! Now he's not talking!'

Did this mean he had already killed the hostage?

Mr Tunn, inquisitive about what was going on over the road, decided to use his need to call on Mrs Chesney for his money, as an excuse to get a closer look at the situation, and maybe even ask one of those flak-jacketed officers.

He quietly opened the front door, stepped out onto his doormat and pulled his door closed.

Unfortunately, to Mr Cunningham's ears, the door latch sounded not unlike a round being chambered, which changed the ball game.

The bullet from number 7 tore right through Mr Tunn's chest, rendering his note for the milkman less than readable, and dropping him dead on his roses.

The shot was like a starting pistol and the ARU were off, taking out the bedroom window, surrounding brickwork, Mr Cunningham, and as luck would have it the Andean wind chimes at number 5.

Adam had walked into town from the McGregor's before Ben had left for work. He had told them he needed some air, but would pick up a taxi from Central Station. However, truth be told, he was in no hurry to get back home to the scene of crime. He found himself walking north east, out through Ponteland, where he had some lunch. Leaving Ponteland he stuck out a thumb and started hitching.

Hitching was rarely done these days, because there were so many dodgy people about, hitching or offering lifts. So it took him a while to get a lift. The first lift only got him so far though. Two further lifts later he had to walk the final five miles. That's what you get for living in the back of beyond. Mind you, he might have got a lift to the door if he hadn't opened up about what had happened with Toyah, to all of them.

It had rained at some point because not only were the forensic tent and marker flags gone there was no trace of his spilled blood. Toyah's car had been taken away, but tyre marks were left in the gravel from the recovery vehicle. Adam sighed. At some point he was going to have to visit Toyah's parents. His stomach began to churn and instead of going into the house he went round the back into the garden.

He found himself battling his way down the overgrown path beyond the lawn, which led to the river and Obsession. When he caught sight of his barge his heart sank further, if that were possible.

'Shit.'

Boarding his tilting vessel he immediately slipped on the algae coated decking and landed on his arse.

'Serves you right,' he cursed himself then patted the decking. 'Sorry old girl.'

Getting to his feet he knew there would be days of work here to get her right again, but first off he needed to get her bilges emptied. For that he needed her keys, which were up in the garage.

Walking back through the garden he decided that between *Obsession* and work there should be enough to keep his mind occupied and off the tormenting replays of Toyah's death.

Inside the garage he went across to the wall where he kept various keys and spotted the wrapped Flintstone on the bed of the milling machine. He hesitated for a moment then picked it up. His hand began to tremble like he had trapped a nerve.

'Do I *really* need this right now?'

Adam *never* needed it, but it didn't stop the stones appearing. He untied the string then unwrapped the newspaper. Turning the stone over to reveal the verse etched into the black flint beneath the white limestone, he read out aloud.

'Too late this time
The murder of your lover,
Don't delay a Flintstone
When you get another.'

Adam's first thought was that if only he had read the Flintstone as soon as he found it, Toyah might still be alive. But then he considered that probably was not true. This was the first time a Flintstone had referred to a past event. Then he wondered whether it would have carried a different message had he read it when he was meant to. Possibly. The whole Flintstone thing was still a mystery to him after all these years.

13

Adam rang Ben the following morning to say he felt he needed another day off, so could Ben continue with Mrs Chesney's extension.

Ben seemed understanding, though he now wanted *crazy woman's* job over with asap. For that he needed the van load of tools to make much progress but didn't feel he could pressure Adam much more.

Though work might have helped Adam keep his mind occupied there was a consuming sense of guilt over the state of *Obsession* and he wanted to spend the day cleaning her up instead.

Placing all the cleaning gear on the bank, Adam gingerly boarded the stern. Even though the decking was now level since he had emptied the bilges the day before, there was still the film of algae to take care of. A mop wouldn't do, he had to get down on hands and knees to scrub the surfaces clean.

Taking a break, halfway down the barge, sitting on the roof and looking out at the river, he remembered the day he had seen a suitcase floating down the river. He had fished it out with one of his pole hooks. Inside had been a Flintstone. These messages appeared by all sorts of means, in all sorts of places, and it was a constant frustration that he could not explain how, or why.

Prior to the Flintstone through the garage window, the last one had turned up while digging out the foundation channels from what had been Mrs Chesney's kitchen garden. Wiping it clean, confirming there was a verse etched into it, but trying not to act strange in front of Ben, because these stones defied rational explanation.

It read:

Gun in hand
He enters the barn,
Suffer no more
Intent to harm.

Making his excuses to Ben, Adam had taken off with the van heading for the nearest place he might expect to find a barn. However, he knew that there was no real need to rush. He had learned in his youth that whatever the situation was it would happen as it was meant to happen. Nevertheless, he always wanted these situations over with.

The third barn he had come to, somewhere out near Chopwell, had the latest model VW beetle parked on the lane outside, which he pulled up directly behind.

There had been nobody at the other two, but this one promised to be different. It was an old wooden barn, quite romantic looking. So romantic in fact that a young man and woman already rolled around naked and giggling in the hay-loft.

Their giggling hushed though, as the scraping of the heavy door alerted them to another's presence entering the barn.

In the loft they froze, the young man losing his erection even before he could raise his index finger to his lips. The young woman's eyes were wide as she unconsciously drew a lock of long blonde hair from her mouth, while searching blindly behind her for her clothes.

'Don't do it,' pleaded a voice from outside.

'Who do you think you are? Barging onto my property? I don't know you from Adam,' demanded the second voice.

'I *am* Adam. I want to help.'

'It doesn't take two to fire a shotgun. Now run along, there's a good chap.'

'I'm not going till you calm down.'

'I'm done with calm. I'm putting an end to the shamefulness.'

'What shamefulness?'

'Munchausen's Syndrome by Proxy.'

'Look. Legal problems can be resolved without making them worse.'

'Legal Problems?! Have you any idea what Munchausen's Syndrome by Proxy is?'

'Not…exactly.'

The two in the hay loft listened to the bizarre conversation unfolding below.

'Our first child fell dreadfully ill when only a few months old, my wife and I did all we could for our little daughter. The doctors were all at a loss. Pat couldn't have given little Ellie more attention, but our child died.

'The doctors and nurses all commended Pat. We had a second child. Lightning never strikes twice and all that, but she fell ill just the same, the whole nightmare replaying itself.

'The doctors could see there was something wrong. The fever, the gagging, but could do nothing to stop the sickness. Millie was actually on the mend in hospital, but as soon as she returned home her health deteriorated rapidly.

'I thought it might be some sort of allergy. I checked her toys, the paint on the walls, the pillows. I even vacuumed her room every day. But she died.

'Then our little boy, Tom, died recently. But now we know what the problem has been.'

'Well isn't that a good thing?'

'I found out my wife was poisoning his meals! She said she craved the praise she received, for the attention she pretended to be giving the children. I'd never questioned it before. All my little children died because I never questioned her!!'

The barrels were in his mouth and a shot fired before the deeply shocked Adam could do anything. Brain matter flew from the top of the falling man's body, and screaming filled the air as two naked, but blood-splattered and shot-peppered bodies tumbled from the loft.

These Flintstones were like obligatory invites to real-life horror shows, which Adam could do little about, unless it was fate that he should do so. However, even on those occasions when he decided he would run away, for fear of the verse, the knowledge that his attention was required always drew him back. It seemed to be some sort of preordained balance for the luck he experienced in other ways.

He had once had a small win on the lottery which had helped him set up his business. He had escaped being involved in a multiple pile-up on the M6, and once dug up a leather pouch filled with old gold coins. But maybe he was fooling himself maybe that was the sort of random luck everyone had.

Adam considered that maybe it was time he sought help. But who should he turn to. Ben?

Adam decided to go below deck and make himself a cuppa. Reaching the galley, he was disturbed to see, inside the pint glass he had placed in the sink after its weathering by the wheel, there was now another Flintstone.

'No…So soon?'

Gathering strength to confront the verse, Adam reached into the glass to retrieve his next *calling*.

He just wished it would be something positive for a change. Or even something that now pointed at Toyah's killer.

Ashes to ashes
Dust to dust,
Look out on Whitley Bay
With Ben you must.

14

Ben had done all he could now without the tools required for the rest of the job. He hoped Adam wasn't going to need more time off. He was considering calling it a day when Mrs Chesney called from downstairs.

'I've got some corned beef pie down here if you fancy some lunch, Benjamin?'

'It's not…' Ben found it irritating when she called his name wrong. He groaned.

'It is, a little bit out of date, yes. But should still be good for another week, or two.'

'I'm okay thanks.'

'Well I've got the kettle on.'

'Right. I'll have a coffee,' he said as he clumped down the stairs.

'No you won't.'

'What?'

'I'm out of coffee.'

'But I only just bought you some.'

'No. What you bought me was this.' She showed him the large jar.

'Yes?' Here we go, he thought.

'B I S T O,' she spelled it out, running a finger across the brand name.

'I can see that. But where's the coffee I got.'

'There wasn't any coffee and since I didn't ask for gravy granules I assumed you got this by mistake. Now either you're not thinking straight with Aiden off sick, or…'

'Adam.'

'Yes Adam. Which reminds me. I was thinking that this street has turned into a war zone while your boss has been away. Is that just a coincidence?'

'What else would it be?'

'A number of my neighbours have died, and not one of them a Kendal.'

'Well maybe your neighbour is up to something.'

'Could be, could be. However, if that were the case you would think I would be top of the list.'

'I wouldn't know.'

'No I think something else is going on here.'

'So tea then?' Ben tried changing the subject.

As Mrs Chesney poured the water onto the bag in the mug she raised another issue. 'That device I took delivery of and asked you to set up for me in the spare room.'

'Yes?'

'You plugged it in.'

'I did.'

'In Frank's room.'

'I thought it was your daughter's old room.'

'Don't let him hear you say that. I never had a daughter.'

The doorbell rang. Mrs Chesney handed Ben his tea in passing as she rolled to the door.

It was Adam.

'Feeling better?'

'Better?' Adam looked to Ben who was coming out of the kitchen mug in hand. His face gave nothing away as to what Mrs Chesney had been told.

'Yes. A little better thanks.'

'That's what I like to see. Someone who gets back to work as soon as they can.'

'Actually Mrs Chesney, I came to pick up Ben.'

'Not going to another job I hope.'

'Not exactly.'

'I wouldn't be happy if you were starting another job before finishing mine.'

'No, of course…We'll be back in the morning to get on top of things.'

As Adam drove them out of Gateshead they sat in silence. Ben had decided that all things considered it might be best to let Adam speak first, in his own good time. However, as they passed through Newcastle and onto the coast road, and beyond where Ben lived, he couldn't hold back any longer.

'Where are we going exactly?'

'Whitley Bay.'

'What for?'

'There's something I need to tell you. Something big.'

'You're letting me go.'

'Letting you go? Why would I let you go?'

'Because you are grieving, you have PTSD and you need to get away from here.'

'No. That's not it at all. I need your help with something. I'm still trying to decide how best to tell you.'

'It isn't about Toyah's murder then?'

'Actually it is all linked somehow.'

'I don't understand.'

'Well you wouldn't. I haven't told you yet.'

'No you haven't. You've left Meg and I guessing how Toyah died. The only clue we've had is that it must have been pretty gory going by how Mr Tanner reacted when he looked inside the forensic tent.'

'Mr Tanner?'

'Yes. The neighbour who gave Meg a lift and then brought you back to ours.'

'Oh yes, right. Well I don't know what *he* saw. The closest thing to gore would have been the blood from my wounds.' Adam raised his right hand slightly from the steering wheel for emphasis, in case Ben needed it to make the connections.

'Oh. So why did you turn that funny colour when you looked at that bacon the other morning?'

'Bacon?'

'Yes. When Meg said she would make you a bacon sandwich.'

'Right, no. It was the cling-film on it.'

'You've lost me.'

'Toyah was smothered to death by polythene.'

'What?...How? Was someone in the car with her?'

'No. She did it to herself.'

'But that's suicide then.'

'I know it looks that way but it was murder, and I have proof now.'

'So what are the police doing about it?'

'Nothing.'

'Why?'

'It's something I, *we*, have to get to the bottom of. Look, I'll explain it all, if I can, once we are through this traffic and on the promenade.'

15

There seemed to be quite a few people on the promenade for the middle of the week as Adam led Ben east from where he had parked up at Cullercoats.

Ben noticed that Adam's behaviour seemed to have turned more anxious. He kept looking around, up and down the street, and across the beach. The tide was on its way in so there were more people on the promenade than down there.

'Are you going to tell me what all this is about?'

'I will when we get to a secluded spot.'

'You are acting quite paranoid, you know.'

'I don't doubt it. I just hope you can take in what I have to tell you, and trust me enough to help.'

'Is it some government conspiracy? Was Toyah working for MI5?'

'No.'

'Or the KGB?'

'No, no. Nothing like that. She was just an accountant.'

'Who got mixed up with organised crime?'

'No. Stop trying to guess. She was an ordinary person.'

'So this was a random killing?'

'I don't think so. But we need more evidence to work out who is responsible.'

Adam brought them to a halt at a quiet spot; a section of promenade that was below the road. There was no one around except for a well-dressed woman in boots down on the rocky beach below, collecting things from among the boulders.

The moment had come to share with Ben what he had once confided in Toyah, he didn't expect Ben to be as open minded as her though. He procrastinated, slipping his day sack off his shoulder.

'Come on, spill the beans.' Ben was growing impatient.

'In a minute.'

'What's the problem? I'm all ears. There's no one else around, except that woman down there. Maybe she's a *spy*.'

'Don't take the piss Ben. This isn't easy for me. I don't think you will believe what I have to tell you and you're making it all the more difficult.'

'What, after all those stories you used to tell at Admissions?'

Adam reached into the bag and pulled out two cans of coke.

'*Now* who's taking the piss? Coke? Where's the beer?'

'I'm driving.'

'Yeah well *I'm* not.' Ben was thirsty so he opened the can and took a few gulps.

Adam was not so fast. He was more concerned about what he had to say.

'Since I was a young lad I began finding stones in odd places. Flintstones. The stones were etched into in such a way that the limestone revealed the dark flint below.'

Though Ben said nothing Adam hoped he had taken that much on board.

'What was always etched into one side of each Flintstone was a verse, a warning that rhymed.'

'Who etched them?'

'I don't know. The rhymes often concerned the fate of others, as if looking to me to prevent each fate.'

'So you became a secret hero.' Ben took a few more gulps.

'No. This isn't some fantasy. It's a very real nightmare. Most people I try to help die, or at least get badly hurt, despite the warning. As if I am only intended to witness what happens.'

'So you think with my help you might change that?'

'Yes. I hope so. Before Toyah died, I found that one of these Flintstones had been hurled through my garage window. Not thinking in a million years it was anything to do with Toyah I ignored it because I didn't want its message to ruin our anniversary.'

'She put it through your window?'

'No.'

'Well why don't you and me wait around for who brings you the next one?'

'It's really not that simple Ben. They never appear in the same place twice. And whoever places them must be watching my every move and know exactly where I will be and when.'

'Why would anyone go to all that trouble?'

'Beats me.'

'Have you brought the stone from the garage?'

'No, I should have, shouldn't I.'

'D'you think?'

'However, I have brought one that has appeared since.' Adam reached into his bag.

'Have you got another can of Coke in there?' Ben asked, crumpling his empty and looking round for a bin.

'Sure.' Adam tried to hand Ben another can but watched as Ben walked over to the lifebelt and tried to find an opening to put the can into. 'That's not a bin, Ben. It's a lifebelt station.'

'Oh.' Ben came back for the second can handing Adam the crumpled one.

Putting the rubbish in his bag Adam continued, 'The message on the Flintstone in the garage which I did not check till after Toyah was dead said *Too late this time The murder of your lover, Don't delay a Flintstone When you get another.*

'That's the first time ever I received one that made reference to the past. Which suggests that…'

'…Whoever is watching you Adam, they knew that you wouldn't read this one till after Toyah had died. How could anyone know that?'

'Exactly. Like when we were digging out the ground for Mrs Chesney's foundations and I had to rush off. I'd unearthed a Flintstone warning of a suicide in a barn. How could anyone know it would be me digging there, and not you? Have you ever come across a Flintstone when you were with me and just never thought to mention it Ben?'

'No. I'm sorry Adam. It's surely some sort of delusion, otherwise I'd have to say it sounds like David Blaine has got it in for you. Maybe that's it, you're going to find it is some long-term prank and they are doing a whole TV show on you. Hidden camera's everywhere.'

'What? And killing people? Now *that's* delusional.'

'Unless they are only special effects dead.'

'Ridiculous.'

'Yeah, sorry.' Ben gulped down a few more mouthfuls of his coke and turned to look across the beach. The woman had moved further out and got up on top of the concrete outflow. Heading down towards the waves, she was walking awkwardly. 'So have you got one of your Flintstones in there or what?'

'Yes.' Adam pulled out the stone and handed it to Adam.

He rolled it over and saw markings on the side. He ran his thumb over the texture, but that's all it was to him. He couldn't read what it said. He would have to trust Adam. 'So what does it say?'

'Oh, of course, sorry…It says:

Ashes to ashes
Dust to dust,
Look out on Whitley Bay
With Ben you must.

'Sounds like it was written by Yoda. Maybe you have the force young Underwood.'

'Be serious Ben… What is that woman up to?'

They both looked at her stumbling further out along the outflow.

'Hey! Lady!' Ben bellowed, but she continued towards the waves oblivious.

'I think she might be going to jump in Ben.'

'Not if I can help it,' Ben promised as he went into action. He dashed to the lifebelt and tore it loose. It felt round so it had to be the right bit. Wasting no more time he started to run alongside the railings. He couldn't see steps or a ladder. Maybe they were there, maybe they weren't. How did the woman get down there?

There was no time to wonder, the surf was lapping at the woman's boots. She only slowed momentarily.

Like an action hero Ben just leaped over the railings and dropped a good five metres to the beach, attempting a para-roll at the bottom. He cracked his head off a boulder and lost grip of the lifebelt. Picking himself up, dazed, he looked around for the lifebelt, blinking. Where was the ring among the boulders? Focusing on the colour orange he got it then rushed stumbling across the slippery rocks towards the woman, now up to her thighs in the sea.

Then it happened. The jolt from the long drop and roll must have set off a chain reaction with the two cans of coke as sure as if he had swallowed a Mentos mint along with it. Coke roared up Ben's throat and shot out of both nostrils like rocket thrusters. His nose and eyes burned. He couldn't see. He stumbled blindly and fell.

Watching from the promenade, feeling useless, leaving a man with cognitive challenges to play the hero, Adam wondered what was going on now. There seemed to be no way Ben could get to the woman in time. He might be ex-SAS but it was like fate was obstructing the rescue.

Emptying the contents of his stomach to prevent a repeat eruption and blinking to clear his eyes, Ben scrambled desperately for the outflow. Getting up onto the concrete he could still see the woman ahead. There was still a chance.

Ben raced along the outflow and into the surf carrying the ring and calling out. Then she was gone. She must have stepped off the side of the outflow he realised. She had vanished like a stone.

Ben started to swim to where he thought the woman had gone down. There was no bobbing head. He abandoned the ring and tried diving down, but he could see nothing in the dark water.

After some minutes, with the tide continuing to come in, Ben knew there was nothing more he could do.

He came out onto the beach and finally found a way back up. Stepping onto the promenade he could see flashing blue lights arrive. Adam had called the emergency services when Ben had jumped from the promenade. It was up to them to take it from there.

When Ben was dropped off at home, still soaking wet, he just had time to get a hot shower and head back out to collect Robbie from school. The wet clothes had reminded him of being on tour in Ireland.

He picked up his son without any trouble. The trouble started when he got back, or to be more precise when Meg got back.

'Hello Luv,' she greeted as she passed the lounge, heading for the kitchen with Beth in tow.

'Hi,' Ben called back from the sofa. He heard her turning the fan-oven on then unpacking shopping and putting it away. He continued watching the TV.

Meg growled and started cursing and shortly came into the lounge. Turning to look he saw her expression change from one of frustration to concern. She reached out to his head. Ben had a welt over his right brow. 'What happened to you?'

'Oh I ur…nothing.'

'Don't *nothing* me Ben.'

'Well you know how it is. I walked into a window frame thinking it was a door.'

'Ben McGregor!' It sounded more accusatory than sympathetic.

'What?'

'You're lying.'

'No Luv.'

'I can see it in your face.'

'I don't know what you mean.'

'So why are there work clothes, lying sopping wet, in the oven?' Robbie and Beth came into the lounge to watch their dad, not the TV.

'I…didn't want to worry you.'

'Worry me? You always worry me. The truth this time and it better be good.'

'Dad got hit on the head chasing a woman on the beach,' said Robbie unhelpfully.

'What?!'

'No! It wasn't like that,' Ben glared at Robbie. 'I mean, Dad was doing lifeguard rescue but fell.'

'Robbie, shut up!' Ben and Meg said at the same time.

'A woman was walking into the sea. I had to jump off the promenade to save her but hit my head on a rock, then coke came out of my nose and by the time I got into the surf she had drowned.'

Meg stood there, mouth gaping, trying to decide whether this was the truth.

'You never told me she died Dad. Or that you'd been doing coke.'

'Coca cola.'

'Oh.'

'What on Earth were you doing at the beach?' Meg managed to ask.

'Adam took me there for a chat.'

'A chat? What about?'

Ben reckoned that if Meg had trouble believing the rescue story, there was no way she was going to go for the Flintstones. He was still cynical about that himself.

'Have a heart Luv, Adam's still grieving.'

'Of course. Sorry…So you just *happened* to be there when this poor woman drowned herself?'

'Yes.' It seemed best to just agree.

16

The sand beneath Adam's feet was toasty warm. Led on by Toyah's hand and seductive laughter they raced across the beach into the clear blue Mediterranean. The contrast of the cool water woke him.

The duvet had slipped off. As Adam reached out for it he realised the bed next to him was empty and reality hit like a train. Adam wept like a child. He missed Toyah so much.

He had kept things bottled up the best he could, by keeping busy with the barge and work, but it kept bursting out of him, with screams and tears. At least he wasn't waking anyone else with his grieving and thankfully he had not dreamed of her dying this time.

He sat on the edge of the bed, face in his hands chest heaving with the pain. He considered whether it might be better to go back to living on his barge. Just for a while anyway, to escape the constant reminders of Toyah in the house.

He knew that wasn't really going to work though. He had promised Toyah's elderly parents that he would sort all her stuff out, at his and at hers, so that they only had to come up for her cremation.

Calming himself and wiping away the tears, Adam looked at his watch on the bedside table. 2:33. No time like the present, he thought, since he wasn't likely to get back to sleep now, after that outpouring.

He shifted to Toyah's side of the bed and switched on the lamp. He took a paper hanky and blew his nose, then opened the draw in her bedside table.

It was a very tidy draw. The items were organised to some logic of Toyah's no doubt. There was a jar of Vick's and a pack of Honey and Lemon Strepsils at the back, a pencil and pad in the middle and some business cards to the front. Picking out the cards, Adam thought they were likely all accountancy clients, but noticed one of them was a contact in mental health services.

Were they an accounts client also, or had Toyah finally been seeing someone about her claustrophobia and OCD? She had never mentioned it if she had.

Adam examined the top sheet of the pad, but there was nothing there. Then he thought to turn the pad over. It looked like something had been written on that side and the sheet removed. He took the pencil and lightly scribbled from one side of the pad to the other and back. It revealed a name and mobile number.

He had never heard Toyah mention a Nadine before. She could be anyone, and it was far too early to be ringing her anyway.

He tore off the sheet with the details on and put it on his bedside table. Then he got up, put his dressing gown on from behind the bedroom door, and went in search of an empty box for Toyah's belongings.

Mrs Chesney was glad to see Adam return in the morning with Ben.

'Did you get your other client sorted?'

'What other client?' Adam frowned.

'The one you had to go see yesterday.'

'She wasn't a client.' Ben said without thinking first.

'Who was *she* then?'

'Urr,' Adam stared at Ben, 'A maiden in distress.'

'Yeah. Up to her armpits in water.' Ben stared back at Adam and shrugged an apology for not shutting up.

'Sounds like she needed a plumber,' suggested Mrs Chesney.

'More like a lifeguard,' said Ben.

'Ha ha ha! You lads crack me up.' She rolled down the hallway into the kitchen but span around as she reached the lino flooring. 'Oh, Adam. When you have a spare moment I want a word.'

'Okay, Mrs Chesney.'

As they headed upstairs with their tools Ben offered, 'If she wants a word, I can think of a few choice ones.'

'So what is it Mrs. Chesney?' Adam finally asked as he came down to put the kettle on.

'There's no coffee.'

'Oh.'

'Would you like some gravy instead?'

'What?'

'What sort of education has young Benjamin had?'

Adam frowned again. 'I don't follow.' It sounded like she was talking about someone he didn't know.

'Are you aware that your partner cannot read?'

'Oh I see. Ha yeah, right…He has brain damage.'

'Brain damage? From birth?'

'No. An accident…We think.'

'You think?'

'None of us are sure exactly what happened. He had retrograde amnesia following a cracked skull. They had to put a plate in.' Adam tapped the side of his head.

'Poor lad. You never said.'

'No, well, he's a hard worker.'

'You mean you can't be seen to discriminate in this day and age.'

'No I don't think I mean that at all.'

'Well he must require a lot of supervision.'

'What makes you say that?'

'When you were away I sent him shopping. When I saw what he had bought I might as well have sent him to bingo.'

The next day Adam and Ben laid the carpets in the extension, upstairs and down, and the job was done.

'What do you think Mrs Chesney?'

'Excellent job.'

'Right well I'll put the invoice in the post. Would you like us to move some of the furniture in while we're here?'

'No, no. It's fine just as it is.'

'What?'

'We'll be off then.' Ben gestured with a swing of his head as a prompt to Adam not to get involved. Then Ben reached down for the toolbox, which he had left resting against his leg so that he would remain sure what it was.

Climbing into the van, Adam looked at Ben. 'So what was all that about?'

'Mrs Chesney is a regular fucking head-case, that's what.'

'Why didn't she want any furniture moved in? Is she getting new stuff?' Adam sensed not.

'This whole job has been about devaluing the neighbour's property in revenge for breaking her back. Nothing more.'

'Well, as long as she pays the bill. And as long as her son is no worse.'

'Frank? Why?' Ben remembered what he thought of Frank's bedroom.

'Mrs Chesney has suggested he might be putting some work our way.'

Encouraged by his mother's account of Ben and Adam's professional shortcomings, Frank Chesney rang Adam on his mobile and arranged a meeting in the bar at the Baltic Gallery, to discuss another job he had to offer them.

That evening he described the *Eco Beech* project, which he had been subcontracted to complete by *Earth Calling*, an Ecological Architectural firm in Durham.

The building site was near Hamsterley Forest, surrounded by beech woodlands to the East, and looking out onto the rolling moors to the West. The project was over-due and already over budget, which was good news for Frank and his boys. However, the site manager wanted to avoid further embarrassment with *Earth Calling*. He asked Frank to get more labour on site, in order to catch up on the deadline.

In hindsight, *Earth Calling*, who were new to the game, should have had completion penalties written into the contract, but their contract had naively relied upon trust.

Frank clearly loved his work but chose not to discuss the finer points of his business plan with Adam and Ben. Instead he encouraged them to come and see the project themselves in a day or two. The evening then slipped into Frank telling yarns about his mother and him.

The story telling and the beers reminded Adam and Ben of the old days. Although *Admissions* had gotten out of hand with dire consequences, there had been fun along the way. On a high from the drink and the apparently pleasant company, Adam and Ben accepted the offer of further work and shook on it.

Frank put on a cheerful business smile as he visualised his problem client, once again in check.

17

Adam was surprised by how soon it was after he had contacted the Mental Health Services on Toyah's card that he was given an appointment. He had expected more than the three week wait it would typically take to see his local GP.

Two days later he was welcomed into a building on the edge of Newcastle University campus.

'Hello, I am Professor Henderson.'

Adam shook the Professor's offered hand. 'Professor?'

'Yes. I'm an academic.'

'Oh. I thought you would be a Doctor.'

Adam was shown into a lounge-like room.

'I'm a Clinical Psychologist. Please, take a seat.'

Adam sat in a comfy chair and immediately noticed a mirror taking up a large section of the wall to his left.

'I want you to relax, Adam. We are here to listen and help.'

'We?'

'Yes. A number of my students are behind the mirror, taking notes. We hold a confidential discussion of cases afterwards. As well as this being part of their learning it has been found to be quite an insightful process. The sharing of different perspectives, has sometimes led to better tailored counsel being provided to clients. However, I still have the final say on how we proceed with cases. You will never meet any of my students. Your sessions, if you agree to proceed, will be just between you and I. Are you comfortable with this arrangement, Adam?'

'I'm not sure that I like the idea of being watched by *unknowns*.'

'I assure you the self-consciousness wears off. However, if you choose to decline our offer of support you can of course arrange private support elsewhere, but that would be a service with a payment plan and there are long waiting lists for many local services.'

'Right well maybe it would help if you describe how you intend to proceed with me.'

'Okay, well initially we require some background. So this first session would provide us with a sense of you as an individual, as a backdrop to the problem or problems you are experiencing.'

'Do you mean like personality tests?'

'Not exactly. We get a sense of who you are by how you talk about yourself and others. Also by watching your non-verbal communications, like body language, facial expression and such.

'If you describe more than one issue needing resolution we look to agree a priority order for addressing these, so that we are not trying to deal with too many things at once.'

'But what if issues are closely linked?'

'If they cannot be teased apart then, of course, we would have to deal with their interrelationship.'

'Right. And what happens if you don't believe I'm being honest with you in what I describe?'

'Well it would be unhelpful if you persisted in false responses and would waste all of our time. However, it is commonplace for people to be somewhat untruthful at the start of opening up. Some people don't even realise that they are lying to themselves and others about certain aspects until some way into their journey. So Adam, what would you say brought you here?'

'Grieving for my girlfriend, particularly because of the circumstances of her death. I am tormented by nightmares. A friend suggested it could be PTSD.'

'PTSD?'

Adam could not read the Professor's poker-face but her query suggested an assumption might have been made on his part.

'Yes, but *I* wouldn't know. It just feels like it could be the final straw.'

'The final straw? So you are saying there are some issues that precede your partner's death?'

'Definitely.'

'Can you elaborate?' The expectation was that Adam would now describe something of his relationship with Toyah.

'Since I was a child I became aware of a sort of yin and yang to my life experiences. I have incredible luck at times, which has saved me from injury and even death, and helped me to win things. But this has come at a cost. I have had to witness a significant number of traumatic events, mostly involving strangers.'

'And that would be the bad luck.'

'Yes. The worst luck was finding my girlfriend suffocated to death. I cannot get the images out of my head. It was made to look like a suicide but I'm convinced it was murder.'

'Do you feel to blame in any way for her death?'

'To blame? No!'

'Sometimes the mind can remember experiences differently, to ease the pain, or hold to a belief.'

'No. The Flintstones confirmed it was murder.'

'I'm sorry, the Flintstones? Cartoon characters?'

'No, no. This is the bit I do not expect you to believe. I find pieces of flint that have verses etched into them, telling me to do things.'

'Telling you to do things? Like what?'

Saying this out loud under observation it struck Adam that it sounded like a version of *voices in my head*. 'Directing me to find someone before it's too late. Only…every time I get there, nothing I do seems to prevent their death. It's like I am meant to equate my good luck to the cost of other's lives.'

'So let me get this straight. You believe that every time you have a bit of good luck you then receive a Flintstone requiring you to witness a death?'

'Not quite. Neither the instances of luck or the appearance of Flintstones appear closely linked. They seem random. I guess I have chosen to believe over many years there is a yin and yang balance of these instances.'

'I see.'

'I *can* create demonstrations of my luck…Do you have a kitchen here?'

'We do.'

'Do you have a chopping board and knife?'

'Mr Underwood, you don't seriously expect me to provide you with a knife?'

'Oh, okay, look I will describe what happens and let you decide. First we drop the knife onto the board to test its weighting, to see that the blade sticks into the board, that it doesn't turn as it falls. Then I place my hand on the chopping board. Palm down, fingers spread. I hold the knife above the back of the hand and drop it. The blade always falls between the fingers. It never results in injury.'

'Sounds like a party trick. What if you close your fingers together?'

'Then the knife turns and the handle hits the hand.'

'But you said the knife would be tested and found not to turn over.'

'I know, right.'

'What if you lower the height the knife is dropped from?'

'That's where it gets freaky. The knife can be seen to move sideways as it falls.'

Professor Henderson tore the top sheet off her note pad and offered it to Adam with her pen. 'What if you use these?'

Adam shook his head, not even attempting to take the pen and pad. 'It won't work. It only works where there is potential for physical harm to me.'

'I see. But you also said it sometimes involved winning. What if we get you a scratch card?'

Adam shook his head. 'Again. The winning only works if it resolves potential for physical harm to me, or enables destiny.'

'Only you? I see. So you can never use your good luck to save the people you witness die?'

'Unfortunately, that is correct.'

'Did you ever try putting yourself in harm's way so that the person was saved?'

'Yes. In one case, a young man jumped in front of a Metro train, off a station platform. As I was prepared for something of this nature by the Flintstone I jumped after him and yanked him over to the clear tracks on the other side, just as the train pulled in. But the lad had a seizure and died.'

'Are they always suicides?'

'Often but not always.'

'Have there been suicides in your close family, Adam?'

'No. Only death by natural causes. Father to cancer, mother to heart attack. No brothers or sisters.'

'You seem quite sincere about everything you have told me so far, though certainly aspects of your experiences are difficult to accept. However, one way of looking at this is that by the distribution of probabilities some people have much luckier or more unlucky lives than others. In your case, this being rather extreme, it has created a sense of the abnormal.'

'Well it certainly isn't *normal*, is it?' Adam reached into his jacket pocket, noting a possible flash of concern in the professor's eyes. 'This is one of the Flintstones.'

It was the stone Adam had shown Ben at the coast. Professor Henderson turned the heavy stone over and examined it closely.

'I don't know much about the likes of art and design, Adam, but couldn't this be created in a workshop?'

'Possibly, but by whom? And more to the point, since I have dug some of these up from the ground, how long ago were they placed there? And how was it known that I would find each Flintstone at the right time?'

'I don't believe such a thing can be possible, certainly not in any repeatable sense. What I might suggest is that the way you are experiencing and remembering these instances must surely be at odds with what has actually happened.'

'Are you saying I'm going mad?'

'Let's not get into labelling, Adam. You *are* clearly disturbed by your experiences. That's why you chose to come here. What we intend to offer is a process for getting you through this, to a happier place.'

Adam relaxed a little, with a sigh and a nod. 'Well as long as you don't think I'm a hopeless case.'

'No, Adam. While you remain open-minded there is hope. Let's meet again in two days.'

As Adam left through reception, having booked his next appointment he was struck by the thought that Professor Henderson was wrong. There was only hope of resolving this if *she* remained open-minded.

18

Adam took Ben to the *Earth Calling* meeting at Hamsterley Forest, where they met Frank again. Cameron, the Site Manager first took them to an area of raised ground. From there they viewed the extensive site and listened to Cameron's description of the *Eco Beech* project.

'The concept of *Eco Beech* is to use both woodland and moorland to provide a number of first-hand experiences of the ecological relationships present in such terrain. There will be a range of activities for all ages around the park, and in the visitor centre we will have a cinema. It will loop a film showing how humankind can better integrate with nature without damaging the ecology. It will involve environments around the world from inner cities to small-holdings. It is intended to be an uplifting experience for visitors, providing a sense of hope for our future in these dark times.

'The visitor centre will demonstrate many aspects of the latest in green architecture and technologies. To inspire more responsible ways of thinking about the environments we live, work, and play in.'

'So which bit would we be working on?' Adam asked. 'Landscaping in the park area?'

'No. The most urgent priority for *Eco Beech* is completing the visitor centre. The ecological edutainment park is slightly longer term. We need the centre completed asap so that we can get staff in and trained up.'

'So what key skills are you short of here?' Asked Ben, concerned by his shortcomings and feeling out of his depth with the size of this project.

'Oh Cameron just needs extra hands-on.' Frank jumped in.

'I guess so,' Cameron nodded, 'Though someone with experience of thermal power would be a real bonus. Our thermal engineer has been off sick ever since she returned from her visit to a thermal power plant in China.'

'Should have gone to Iceland.' Frank laughed.

'You're probably right, but the Chinese have a share in this project.'

'Really?'

'Yes, they still have plenty of money to invest.'

'Great.' Frank's eyes lit up.

'Let's go take a look at where we're at with the centre, then grab a coffee and deal with any questions your lads have.'

Later on that morning, having picked up something for lunch along the way, Adam enlisted Ben's help in finishing repairs on the *Obsession*. They had agreed to start work at *Eco Beech* once the new construction materials arrived on site. That delivery was expected in two days.

Ben followed Adam into the garage as Adam sorted what tools they would need. Ben left him too it, he knew it would be quicker that way. He leaned against the miller and happened to turn to see something on its bed. He picked it up and only then understood it was a Flintstone. He ran his thumb over the etched verse, and started to wonder. He ran his fingers along the grooves in the bed, checking for splinters of stone. The bed was clean.

'Right. You take this bag, and I'll carry this.' Adam led Ben out and down the garden to the woods.

Ben had seen the *Obsession* once before, some time ago. The path down to the river needed a lot of attention now, he thought, as brambles snagged at his legs.

Once aboard, Adam set Ben the task of stripping all the curtains and cushions. They would need washing. There was mildew on some of them. Adam turned his attention to the plumbing.

'Where do you want this pile of washing put?' Ben asked, task completed, but clearly in the way.

'Take it up to the house. Don't worry about the washing machine. I'll sort that.' Adam had heard from Meg that Ben was liable to put washing in the oven. Adam delved into his pocket. 'You'll need these.'

Ben caught the key chain and looked at the number of keys on it. 'You're kidding right?'

'No. You can do it. The one you need is the only one with the black and orange plastic cover.'

'Urr…this one.'

'That's it.'

'Right then.' Ben stuffed the keys in a pocket then stuffed the washing into two seat-cushion cases and left.

Ben's days of tracking were over but it wasn't too difficult to follow the trail of damaged undergrowth back to the garden. He soon had the load of washing placed on the kitchen table and was back out of the house, but there he paused.

Ben walked round to the garage and returned to the miller. He picked up the Flintstone again then bent down and opened the door under the bed. There was a shelf there. He felt along it and picked up something wondering if it was a milling bit. It felt more like a pen. Then he found a small plastic case. He lifted it out and up onto the miller bed.

Putting the stone down and opening the case up Ben discovered a number of shiny rods that he hoped were bits. He lifted one out and felt both ends. Flat. He replaced the bit then checked another, then another before coming across one he felt a point on.

Ben put the point to the etching on the Flintstone. The point followed the course of the text, but felt too large for the job. Ben selected a much finer bit placing it again into a groove. This one felt better but he couldn't be sure this is what had been used.

Putting the bit and stone back down on the bed, Ben felt around the machine determining where the switch was and then the power cable which he traced to the wall.

First he made sure the power was off at the wall then remembering his metalwork lessons at school he searched for the chuck key and put the chosen bit firmly into the mill chuck. Putting the key away he manually lowered the chuck towards the bed to guide where he needed to place the Flintstone. Then he searched for the bed clamps which would be set to grip the stone in place.

With everything in place, and the Flintstone gripped firmly, clean white surface faced the mill bit above. Ben switched the power on at the wall then pressed the green button on the side of the miller. He knew the miller could be set to run at any number of speeds, but it didn't spin at all.

Feeling the control panel his fingers detected what could be a key hole. Quickly Ben lifted Adam's keys and tried inserting one after another. Finally one fit. He turned it and there was a promising click of a circuit breaker, then he pressed the green button and the chuck span.

It sounded fast, but that seemed right for this job. Ben knew the miller was intended for metal, wood and plastic, but if he took it careful it ought to work with stone.

He lowered the bit until contact made a gritty sound then made a fine adjustment. Dust flew out. He should have been wearing goggles he thought, but no time for that now. He had to get on and get back to Adam before he came looking for him.

Ben used a transverse wheel to guide the bit slowly across the chalky surface of the flint. He could not see the working edge clearly but the cut was not smooth but crumbly. He lowered the bit further and the tool started to squeal nastily as it attempted to cut into the harder dark stone beneath. Now Ben thought ear defenders wouldn't have gone amiss either. Adam was bound to hear this, but what the hell.

Ben drew the bit back along its initial cut and the bit complained shrilly then the stone began to vibrate followed by an angry crunch and a bang. The Flintstone broke in two, one half hitting the wall before falling to the floor. At the same instant the bit sheared in half and flew off into the garage somewhere, luckily missing Ben. Ben slammed the red button off.

'Fuck it!'

There was no sense cleaning up this mess. Adam would know what Ben had tried to do as soon as he saw the broken Flintstone. Unless…Ben considered…he got rid of the stone, and then denied any knowledge of its disappearance. No, that wouldn't work, not with a broken mill bit.

Ben lifted up the broken stone from the floor and removed the other half from the bed, comparing both halves. They were flint all the way through. He ran a thumb over the satin finish of the fracture, then over the mark he had made. The fine edge of the bit cut was much rougher. Maybe it needed to be done at a different speed or using a proper masonry bit more likely, he considered.

Ben turned the flint round in his hand and ran his thumb over an exposed edge of verse text. Though still a fine edge it felt smoother than the fracture surface, almost glassy.

He'd had enough of this puzzle for today. When questioned, Ben decided he would say that he was proving that Adam had not simply made the whole story up. He clearly hadn't milled the verses into these stones himself.

Ben dropped the pieces of Flintstone on the bed by the clamps, removed the keys, switched off at the wall, turned and headed back to the barge.

Ben was expecting to see Adam on deck as he returned and to then be questioned about the noise. Instead he saw an attractive redhead on the opposite bank, having a picnic.

'Hi.' Ben beamed a smile her way as he stepped aboard the *Obsession*.

Her mouth full she simply waved back.

As Ben ducked his head to go below he spotted Adam on his knees in the galley, monkey wrench in hand.

'Who's the girl?'

'What girl?'

'The pretty redhead having her lunch on the opposite bank.'

Adam got up and peered through the window. Then he went up on deck with Ben in tail.

'Hello. I'm Adam.'

'I know.'

'Oh. Are you my new neighbour? I didn't think old…'

'No.'

'Oh. What are you doing there then? That's not a public right of way.'

'At the moment I'm finishing my lunch.'

'Well, old Beaufort doesn't take kindly to trespassers, as I found when I had to attach pulleys to some of his trees, getting this barge up river from the bridge.'

'Well I don't let things bother me.'

'Don't you now?'

'I do what I do then move on.'

'What a carefree life you must lead.'

'I guess so. I used to care once. Not long from now in fact.'

'You speak…oddly,' Ben commented. 'So where are you from?'

'That's a difficult one to pin down.'

'You move about a lot, I got that, but originally.'

'I um, don't think you'd have heard of it. Tormidier.'

'I guess that's a town in American going by your accent.'

'Well you can guess what you like. We can't stop you.'

'I'm Ben by the way. We were about ready to have our lunch too.'

'I'm Dawn Summers, but it's time I was back at The Apple.'

Adam didn't recognise The Apple as a local pub or shop for that matter.

She reached into a hamper and brought out an apple and under-arm threw it to Ben. He caught it as she made a second under-arm throw to Adam.

What crossed the river this second time was not an apple. Adam could see it was larger and by the way it moved it was heavier. His

114

subconscious knew what was coming at him, raising the hairs on his arms and legs before it arrived heavily into his hands verse-side up.

In that moment Adam was certain Dawn knew who had murdered Toyah. Looking back at Dawn he saw she was leaving.

'Where are you going?'

'I told you, The Apple.'

'I don't know where that is.'

'Well nobody is supposed to know.' Hamper packed she turned away.

'Wait! Did you kill my girlfriend Toyah Pembroke?'

'No.'

'Do you know who killed her?'

'Yes.'

'Who?!'

'Can't say.' Dawn headed into the trees.

Adam placed the new Flintstone by the wheel then bounded off the stern onto the bank.

'Where are you going?' Ben shouted after him.

'To head her off at the bridge. I bet she's parked there.'

'Right.' There seemed little sense in taking the same approach. 'Here I go again.'

Ben jumped over the side jolting his legs on the bottom. The river, muddy from recent rains, was not deep but it had a strong current and it took Ben's legs from under him. He fought for the opposite bank. Clambering out through stinging nettles and brambles he tried to get his bearings.

He heard a noise and then spotted Dawn. He had to keep eyes and ears trained on her as he smashed through the undergrowth. Ben knew they were onto something big now.

Meanwhile, Adam forced his way through the undergrowth on his property, scrambled over a barbed wire fence then raced across the neighbouring meadow. He headed straight to the gate onto the road then turned left down to the bridge, but there was no car, or bike for that matter.

Wasting no time, Adam clambered a fence into the woods on the opposite bank and headed back as fast as he could, listening out for Dawn.

Adam could hear no one, not even the sound of undergrowth being trampled. Eventually, short of breath, Adam came across Ben, soaking wet sitting on a fallen log looking dazed.

'Ben! Are you okay?'

'I…I'm not sure.'

'Did you see where she went?'

'Yes.'

'Did you get close enough to ask her to tell you who killed Toyah?'

'Yes.'

'Well?'

'She said again that she couldn't say. So I asked her straight *can't* or *won't*? So she turns and says read my lips. Toyah Pembroke was killed by…She seemed to freeze. I reached out to her but she snapped don't touch me, turned and was gone.'

'Turned and was *gone*?'

116

'Into a hole.'

Adam looked around the forest floor. There were no holes or shafts he could see. 'Where was this hole, Ben? Maybe we can get her out.'

Ben shook his head with his dazed expression showing no sign of clearing any time soon.

'Ben? Where was this hole? Just point.'

Ben pointed to where Adam stood. 'Right next to you. In the air.'

117

19

'Ben! What the hell?!'

Meg slid the frosted glass door open to find Ben crouched in the shower tray, blood trickling down his arms under the warm water. He got up slowly, not looking her in the eye; embarrassed.

'It's nothing Meg, just bramble thorns, working in Adam's garden.'

'Don't bullshit me Ben! Robbie told me...'

'Oh fuck, I forgot to pick him up from school, sorry luv.'

'What? No you didn't. He said you turned up soaking wet again. He asked you if you had been chasing women again. You didn't answer him so he asked if this one drowned too. It would seem you said *No she didn't drown*...Is this what we have come to Ben. *You* chasing women?'

How could he tell his wife about the weird shit that Adam had drawn him into. She wouldn't believe a word of it. Perhaps he shouldn't either. Maybe he hadn't really seen Dawn step through a hole in the air. It must surely have been his cognitive problem just playing tricks. Dawn probably stepped behind a tree and he lost track of her. Yes, that would be it. He really needed to get a grip.

'Just tell me one thing Ben.'

Ben looked at Meg. She was shocked. She couldn't remember having seen Ben look so sad, so lost before. This was serious.

'Anything, luv.'

'Is she pretty?'

'What?'

'The woman you are after. Is she pretty?'

Don't answer that! It's a trick question like: Have you stopped beating your wife? Don't be honest. Don't be honest! Don't! Be honest…

'Yes.'

'No!!' Meg burst into tears.

'Fuck.'

Adam was in two minds whether to go to the *Obsession* when he returned home. He had a lot on his mind.

Could Ben have been mistaken about what he saw? After all, object recognition wasn't exactly a trump card of his any longer. Ben had certainly been affected by whatever he had experienced. He was still quite dazed when Adam had dropped him off outside Robbie's school.

Adam knew it was probably best to limit the facts he was juggling to those he had witnessed with his own eyes. That said, hadn't the Professor suggested that everyone's mind can play tricks on how they perceive and interpret experiences?

Dawn had admitted to prior knowledge of Adam, yet he was not aware of them having met previously. He would have remembered someone that attractive. Might he have misunderstood her because of her odd way of talking? However, she had definitely admitted to knowing Toyah's killer. What possible benefit could there be to withholding that information? Did the killer have some hold over Dawn? From the way she behaved however, it would suggest she cared little for what others said or did. Oh it all lacked logical explanation.

Adam walked through the woods and boarded the barge. He lifted the Flintstone and with a sigh of trepidation read it.

Tyne Bridge fundraiser
Certainly will distract,
The scene unfolding
With crushing impact.

There was no mention of Ben needing to be there with him. Maybe Adam should leave him out of this one. Ben looked like he had seen enough today. Ben was tough, but whatever happened in the woods had clearly taken its toll.

Pocketing the Flintstone Adam left the barge for the house. He decided to try and sleep on it. Nevertheless he couldn't just go to bed, he was too wide awake.

In the kitchen he removed the *Obsession's* curtains and covers from the washing machine. He had set them going while he had taken Ben back to Newcastle.

Putting a pizza in the oven, Adam was suddenly seized by a paranoid thought. What if this Dawn Summers had him under surveillance? Was his house bugged? Was

Toyah's bugged? Was Toyah involved in something clandestine? Who was Nadine? He had tried ringing that number he had found in Toyah's draw but it was not recognised.

He spent the evening around the house undoing fixtures and fittings to see if any contained anything untoward. Finally, finding nothing and growing tired, he sat on the sofa with a beer and his iPad checking Google.

The Apple just brought up a cider bar, pubs, restaurants and shops. Then he typed in various spellings of Tormidier but Google struggled to find a match. So he tried Googling Dawn Summers. There had to be a lot of people with that name, so he knew it didn't hold much promise. He was surprised to see it was the name of a character from Buffy the Vampire Slayer. The photo of the actress, though also pretty, didn't look like this Dawn Summers.

Ben had ended up sleeping on the sofa. Not welcome upstairs. He didn't argue. He knew he had to be a drain on Meg with his disability. She had been good to put up with it this long.

As he lay there his mind insisted on replaying the air opening up next to Dawn. He tried to stop frame the image and consider that hole. It wasn't dark. There was light coming from it into the shaded wood. It was difficult to see what was on the other side of the hole because of his angle of view but he thought it had been a room.

It was like something out of science fiction. It had no place in his world. Could Dawn be a time-traveller? Or were there others involved, since Adam said he had been receiving these Flintstones since he was a child.

What a dreadful curse those Flintstones must be for Adam. Was this a punishment, a test, something preparing him for some final deed? If Ben saw Dawn again he'd be demanding proper answers to a number of questions. He just hoped he would be prepared for her answers.

20

Ben woke early but just lay there on the sofa, going over the previous day, once again. He'd convinced himself that Ben wasn't making those Flintstones with the miller. He had nearly injured himself in the process. Then he had seen that woman, Dawn, chuck a Flintstone to Adam. So either she was making them or acting as the courier.

He decided he had overreacted to the weirdness relating to the Flintstones and Dawn. If he had seen this on TV he'd have said he'd seen it all before. Nevertheless, seeing time-travel, teleportation, or whatever the hell it was in real life, was unnerving. It wasn't natural. It was the same feeling that well-executed magic tricks created. The observer needed to rationalise what was witnessed against the physical laws everything was believed to hold to.

He was just starting to consider what it would mean if people *could* just pop in and out of the world when he became alert to the sound of Meg getting up.

The day started off fine. Ben and Meg got the kids up, had breakfast, and watched a bit of the local news. The only difference was that Meg didn't seem to have much to say to Ben. That was a relief for Ben. Maybe she was putting it behind her, he thought. However, when there was a knock on the door Meg went and opened it to find Adam standing there looking excited.

'What is it, Adam?'

'I've come to pick up Ben and…we could drop Robbie off at school…Is everything okay?'

'Okay?' Meg stepped outside, pulling the door to behind her. 'Things are never okay in this house, Adam. You of all people should know that.'

'Sorry…Have I done something…else wrong?'

'You have a duty of care, Adam.'

'Sorry, what do you mean?'

'As Ben's employer, you have a duty of care.' She saw Adam was still frowning. 'With Ben's cognitive issues, I don't want to find out that you are, shall we say, encouraging him to um…'

Adam's expression changed. 'Has Ben told you? I didn't think he would say anything in case it worried you.'

'Well actually it was Robbie who let out the dirty secret.'

'*Dirty* secret? And how does the lad know what's going on?'

'Ben chasing women. Seems Ben let it slip. It's got to stop. Him coming home soaked and acting odd.'

'It's just coincidence…the wet clothes.'

'So there is a woman?'

'Well it's not what you're thinking Meg. Her name is Dawn.'

'Right well I want words with this *bitch*.'

'Ha. Join the queue. Ben and I are finally onto something which will prove Toyah, and possible others in the area have been murdered. Dawn is our lead.'

'The police should be dealing with this.'

'Well they're not. They've closed the case as a misadventure.'

'Do they know about this woman?'

'Well no. We haven't told them about Dawn, yet.'

'Why ever not?'

'She urr...disappeared. We don't know who she works for, or where she lives. She said she was from The Apple, but I was Googling everything I could think of last night, and getting nowhere.'

'And what makes you think this woman knows anything?'

Adam didn't want to lose any more credibility by mentioning the Flintstones at this point, so said 'Ben told me that Dawn told him, she knew the killer.'

'Adam! I was starting to believe your story! So now you're saying Ben's chasing this woman, telling you it's okay because she will have all the answers to how Toyah died. So he's trying to fool you too. Is that it?'

'No it's not like that.'

'Oh wake up and smell the coffee, Adam. My marriage is falling apart. I've tried so hard to support Ben through these difficulties but he's clearly developing interests elsewhere.'

'Look, it will be over soon, I...'

'I thought we were friends.'

'We are, Meg.'

'Well quit covering for him with this bullshit. I need him with me, not drifting away.'

Before Adam could say another word Meg turned unlocked the door, went inside, and closed the door after her.

Adam waited for Ben to come out but when he didn't Adam knocked again.

This time Robbie answered the door. 'Hello Uncle Adam.'

'Is your Dad ready yet?'

'Will you be chasing more girls today?'

'Not exactly, Robbie. You're dad it trying to save lives.'

'Like in the old days?'

'Kind of.'

After Robbie was dropped off at school, Adam mentioned that Cameron had texted him earlier. The materials and equipment delivery had been delayed and so there was no need to come to the site until after lunch. This suited Adam fine because they had to go and check out what was happening on the Tyne Bridge.

Adam parked the van in the multi-storey on Dean Street which had an upper exit onto the bridge.

As they reached the pavement, Ben asked 'How do you know the *situation* will occur this morning, Adam? Did the Flintstone say so?'

'No, Ben. The Flintstones rarely specify time and are not always specific about place either. The situations always develop after I arrive wherever I'm supposed to be.'

'So what's the clue this time?'

'A fundraiser.'

They didn't have to walk far to spot what they would be dealing with this time. 'Look, some people are gathering on the other side of the road. Let's cross.'

Crossing wasn't easy, with so many angry motorists hooting because they wanted to speed across the bridge, hating the fifty miles per hour limit.

It turned out the event was to be a charity bungee-jump. The organisers were just finishing setting up and preparing to do the safety checks.

It seemed obvious to Adam that what was going to happen here was that someone was going to fall to their death. It was tempting to try and tell the organisers that someone was going to die and that they should postpone, but he knew he would just sound like a mad man and get totally ignored.

To work out what was best to do Adam decided to ask some questions.

As he and Ben watched the people setting up, it became quite clear which of them the event manager was.

'Excuse me Miss.'

'Yes?'

'I'm curious. Why's the jump platform set up over the paving below rather than the river?'

'That is in case there's any unscheduled river traffic. We have better control on the ground.'

'I thought you might be getting people to splash into the Tyne.'

'Not today. We have a list of quite well-to-do folk who I don't think would be up for a soaking.'

'No, I guess not.' Adam needed to know more. 'I've always wondered how you ensure the safety of a bungee line. Jumping looks pretty risky.'

'Yeah it looks it but it's all quite safe really. We weigh each person after we prep them and harness them and that tells us what length of bungee to set the winch too. Are you thinking of doing a jump? It's a hundred pounds per jump. It's going towards local domestic abuse support.'

Listening to this, Ben could almost hear Adam say *'No, but my mate will do it.'*

However Adam declined, 'We're happy just to watch for now, thanks.'

'Fine. There's a donations bucket over there if you're feeling charitable.'

'Okay, right.' Adam took Ben aside. 'This is what I think we need to do. One of us needs to keep an eye on the jumpers from up here, to spot anyone acting odd or suicidal…And you need to go down to the street below and watch from there.'

'Me? Why me?'

'That's where you would be most likely to save someone?'

'How d'you figure that?'

'Well if it's death by impact, it must involve the paving below. Right?'

'I suppose.'

'You are stronger than me…'

'Whoa. Hold on a minute. Are you trying to get me killed? I may be cognitively challenged, Adam, but I'm not stupid enough to stand under a falling body.'

'No, no. Hear me out. Look, if for instance the bungy broke, or was cut, I would expect you to step out of the way, of course. However, with these safety measures the only thing I can think might go wrong is miscalculation of weight. In which case the jumper would either not go down far before the elastic slows them and brings them bouncing back a way. Or, it will slow them but not quite enough and then they make contact with the paving. If it looks like they might reach the ground, *and* would be slow enough, you could maybe catch them.'

'I see what you are suggesting, but I'm not happy about this. I'm getting the feeling you are starting to treat me like some side-kick who does all the tough stuff.'

'You're SAS Ben.'

'Was SAS. Was!' Ben stomped off to make his way down.

Megs earlier lecture about *duty of care* forgotten, Adam turned back to the proceedings. There was already someone being checked off the list and emptying his pockets before being helped into the harness whilst listening to *the talk*.

The lad, in his designer clothes was smiling at the young woman in charge but looked attentive, nodding his acknowledgments. Adam judged that the lad certainly didn't look the sort to do anything silly.

Shortly the lad was weighed and then with the bungee connected to his harness he was directed up the short ladder onto the jump platform.

A photographer started taking shots. The lad began to look a little nervous but was clearly determined not to back out now with his mates watching.

The event manager continued to talk the whole time, to put her first jumper at ease. She had done this so many times now, it all felt rather ordinary for her, just a way of making money.

Meanwhile, Ben made it to the road below and crossed to the pavement where another photographer waited. A man with a walkie-talkie gestured for Ben to keep clear, so he went and stood aside to watch what was happening above them.

The lad who was up first finally turned to face out and with almost no pause went into a swan dive. Half way down he gave out a whoop to clapping from his small audience above and below the Tyne Bridge.

After he had stopped bouncing, the lad was winched back and the next person was prepped.

Ben saw that the next person was a young woman. He began to wonder if all the victims would be women. There was some delay before the woman jumped, and on her way down she screamed.

Ben thought she was coming faster than the lad had. Was this it? He stepped forward, still trying to judge the situation. Time seemed to go into slow motion.

'Hey keep out of shot!' cried the photographer.

Then the young woman was going back up, her scream having change to laughter supported by applause.

Another wait followed and then a lad jumped. He was quiet till the last moment when the bungee went taught. The lad gave out a groan like someone who wished they'd not had that *full English* against the advice given in the information pack for jumpers.

Next up was a rather large woman.

'Fuck, no!' Ben heard himself say.

He wondered if there was a limit to the weight of people who could jump. Regardless, he decided, he wasn't getting under that, no matter how much the elastic tried to fight gravity.

The air was soon filled with joyful belly-laughs down and up, and down and up again, until the woman could be winched back up to the bridge.

After yet another wait, the next jumper was another young woman. Ben decided this one was nervous as she took longer before stepping out backwards. Ben felt his muscles tensing. He felt in his gut this was the one.

It all happened so fast. The young woman shouted something that Ben could not make out, then stepped backwards, arms flailing and screamed like her soul was being ripped out of her. As she fell it was with despair and loss, not with fear and excitement.

Ben ran underneath.

'Fuck off!' yelled the angry photographer.

Ben ignored him, lifting his arms in readiness, but before the young woman came close she was on her way back up again.

'What the fuck's the matter with you mate? Why don't you just...' The photographer's bravado evaporated as Ben was suddenly in his face, struggling not to hit him.

The dangling woman was almost hysterical now, but as both Ben and the photographer turned to watch, no one seemed to looking down at her.

Ben lifted the phone from his pocket and attempted to speed-dial Adam. All he got was the answer machine. Ben didn't waste time with a message. He ran across the road and on up Dean Street.

By the time Ben got back to the bridge the traffic was stood still and there was a crowd of gawpers. The young woman, still sobbing uncontrollably, was just being helped back onto the platform by the event manager and her assistant. Ben looked around at all of the heads for Adam as he pushed through the crowd.

Then he spotted Adam sat at the curb-side. His hands covered in blood. There was also blood on his clothes and face, but much more on the tarmac seeping from a woman's body under Adam's jacket.

'Adam.' Ben forced his way to crouch at his side. 'Adam!'

Adam was in shock.

Ben spotted Adam's phone on the ground and picked it up.

'Adam. Did you phone for an ambulance?'

'Yes.'

'What did they say?'

'They started the usual questionnaire. I ignored the woman and explained where I was. But as I started describing what had happened, she hung up on me.'

'What?'

'It was like she didn't care.'

Ben wondered whether they should just leave the scene and get Adam cleaned up. He didn't know for sure what had happened, though a truck had clearly run someone over, but there was nothing they could do for this woman now.

Then the siren of an emergency vehicle could be heard trying to push through the grid-locked traffic.

The sobbing woman pushed through the crowd to lift Adam's jacket and look at the body beneath only to renew her wails of grief.

Ben turned to see two men peering down at the scene. Adam then turned and recognised them with a groan.

'Caught red handed this time Mr Underwood,' said DI Jenkins.

'What?' Ben answered for Adam.

'And you. Whoever you are,' said DI Carmichael. 'You're coming back to the station for questioning. You're both clearly involved.'

21

Ben was taken to a separate interview room to Adam. After quite some time, the officer who identified himself as DI Jenkins entered with a rather uncomfortable looking WPC Hanley in tow. Jenkins sat in front of Ben, while Hanley stood at the door. Jenkins then stated the date and time and identified everyone present for the purpose of the recording.

'So Mr McGregor, before I tell you what happened on the Tyne Bridge this morning. Is there anything you would like to tell me?'

'Let's see.' Ben pretended to look around the room for inspiration. 'I don't think so.'

'Okay then. I see from my notes that you were involved in the drowning of one Patricia Maris.'

'Who?'

'Come, come. Witnesses said they saw you and Mr Underwood fill her boots and pockets with rocks and throw her into the sea from a concrete outflow.'

'What?'

'There's no use denying it. Your mate Underwood phoned it in while he had you go for a swim to convince the services when they arrived that you had tried to save her.'

'You've got to be pissing me!'

'You see, for some time now the emergency services record all incoming call numbers. Underwood's has come up three times recently, what with today's call. Emergency service call centres are making a stand against hoax callers, by way of a questionnaire and call registry. Only, today we find you and Underwood are not hoaxing, are you?'

'No.'

'No!...You've been going on a bit of a fucking killing spree no less. First you smother Miss Pembroke then drown Mrs Maris…Now you've shoved one *Marie Sutton*, an identical twin, under a truck. An identical twin! Are these random killings or did you know it would be extra painful to separate twins?'

Ben turned to WPC Hanley. 'Is this guy for real luv?'

'Yes, I'm afraid he really *is* a Detective Inspector, Sir.'

'So, is there anything you would like to tell me *now*?'

'Yes, there is.'

'Good. Let's hear it.'

Ben leaned in closer to the recorder. 'In the real world of *adults* I have a job to get to.'

Jenkins launched forward out of his chair, intending to make more shocking fake claims up close with teeth bared like an attack dog. However, he didn't even get as far as his first word.

In one swift and powerful motion Ben took Jenkins by the front of his jacket, lifting him over the top of the desk. Jenkins passed over Ben's head and down to the floor behind, like a rag doll, without Ben leaving his own seat.

Jenkins cried out as he crumpled into the corner of the interview room.

Ben's chair screeched as he shifted to look, aware that Hanley had stepped forward for a better look too.

'My shoulder!' Jenkins whined as he got back to his feet, his right arm swinging limply. 'You're in trouble now son!'

'Me?' Ben feigned surprise.

'Yes. Assaulting a police officer. You saw that didn't you Hanley.'

'Yes sir. From where I was standing, Mr McGregor made a smart remark which made you snap and launch yourself at him, only you ended up on the floor.'

'What? No! You stupid bitch. You weren't paying attention were you. Probably thinking about going shopping for more shoes.'

'I don't think that's fair, but then everyone in the station knows what you're like, Sir.'

'What's that supposed to mean?!' Jenkins was trembling with rage rubbing at his shoulder.

'Well, you being a pathological liar, Sir.'

In an interview room a few doors down, having been allowed to clean himself up first, Adam sat listening to DI Carmichael.

'You've called emergency services three times in the last month. In each case it has involved the death of a woman. You realise it is not looking good for you, Adam.'

'Sure, but what you need to understand is I wanted to save them.'

'No, what I need to understand first is your link to these women. Were you dating them all?'

'What? No! Just Toyah.'

'One death by misadventure is unfortunate. Two is something of a coincidence. But three is no coincidence at all…So what is the link?

'I don't think I can tell you.'

'The second death, a Mrs Patricia Maris, looked more like a suicide. She was found to have large pebbles in her boots and pockets to weigh her down. There were no witnesses to dispute your report that she just walked off the end of the outflow.

'The third death, a Miss Marie Sutton, to all intents and purposes looks to have been an accident. Her twin sister, Justine, reported seeing her step back into the path of a speeding truck while trying to take her photograph.'

Adam shook his head. He remembered Justine standing there on the platform suddenly scream a warning to Marie. That was immediately followed by the screech of brakes and the sickening thump. In a state of shock Marie fell backwards off the platform screaming. By the time Adam turned round it was too late to save anyone, once again. Why was he always too late? Why did he have to be there at all?

'I'm going to level with you, Adam. I believe you are genuine, but I also believe you are somehow caught up in some seriously weird shit that I cannot figure. I also think if I let you

137

walk out of here today I'm going to find you are involved in more deaths. Am I right?'

'Probably.'

'So are you going to tell me what is really going on here?'

'I don't think that will help, Detective Inspector. You're just not going to believe me.'

'Try me. I'm not going to let this one go, or else I'll be losing sleep over it.'

'Okay, on the condition that you bring Ben in here and that large stone you took off me during processing.'

'The stone?'

'Yes.'

Carmichael turned to the PC at the door. 'Trent can you go and round up Jenkins and McGregor and bring this gentleman's *stone* in here please.'

'Sir.'

PC Trent returned with the Flintstone and McGregor but no DI Jenkins.

'Is Jenkins coming, Trent?'

'No Sir.' Trent passed Carmichael the Flintstone. 'The duty Medic has sent him to hospital, Sir.'

'Hospital?'

'Yes Sir. Suspected broken collar bone. WPC Hanley says he flew at Mr McGregor and um…slipped.'

'Idiot!' Carmichael shook his head then turned to Ben and gestured that he take the seat next to Adam. 'Right, to recap for the recording and for Mr McGregor's benefit, Mr

Underwood has now agreed to come clean about what has been going on.'

DI Carmichael looked at the stone, turning it over and reading the verse before placing it in the centre of the interview table.

Adam was saying nothing. DI Carmichael thought Adam was either going back on his word or didn't know where to start. 'Over to you then, Adam.'

Adam exhaled between pursed lips. 'Okay...I have been finding these Flintstones since I was a young lad. Although I have dug some of them up, many of them have been placed in or on things where they are easier to spot.'

'So do you think there may be more of these around and others have found them instead?'

'I used to wonder if others would find them, but I have come to believe that whoever places them knows my moves exactly, ensuring only I find them, no one else. There must be other Flintstones out there right now, buried until the right time for me to find them.'

'Surely whoever is behind this can't get that right every time.'

'You'd think.'

'Do all of these stones carry verses?'

'Yes.'

'Cryptic predictions?'

'Yes.'

'Have you still got all of these stones?'

'No. I do still have quite a few. They are in a box in the garage. But I've thrown a lot of them away over the years. I used to get so angry that I was receiving them and worse still having to witness their terrible events.'

'So other people may have found those discarded ones.'

'I guess so.'

'Did you ever get to a destination and find anyone else waiting with your Flintstone or dare I say one of their own?'

'No, never.'

'So who has been doing this? Your parents?'

'Nope. Parents are both dead now.'

'Well. Adam.' Carmichael looked at the etching more closely. 'It does look to me like something you could make yourself, with the right tools.'

'I had thought that,' Ben interjected before Adam could respond. 'In fact, before Adam was given that stone there I tried to use his miller to cut into the back of another, in his garage workshop.'

'What?' Adam turned to Ben wondering if this was just a line of defence Ben was feeding Carmichael.

'Yes, sorry Adam. I broke one of your miller bits. It seems it's not possible to just machine those things.'

'Of course it isn't. The surface of a flint is not even. To get the writing on such a surface so that the lettering is consistent, you'd have to use a hand tool like palaeontologists use to reveal fossils. Or a computer aided miller using 3D scanning lasers or something. The depth of chalk to the flint varies but these verses are always so neat. They look like the work of a master craftsman. If done by hand it would take many hours, and they didn't 3D scanning, when I was a kid.'

There was a pause as everyone in the room found they were giving this crazy story some serious thought.

Carmichael broke the silence. 'So do you have any idea who is behind this?'

'We do now. At least someone who I believe is involved and must surely know more. She said her name was Dawn Summers. It was the first time a Flintstone has been passed to me by a person. Ben was there. He saw her.'

Carmichael turned to Ben. 'Is this true?'

'It is but I wish it wasn't.'

'What do you mean?'

'I don't like the thought that this isn't just a prank of Adam's.'

'A prank?'

'Yes. We used to prank people.'

'For God's sake Ben that's not helping!' Adam put his head in his hands.

'No, sorry. Forget that. It's what happened next that's important, but you're not going to like it.'

Carmichael turned back to Adam. 'So what did this person do, Adam?'

Adam lifted his head out of his hands but only to say 'It's best if Ben tells this next bit because when Dawn left only Ben managed to catch up with her.'

'Over to you then Ben.'

'You won't believe it and I don't blame you…Dawn was on the opposite side of the river to Adam's place. We were on his barge. She seemed very familiar with Adam.'

'So they knew each other?'

'From Adam's reaction to her I believe he had never seen her before. Nevertheless, she spoke like she knew him well. She didn't answer all of Adam's questions and started to leave. As Adam headed down the river bank hoping to head her off I crossed the river and went through the woods after her.' Ben's eyes seemed to be searching as if he was starting to relive the episode.

'And...?'

'I caught up with her, *almost*. Enough to speak to her again, at least. I asked her again if she knew who killed Ben's girlfriend, as before she just said yes. When I asked her who it was she couldn't say.'

'What do you mean she *couldn't say*?'

'It was strange. I watched her try but the name wouldn't come out.'

'So she couldn't recall the name, but maybe remembers the face?'

'I guess, but it seemed as if she knew but something was stopping her.'

'Like she wanted to tell you but was too concerned she would put herself in danger telling you?'

'No, not at all. This woman seemed very confident, she even claimed she wasn't bothered by anything.'

'So what then?'

'I don't know. It was like some bloody Harry Potter spell was on her voice.'

'Now you're being ridiculous.'

'That's not even the most ridiculous bit, I tried to grab her. I thought I maybe could snap her out of it. But she was certainly bothered about me touching her. She turned and disappeared.'

'Into the woods?'

'No. This is the bit you won't like. This is the bit that spoils the credibility of the story.'

'Come on Ben, spit it out.'

'A hole opened up in the air next to her.'

'Bollocks.'

'I've been trying to explain it to myself ever since. She stepped through the hole into what I think was a very bright room and then the hole closed up after her. It sounds like science fiction doesn't it.'

DI Carmichael sighed. 'The problem with your story is that the police deal with facts not fantasy. I need to know what *really* happened.'

'So do I, mate.'

'Look,' Adam suggested, 'What if the next time I receive a Flintstone I call you and you come along with us.'

Carmichael gave a protracted groaned as he thought about the suggestion. 'Okay. But when you see the next stone I want you to leave it in place for me to see how you found it, don't just bring it in.'

'Sure. I'll ring you, but you'd need to come right away. These incidents which the verses refer to are usually imminent. I ignored the one that referred to Toyah's death, only read it when it was too late. It referred to her death in the past tense.'

'But that would mean that this Dawn knew you would not read it till after Toyah had died.'

'I know, right?'

22

Adam and Ben arrived at the *Eco Beech* site later than agreed.

'You're late!' Cameron was not impressed.

'Yes, sorry. There was an accident on the road and the police needed us to make a statement.'

'Right. Well I guess *that* won't be happening again. You need to get round the back where the others should be unloading and sorting the delivery.'

'Okay.'

Ben followed Adam round to the rear of the visitor centre. When they got to the truck they saw two burly men just standing chatting and smoking.

'Hi, we're Adam and Ben.'

'You're late.' The slightly shorter of the two announced the obvious, but with a half smirk.

'There was a...'

'Whatever,' He waved Adam off, not even bothering to complete introductions he explained. 'The forklift won't start so we have to unload this by hand.'

'Would you like me to take a look at the forklift?'

'No Adam, I've checked it. I understand vehicles. I was in the army.'

Adam glanced as Ben and back at Frank's men. 'Is there anyone else free to lend a hand?'

'Nope. And the driver is pretty pissed off, so I wouldn't talk to him.'

'What's the load?' Ben enquired stepping to the side curtain nearest the building, and pulling at the fastening.

'A mix of stuff on shrink-wrapped pallets. Plasterboard, tiles and shit.'

'Well then, we'll take the plasterboard and tiles if you want to take all the shit.' Ben was hoping to get a laugh but neither of Frank's men even cracked a smile.

After fully opening the side curtain and removing the shrink wrap the four of them started the unloading. They took it in turns to either pass materials down off the bed of the truck or the shifting of materials to where they were being stored inside.

Considering how strong Frank's men looked they seemed to Adam to be taking it easy. After a while the short one started to look cross.

'Hey, you two. This isn't a race.'

'I don't understand.' Adam had no intention of racing anyone.

'You're going too fast.'

'Too fast? The driver will be wanting to get away.'

Ben got back to the truck to see an argument kicking off. 'What's up?'

'Apparently we are going *too* fast.'

'You'll wear yourselves out and then Max and I will be left to do the rest.'

'Listen, Min…' Ben started.

'It's Mic.'

'Close…Adam and I are pacing ourselves. We're not new to this.'

Adam sensed something was wrong here and things might get out of hand. 'It's a shame that *Earth's Calling* didn't arrange for a delivery truck equipped with a crane. But let's keep going at our own pace so that we can get on with the next task.'

Mic mumbled something to Max and everyone got back to unloading.

When Ben arrived home it was to the sound of Beth crying over something. Before he could ask his daughter what was up, Meg was onto him.

'Have a good day?'

Ben felt an undertone of sarcasm. 'Not particularly.'

'Not had any women to chase then?'

'No, I failed to catch one this morning.' Ben mirrored his wife's sarcasm.

'Oh grow up.'

'Hey, I really don't deserve this confrontational attitude, luv.'

'No?'

'No.'

'Even though you are letting Adam draw you into chasing women?'

'If it wasn't for Adam I wouldn't have a job and we would be struggling even more.'

'I *do* realise that. It's just…'

'Just what?'

'I'm worried about you.'

'Thanks but I think I've learned how to look after myself.'

'If you get arrested, or injured, how will I…'

'Oh I see. It's the *money* you are concerned about *not me*.'

Beth continued to cry.

'I was going to say, how will I ever forgive myself for not doing more to stop Adam using you like he is?'

'Look it's just a mate helping a mate. I won't be doing anything I don't think I can handle. And it should be over soon, as soon as we come across this Dawn Summers again. The police are involved now anyway, so it's all above board.'

'The police, really?' Meg sounded relieved to hear that.

'We had a lunchtime meeting with them, and once I smoothed out a bit of a wrinkle, we came to an agreement.'

'A wrinkle.'

'Yeah. One of the detectives was being an arse, and ended up in hospital.'

'Ben!!'

Adam took the comfy seat in the room with the one-way mirror.

'So, Adam. Have you had any further thoughts since our meeting the other evening?' Professor Henderson enquired.

'Oh yes, some headway has been made. My colleague Ben and I believe we have found out who is responsible for the Flintstones, and she knows who killed my girlfriend. Plus the police are now involved.'

'I…see.' The Professor paused to take that in. 'So what about the trauma over your girlfriend's death?'

'Well I'm still getting some nightmares so my sleep is disturbed. It's like having a recurring dream of falling over, where your leg kicks out and wakes you up. In my case my arm keeps lashing out trying to break the window, although things don't always happen in the same sequence, or place.'

'If it's any help, the brain often comes to terms with traumatic incidents by replaying the scene in order to accept that nothing could have been done differently. Sometimes the dreams serve to help learn to cope with the experience, possibly to be better prepared in the event something like that happens again.'

'I bloody hope not.'

'Can I ask how serious your relationship was with Toyah?'

'I believe we were becoming more serious, more open. Toyah seemed keen to change my ways.'

'What ways would those be?'

'I guess my being happy with the status quote, with no particular life goals. I sometimes thought she might want to get married, but I was happy as we were.'

'Well these days marriage is really no measure of how serious a relationship is. Would you say you had become emotionally dependent on Toyah in your time together?'

'How do you mean?'

'Did you need Toyah in order to feel happy?'

'I certainly felt happier when I was with her.'

'But did you need her there to support you?'

'I…don't…think so. I just enjoyed her company…a lot.'

'So how would you rate your grieving over her death, where one is at peace with it now and ten is inconsolable.'

'Are we saying the fact that she is dead, or how she died?'

'The fact that she is dead.'

'Well I miss her but I'm not feeling suicidal about it, so I guess four or five.'

'So between one for coming to terms with the way Toyah died and ten for believing you will never be rid of the traumatic memory, how do you feel presently.'

'I don't know, seven, eight? I'm only here because I think I need support, to find a way through. I think it will also help if I find out who killed Toyah and why.'

'I could also suggest that what may help is to reframe your memory of the event.'

'Sorry, I don't understand. *Reframe*?'

'To see what happened in different terms, from other angles.'

'I still don't understand.'

'People can be involved in behaviours which they find pleasure in, which they may want to share, but have difficulty talking about because for whatever reason they feel it is not normal and they feel ashamed.'

'I'm still not following.'

'Fetishes…'

'Fetishes? You are sounding just like DI Jenkins now!'

'Are you sure Toyah was not an asphyxiaphile?'

'Of course I'm sure.'

'What if you are wrong? What if this wasn't a terrible murder, just a tragic accident?'

'It didn't look like an accident to me.'

'She could have had an unexpected complication, and then suddenly what was meant to be a bit of fun all went wrong.'

'No. It wasn't like that. How would that explain all the other deaths?'

'Other deaths?'

'I've had enough of this.' Adam got up and left.

Crossing the street to the car park he heard the rushed clatter of heels. Reaching the pavement he turned to see a young woman.

'Adam. I think I can help you.'

'Sorry, I don't know you. Are you a friend of Dawn's?'

'Dawn? No, sorry. I shouldn't *really* be talking to you. I'm a psychology student. My name is Candice. I'm one of the observers from behind the mirror.'

'I see.' Adam noted that Candice was certainly easier on the eye than the Professor.

'I think I can help you with your trauma problem. I'm doing an MSc, investigating a new approach to hypnotherapy, specifically to resolve PTSD.'

'Well maybe when you're qualified if I'm no better I'll come and see you.' Adam turned to continue to his car.

'I know I only have my BSc, but I've already helped a number of people, and the more people I help the more data I have for my study.'

Adam turned back to face Candice, intending to decline, but the student had a sweet manner about her and an attractive smile, which looked even more attractive when he found himself saying 'Okay, tell me more.'

23

Adam had intended to hear Candice out and then head home. However, as he sat listening to her in his car he felt at easy with her and interested in what she had to say.

'Hypnosis should not be viewed as some magic trick to make people do something against their will for the entertainment of a crowd, Adam. It is a state of relaxation. It is even possible to achieve a hypnotic state on your own. The role of a hypnotherapist is simply to help their clients put *themselves* into that relaxed state.'

'And once they are relaxed, what then?'

'Session goals have to be agreed beforehand of course.'

'Well my goal has to be to stop these traumatic replays of my girlfriend's death.'

'Initially yes, but I believe there may be more to resolve. Back there you were talking about these Flintstones. Their meaning could also be explored in a relaxed state.'

'Would this be done in the room with the mirror?'

'No. I would need to do it at my flat.'

'Don't you need a supervisor present?'

'Not any more, no.'

'When are you free, Candice?'

'Whenever you feel you are ready. We could even make a start this evening if you like.'

Adam looked at his watch, 'Well I did rather cut short that session back there didn't I.'

As Adam got settled on Candice's couch she continued to talk in her soothing tone.

'It is important that you relax, Adam. Some people find it helps to have a drink or even do some downers to relax but I prefer it if people start off without any of that.'

'Fine, I'm okay. Besides, I'll be driving home afterwards.'

'Sure. So the importance of being relaxed is to enable the subconscious to communicate hidden information via the right brainwaves. Do you understand what I mean by brainwaves, Adam?'

'I think so. Ideas.'

'Well not really ideas. There are different wavelengths of nerve signals. Alpha waves are what we are after. They feature heavily in dreaming.'

'Right. So you need me to relax so much I might fall asleep.'

'That's one way of looking at it.'

'Not sure I can do that being in a strange place, with a stranger.'

'Sure but this is just the first time. When we do it again it should be easier. So let's start with the breathing.'

'My breathing?'

'Yes, to help clear your mind, take deep breaths in and out, slowly. Think about the breath going in and out of you. Think about relaxing the muscles in your toes and fingers, legs and arms, back and neck. You are starting to feel light as if you might float away. You're becoming so relaxed you want to close your eyes. You are still thinking about your breathing and how soothing my voice is as I guide you into your trance state. You feel you are slipping in deeper, and deeper, and now you are in. You are still conscious of my voice and can talk to me, can't you Adam?'

'I…Yes I can.' Adam sounded half asleep.

'Good. I would like you to cast your mind back to the moment of Toyah's arrival at your house on that fateful night.'

'Okay.'

'Now it isn't going to be like being there, so it won't hurt as much. It will be like watching it unfold on video. We will be able to pause and rewind, if we need to. Okay?'

'Okay.'

'So where are you Adam?'

'I'm in my kitchen.'

'Good. I want you to start describing what you see and hear.'

'I'm preparing dinner for my date with Toyah. I hear the sound of her car coming up the gravel drive. At first I continue with the cooking but I can't resist seeing her and go into the hallway to look out through the window at her.'

'How does she appear?'

'She seems…preoccupied. She's not looking at me.'

'Pause that view frame, Adam. Why isn't she getting out of the car?'

'She appears to be putting hairspray onto her hair.'

'Does her hair look different?'

'Yes, it...seems shorter or thinner, tighter. Only the spray can isn't a can. It's too long and thin. It's a tube, a roll, it's cling-film. She's winding it round her head. It's so obvious! Why would I think it was hair spray? I must be the stupidest man alive!'

'Easy, Adam. Your mind presented you with the most plausible interpretation at the time.'

'I should have been helping her! Instead I turned away and went back to the kitchen! I turned my back on her!!'

'Calm down Adam.'

'It's my fault she is dead!'

'It's not your fault, Adam.'

'I'm a complete idiot! It should have been me...'

'No Adam, no. The image is fading, you only have to think about your breathing. In and out, in and out. Deep slow breaths. You're safe with me. Relax. You need to start listening to the other sounds around you, the ticking of my clock, the sounds of traffic down the street, you are becoming more alert. You are slowly coming out of your trance state now. You are thinking of opening your eyes. You feel refreshed. Open your eyes.'

Adam blinked his eyes. 'Sorry, I guess it will take more practice, Candice.'

'You did okay, for your first go. How do you feel?'

'Quite refreshed actually, like I had a good night's sleep at last. It was worth it just for that. Thanks.'

Candice smiled. 'And what do you remember?'

'A feeling of floating, someplace where everything was okay. I think I dreamed something but I can't remember what. Does that matter?'

'Not at all. Look, I'll give you my number and if you need to talk or to arrange your next session you can ring me.'

That night Adam almost rang Candice but stopped himself in mid-dial. It was too late. It could wait till morning when he would be calmer. After all it had only been another bad dream. That said it had felt worse than the others. He had woken screaming with self-reproach as the scene replayed itself.

The car crunching gravel on the drive. Adam went to look. The Mercedes had *Cling-Film* emblazoned in big letters on the side of the car. The car itself was completely shrink-wrapped. There was no way to get into or out of the car. Toyah could be seen inside, trapped, hammering on the window yet her voice was inside Adam's head, pleading.

'Help me Adam. Help me. Please don't turn away. Adam!'

Adam fought for control of his body, but it was no use. He turned his back on Toyah just as he was destined to.'

24

Adam had called Candice the following evening, having given himself a day of work to reflect on things.

'Sorry Candice I know I felt quite positive immediately after last night's session but I don't think it is going to work for me. I went on to have the worst nightmare yet and now I'm feeling really guilty over Toyah's death.'

'Listen Adam, you are not to blame, and these sessions can take time to find resolution. Clients often report that things appear to get worse before they get better. Similar has happened with other clients of mine.'

'Really?'

'Really. And I happen to think you made good progress last night. I'm sure we could achieve more with a second session. But it's your choice. Have a think about it and get back to me when you are ready.'

The next morning when Adam and Ben arrived at *Eco Beech* they saw Cameron with a couple of men they hadn't seen before. They were standing at one corner of the visitor centre having what looked like a heated discussion. Cameron looked embarrassed while one of the men holding what looked like blueprints was gesturing across the ground.

Adam thought it tactful to pretend they had seen nothing and head straight to Cameron's porta-cabin to check their tasks on the schedule.

Adam had to read out what was against their names. Cameron still had not cottoned on to Ben's cognitive difficulties. Provided they kept completing their tasks there shouldn't be anything to worry about.

'Plasterboards on walls C through E.' Adam stepped over to the floor plan and pointed them out for Ben though he might as well be pointing at a map of Minneapolis for what good it did.

'You lead, I'll follow.'

As they crossed the yard into the visitor centre they saw Mic and Max next to a stack of four-by-eight plasterboards. The men had placed a chippies A-frame in front and with one pull on a restraining strap the stack leaned forward and came crashing down on the A-frame.

'What do you think you're doing?!' Adam warned far too late.

The first few boards broke in half while the next few creased. The damaged boards couldn't be used for the main wall now. More would need to be ordered, further delaying progress.

'What's going on in here?!'

All heads turned to see Cameron looking pretty pissed off.

'These two,' Mic gestured at Adam and Ben, 'need to learn how to stack plasterboard. It is stored flat, not on its end like this. Some of them are damaged now.'

158

'Bloody hell! That's all I need. What is it with you people?!'

'Hey!' Ben yelled, '*We* never stacked those boards.'

'You two come with me,' Cameron gestured to Adam and Ben, and led them outside.

'That wasn't our doing, Cameron.' Adam tried to explain.

'Just shut up Adam, you're both working with me this morning.'

'Right.'

The three of them returned to the porta-cabin. Cameron handed Adam a ball of orange nylon string, half a dozen wooden pegs, a mallet and a Stanley knife. Picking up a two metre ruler and a theodolite he took a set of keys off a rack on the wall and handed them to Ben.

Ben looked at the keys with concern. Was he supposed to guess what these were for?

'You're going to dig a drainage trench this morning which should have been put in when the foundations went in.'

'That wasn't our fault either.'

'I never said it was, Ben. You weren't here then. Go and bring the Bobcat round to the side of the centre.'

'Right.'

Cameron led Adam to where he had earlier stood with the architects. 'This downpipe is just emptying onto the ground. I don't know why I never spotted it before. It's an obvious error.'

'I guess you've just had a lot on your plate, Cameron.'

'Don't patronise me. Just do what I say.' He snapped, handing Adam the ruler.

With hands already full Adam dropped the ball of string which rushed off down the incline unwinding as it went.

Cameron growled.

Ben stood in front of what he hoped were the Bobcats. Small tracked vehicles. He kicked the tracks to check they were not tyres. They sounded metallic.

Holding and feeling the keyring he counted two keys on it. Logic would suggest that both keys would be for the same machine, otherwise only one Bobcat could be in use at any one time. He knew he needed a machine with an excavator on but looking at them he wasn't even certain what was the front and what was the rear. He ran his hands over the two vehicles like they were metal horses.

Choosing the Bobcat with the long neck, the seat indicated what was forward facing, for the cab at least. He sat down and tried a key. The ignition confirmed he had the right Bobcat. Feeling more confident now he thought he better acquaint himself with the controls.

Ben had driven a tank before so knew about brake steering, but he had never used a Bobcat before, or any excavator for that matter.

Adam and Cameron were just finishing up pegging the trench line when they heard a metallic crunch and popping of glass come from the yard.

Downing tools to look they saw Max rush out of the centre and yank Ben out of the Bobcat cab.

'That's my car! You did that on purpose. And now you'll pay for it. We are ex-SAS you dumb motherfucker.'

Max tripped Ben as he made to get up and Ben rolled over and into Mic. Mic brought Ben to a sudden halt with a hefty kick in the ribs.

'Hey!' Cameron yelled. 'Stop this, now!'

'Look what he's done to my car.'

The paintwork along the driver's side of the BMW 4x4 was badly scratched and the wing-mirror was busted.

'The site insurance should cover it.' Cameron offered as Ben got to his feet.

'Fucker.' Max, still angry, lunged forward and threw a punch at Ben's jaw.

Ben simply deflected the blow. Unfortunately for Mic who was attempting to block Ben's retreat, the fist went on to break his nose. Blood poured down Mic's overalls as he groaned through gritted teeth.

'Max help Mic get cleaned up.' Cameron urged. 'Ben, what do you think you were doing?'

'I was bringing the excavator across the yard and must have nudged the controls for the bucket. As I tried to reset them I must have grabbed the wrong one. The cab turned and the arm swung the bucket down the side of Max's car. Sorry.'

'You *have* used one of these before *haven't you*?'

'Oh sure.'

'Adam, you take over with digging the trench. Ben, you come with me. I'll find something else for you to do.'

As Cameron took Ben inside the visitor centre, and pointed him at the first partition wall that required cladding with plasterboard, he said 'If you just focus on getting these walls up the day shouldn't get any worse.'

Adam was making good progress with the Bobcat. The ground seemed to be the perfect consistency for a neat trench, not too hard not too soft. There were occasional looser sections of course where, as the bucket scooped down and pulled back, some of the earth would fall in.

Halfway along the pegged out route, as Adam pulled back the bucket once more, he caught sight of something white. The hairs on his arms stood on end and he stopped the excavator.

He climbed out of the cab and went to make sure he was wrong.

It had to be just a geological anomaly; One white rock where most were among fifty shades of brown. Maybe it was just very pale beige, after all the soil here at Hamsterley was particularly dark.

Adam knelt at the end of his trench and took a closer look. It did look like a Flintstone. If it was the size of the others then only a third of it was protruding from the end of the trench. He reached in to see how loose it was but stopped himself. DI Carmichael had said not to touch it. But what if it turned out it wasn't one of his Flintstones? That wouldn't be good for either of them.

There was no sign of writing on the exposed upper surface. He had an idea, he could go and grab a piece of that shattered wing mirror and use it to check out the underside. Adam got to his feet and looked across the yard then had a better idea.

Reaching into his jacket he pulled out his phone, lay down on the ground and took a picture of the underside.

Examining the image it was a little out of focus but there were clearly some letters there.

Sitting up, Adam rang Carmichael.

'DI Carmichael.'

'This is Adam, Adam Underwood.'

'Sorry Adam I'm in the middle of something. Can I call you back?'

'No.'

'What?'

'I told you, if I called about a Flintstone you would need to act immediately.'

'A Flintstone?'

'Yes. I've come across the next one.'

'This better not be a prank, Underwood.'

'No prank, Carmichael.'

'Have you picked it up?'

'No, you said not to touch it. It's still in the ground.'

'How do you know it's not just a stone?'

'I'm sending you an image now.'

There was a long pause followed by 'Shit. Alright then I'm bringing someone from forensics.'

'Good, but make it quick, the clock will be ticking for the next woman.'

'Okay, okay. Where are you?'

'Hamsterley.'

'What? Off the A694?'

'No, off the A68.'

'Durham? What the *fuck* are you doing all the way down there? That's way off my patch.'

'Sorry but that's where I'm working at the moment. A building site called *Eco Beech*.'

While Adam waited for the police to arrive he knew he couldn't just sit around doing nothing. Cameron was already in a bad mood. So Adam shifted the Bobcat to the other end of the trench route where the drain would empty into a stream and started digging from that end.

He was steadily closing the gap on the section with the Flintstone when Cameron came by.

'What's going on?!'

Adam turned the Bobcat off. 'I couldn't continue with the first half of the trench so I thought it best to start from this end.'

'Oh don't tell me you've hit a massive rock.'

'Well no, not a *massive* rock. Listen Cameron, I've had to call the police.'

'The police?' A look of dawning came over the site manager and he rushed to where the Flintstone lay. 'You found human remains? No, no. That can't be. There's not supposed to be any old burial sites in this area.'

'No it…'

'I can't see any bones, just this…'

'Don't touch it!!'

Cameron froze where he knelt at the edge of the trench.

'The police were adamant that it shouldn't be touched, under any circumstances.'

'But it's…just a stone, Adam.'

'No, it's not *just* a stone. A woman's life depends on it.'

'What?! Are you crazy? What's going on here?'

'I can't explain. It's best if we wait for the police. Once they remove the stone, the trench can be finished.'

'I'm sorry Adam. This is the last straw. I don't know what you and Ben are up to but I can't afford for anything else to go wrong I'm going to have to ask Frank to get me some replacements.'

'You can't be serious. Ben and I are better than Mic and Max.'

'Maybe all four of you need to go then.'

'Let's just put that thought on hold for a moment. I'll call DI Carmichael and see how soon they'll be…'

At that moment Adam and Cameron both heard a police siren getting closer.

A police car soon pulled into the yard, drawing the attention of everyone from the site. No sooner had it screeched to a halt and silenced its blues and twos, than Carmichael was out of the front passenger seat.

The Detective Inspector looked irritable, having had to make his apologies in the middle of another case meeting. What's more, this potentially futile journey had taken longer than expected. To top it all, the first thing that Carmichael saw was Ben McGregor suddenly grasped by a man with a bloodied nose.

'Here he is officer. Malicious damage to property, *and* assault!' Mic shoved Ben towards the detective.

Ben wasn't sure what was going on, but seeing Carmichael and not a local was pretty sure this was nothing to do with his Bobcat mishap.

'Where is Adam, Ben?'

'Urr, round the side, there.'

Everyone looked bemused as Carmichael walked past Mic and Max as if they were invisible.

A younger man got out of the rear passenger seat of the police car bringing with him a case. He rushed after Carmichael.

The driver's door opened and WPC Hanley stepped out. She walked over to Ben and looked across at Mic with a hint of a smile.

'Someone else with a work related accident, McGregor?'

Adam was getting impatient, matching Carmichael's irritability. 'How long is the lad going to be? This isn't archaeology where there's plenty of time for brushes and tweezers. A life is at stake here.'

'I know that Underwood. It would have been so much easier if you had found this on a Newcastle pavement.'

'Wouldn't it just. If I'd known it would take you this long I'd never have called it in. I might have saved this woman by now.'

'The forensic specialist I wanted for this was too busy on another job so I had to grab his assistant from the lab.'

'Does he know what he's doing?!'

'I believe *so*,' said the young man getting up from the trench placing his camera back in the case. 'From the condition of the soil and turf above the stone, there is no indication that it was buried here. There are no prints on the exposed surface of the stone, though gloves could have been worn to force the stone into the soil. However, there is no indication of pressure disturbance around the stone. In fact, as with the neighbouring stones in the trench wall, the soil in contact with the surface of the stone is as would be expected for natural soil covering.'

'This isn't a CSI show lad.' The assistant's tech speak was doing nothing for Carmichael's irritability. 'What are you telling us?'

'The depth of this stone would suggest that it has been here for some considerable time, Sir. Hundreds possibly thousands of years. I couldn't be more specific without a survey of the area.'

'But what about the writing?'

'That is the conundrum of course, Sir. It's typography is too modern.'

167

'Never mind the bloody typography!' wailed Adam. 'What does it say? Get it out so we can read it!'

Quickly the assistant returned to the Flintstone and pulled it free, with quite some effort required to loosen it. Lifting it clear, turning it over and rubbing the caked-on soil away, the verse was revealed.

At Café Noir
She drinks her last,
Waiting for Cotes
The die is now cast.

'What coats?' Adam asked no one in particular.

'That would be me Sir, I guess,' the assistant sounded rather shocked. 'My name's Colin Cotes.'

There was an impressed murmur from the crowd that had now gathered around the trench, as if witness to a David Blaine magic trick.

The blues and twos were off again as Hanley sped Adam and her two colleagues towards Bishop Auckland.

'What makes you so sure it is the Café Noir in Bishop Auckland Mr Underwood?' asked Cotes.

'According to Google it is the nearest one to us.'

'But why must it be the nearest?'

'You have a point. It could be whichever one I arrive at.'

'I don't follow.'

'These events occur wherever and whenever I arrive, *usually*. Although this Flintstone suggests today we will be too late because we were waiting for you, Cotes.'

'But how could the person who engraved the stone possibly have known I would be called to the scene today, thousands of years ago?'

'Exactly!'

Carmichael had the wits to call ahead, and confirmed that an incident was indeed already in progress at Bishop Auckland's Café Noir. The manageress explained that an ambulance might be sent out as soon as her first-aider, Helen, was able to complete the call centre questionnaire.

Carmichael demanded a situational report, so the café manageress started from the beginning.

A young woman, having a coffee on her own, for no apparent reason launched into an impression of the restaurant scene from When Harry Met Sally. Maybe someone was videoing her for a social media post. She certainly looked and sounded like she was experiencing a great deal of pleasure.

As she persisted, drawing everyone's attention, the manageress concluded the young woman must be on something. She had then gone over to her, intending to ask her to leave. However, the woman simply looked back at her with an open-mouthed smile of sheer astonishment at the intensity of what she was experiencing. The manageress gently took the young woman by the right wrist, at which point the woman gasped with further surprise. Then began fitting and collapsed to the floor.

The manageress had then called to Helen, the first-aider. As she came to the young woman's side the manageress dialled 999. She then told Carmichael that as soon as she heard the nonsense questions she quickly passed her mobile over to Helen.

'How is this young woman now?'

'Well Helen has put the phone down and is providing CPR now. The young woman is still smiling, wide-eyed. So I think she is going to be okay. No, wait, Helen is looking across to me now and shaking her head.'

'Okay. I want you to lock the Cafe. Don't let anyone leave, or tamper with the young woman or the contents of her table.'

'What's the matter?'

'Miss?'

'Helen, what's the matter with you?'

'Miss?!'

'Sorry Officer. It's Helen. She's started hyperventilating and groaning.'

25

As Adam left with the police, Ben returned to the partition walling he had been busy with, noting that Max and Mic were following him inside. He had considered taking a photo of them to see if their ex-SAS claim checked out with his buddies down in Hereford but that might have to wait.

'What the hell do you think you are doing, Ben? Frank is going to be pissed with you.' Mic warned.

'What do you mean?'

'You're already on the second wall. You need to slow down.' Max pointed out.

'We don't rush things in this business.' Mic explained.

'Don't worry Mic. It looks like he's put most of them up the wrong way round.'

'What do you mean?' They looked fine to Ben. Anyway, they would soon be painted.

'Yeah, you're right. What a fucking moron. They will have to be pulled back off and replaced. Nice going shit for brains.'

Ben wasn't getting riled by their language, he'd heard far worse in his time, from Meg.

Seeing that the verbal abuse was like water off a ducks back for Ben, Max stepped in close, laying a gentle hand on Ben's left shoulder. 'Let me share a friendly bit of advice with you.'

Max slammed his left fist into Ben's solar plexus. However, Ben's six-pack was so hard and Max's angle of attack a little too shallow, it did more to sprain Max's wrist than wind Ben.

Ben raised Max's right arm and followed through with a blow to the armpit, cracking a rib and bowling Max over.

However, Mic's heavy boot in the back of Ben's right knee brought Ben toppling down onto Max.

Mic followed up with the end of the 2x4 he was wielding, swinging it down for Ben's skull just as Max was trying to twist from under Ben.

Ben bent double at the last moment, removing his head from the path of the length of timber which planted itself in Max's groin.

Ben didn't waste time enjoying the sound of max's increased pain. Frank's men meant business. Rolling aside Ben got back to his feet. He was going to have to deal with them one way or another.

Ben lifted his hands in semi-surrender. 'Listen guys. I enjoy a bit of rough and tumble as much as the next man, but not in the workplace. We're on the same side.'

'Same side?!' Max growled, getting up holding his balls. 'After what you did to my car?'

'I didn't even know it was *your* car.' Ben's smile, intended to help calm the situation, only seemed to make his words sound insincere.

Max grabbed a hammer from the nearby bag of tools and hurled it at Ben's groin. Ben twisted aside, but should have stepped back too, as the head struck him in the thigh giving him an instant dead-leg.

'What will Frank say, lads?' Ben hopped backwards a few paces.

'Frank only cares about his bottom line.'

Max and Mic rushed Ben together.

Ben knew the odds were stacked against him now. Two hard men and him with only one working leg. Time seemed to go in slow motion. His mind raced through his options. He knew there was a rib and groin injury he could possibly exploit, but truth be told he couldn't tell in that instant which of them had had those injuries.

As the two men slammed into him, Ben struck hard and fast, delivering a blow to a throat. He felt cartilage crumple as he lost contact with the ground. A blow to the ribs, right where he had been kicked earlier, sent him backwards onto the low pile of plasterboards.

Mic turned away gagging, holding his throat, bent double, while Max brought his right fist down on Ben's face. Ben turned aside but the blow impacted his jaw making his head ring. There was no time to stop. Ben bolted up, head-butting Max in the face. Blood from Max's lip sprayed into his eyes. Blinking to clear his vision, tracking the blur of Max's body, there was a sudden pain in the back of Ben's head and then a relaxing blackness.

Mic stood over Ben, still holding the 2x4, making ready in case Ben got back up.

Max made sure with a kick in Ben's ribs, then doubly sure with a kick in the groin. Both of which only got slight movement and little sound.

'Right,' Mic gurgled, 'Check the yard is clear and back the car up.'

'Are we taking him to Frank?'

'Frank? No, the fun has only just started.'

The BMW was reversed up and Ben was piled in to the boot. For good measure, before the boot was closed Max gave Ben a black eye.

'So where are we going Mic?'

Some twenty minutes later, travelling west on a moorland track, Ben began to come round. Years of training kicked in. He made no sudden movements or sounds. He kept his eyes closed and listened.

It was clear to Ben that he was in the back of a slow moving vehicle, possibly Max's BMW, going over rough ground. He could smell petrol. It was unlikely that the BMW would have a leaking fuel tank, so there was probably a petrol container in the boot with him. Slowly Ben felt around, opening his eyes.

He was pleased to find that neither his wrists nor ankles were bound, such was the confidence of his captors, who he realised were now speaking in Russian.

Splinters of light were getting into the boot around the edge of the rear cover-board. He located the petrol container and wondered how he might safely use it to his advantage.

Ben continued his search of the interior to see what else he might use to make his escape and discovered a camo jacket. He immediately searched the pockets. They were empty except for a pen, which was better than nothing. He might be able to flip the back latch and roll out of the slow moving vehicle but such an escape would be obvious. His body ached but in testing his muscles he acknowledged that his dead-leg had now faded. Nevertheless, he was unlikely to get far with the two of them in a 4x4 and no idea where he was. Ben remained positive. There had to be a solution to this problem.

The BMW crested a rise and started down a winding incline towards a stream. At the first bend the 4x4 turned into a massive fireball, the hatchback still shut.

Arriving at Café Noir Carmichael took charge of the situation. He assumed correctly that the woman who let them inside was the manageress.

'Hello. I'm DI Carmichael, I believe we spoke on the phone but you didn't tell me your name.'

'Yes, sorry no, it's Pauline Edwards.'

It had become clear from the continued reporting over the phone that Helen had also died though no close examination had risked confirming that. 'Where are they?'

'Just over here.'

'Henley, start taking statements. Cotes do your stuff.'

Most of the customers were looking worried, standing to one side, but one woman was still sitting at a table looking quite relaxed.

'Dawn?'

'Hello Adam.'

Carmichael turned to see Adam walking over to the red-head and followed him. 'Is this Miss Summers?'

'Yes,' Dawn answered.

'What are you doing here?'

'Well since Adam was going to be late I had to watch the woman die. I have to say, if I was to die and could choose how, that would be top of my list of exits. It appeared to be quite…beautiful.'

Dawn sounded unhinged to Carmichael. 'Miss Edwards, do you have an office we might use as an interview room?'

'Yes, follow me.'

'I have some questions for you Miss Summers,' Carmichael gestured that she should follow the manageress.

'I know. I will answer them as I do.'

'Thank you.' Carmichael turned to Adam, 'You best join us.'

The manageress opened her office door. 'Please excuse the mess.' She closed the door after them and headed behind the counter to make herself yet another coffee.

There was only one seat in the office. 'Please sit down Miss Summers. Mr Underwood and I will remain standing.'

'As a position of *authority*?' There was a hint of a chuckle to her comment.

'Do you mind if I record this interview?'

'No, not at all.'

Taking his phone and positioning it for the best possible angle of view Carmichael started the video recording.

'Miss Summers. You have already admitted to watching the victims at Café Noir die. Are you responsible for their deaths?'

'Do you mean am I responsible because I did nothing to save them, or are you asking if I murdered them?'

'Did you kill these women?'

'No. The customer died when she drank coffee she had administered a neurotoxin to. The shop assistant died when she became contaminated with the neurotoxin upon delivering CPR.'

'Did you have prior knowledge of what was going to happen here today?'

'Of course.'

'And you felt no desire to warn these women.'

'I have no desire, no.'

'But you could have saved these women.'

'No I could not, DI Carmichael.'

'Why ever not?'

'This is what happened here today.'

'You are not making much sense. Are you on any…medications?'

'No, we are not.'

'We? Are you suffering from any mental health issues at present? Multiple Personality Disorder, or the likes?'

'No. I'm absolutely clear what I am and what I will do.'

'Will do?'

'Yes. I am a Time-Slave.'

Carmichael turned to Adam, 'I don't think she is going to be able to help us. I think she is insane.'

'Dawn?'

'Yes Adam.'

'Did you kill any of the other people the Flintstones directed me to?'

'No.'

'Are you the maker of the Flintstones?'

'No.'

'Is it always you who places the Flintstones for me to find?'

'Yes.'

'How did you know I would dig that trench today and find that Flintstone? It could have been someone else.'

'No Adam that is not possible. It was you.'

'When did you put that Flintstone there?'

'I dropped it onto a patch of bracken around 700BC.'

'*That* is not possible.' Carmichael snapped.

'Ha. You people are funny. So narrow minded.'

'Okay, so how old are you then, eh?'

'Oh that's not so easy to answer. Dawn Summers, the truck driver, she is not born yet.'

'So you believe you are from the future?' Carmichael might have been amused had he not been feeling so frustrated by Dawn's continued cryptic responses.

'Yes I believe so.'

'And why would it be so important for you to come back here and torment Mr Underwood since he was a child?'

'I don't see my actions as torment. I have been part of his prepping.'

'Prepping?'

'Yes. Adam is not much longer for this world.'

'What do you mean? Are you going to kill me, Dawn?'

'In a manner of speaking, yes.'

'*In a manner of speaking*?...Why?'

'All will become clear soon enough.'

Adam made to place a hand on Dawn.

'Don't touch me…yet.' She warned. 'It is time for me to go now.'

'I'm afraid we are going to have to detain you a little longer Miss Summers.' Carmichael insisted.

'Adorable.' Dawn clapped her hands together, beaming a smile. 'Human over-confidence. You've got to love it.'

Dawn rose from the seat. As she did so a shadow appeared on the wall behind her, as if from an invisible light. She stepped towards the men and was gone.

'What the *fuck* just happened, Adam?'

'I think that might have been Ben's hole in the air.'

26

Above Ben the cover-board in the boot seemed to slide back suddenly but soundlessly. Not to reveal the rear window and ceiling of the BMW but something unacceptable to a rational mind.

Maybe it was another cognitive anomaly Ben considered. However, it did seem very real. Suspended a couple of meters away was a strange ceiling of glowing tubes, almost like a giant brain.

Then Ben saw two figures step forward to look down at him. Ben wondered what the hell was going on. Had the petrol fumes got to him?

Then Ben noticed that one of the white clad figures in the bright white room above was Dawn. She beckoned him to climb out.

Without a word he stood up. The boot seemed even less stable now that he was standing upright in it. He stepped out and onto the white flooring above.

The other figure, a male, drew a weapon from his back holster and shot a bolt of energy into the boot just as the hole in the floor snapped shut.

'This is Destiny, Ben.'

'What's going on Dawn? Where is this?'

'This is the core of The Apple.'

'And where exactly is The Apple?'

'The exact coordinates would be meaningless to you, Ben. Not because of your cognitive issues, but because all you need to know is that we are in deep space, outside of any galaxy.'

'You've *got* to be pissing me.'

'No. See for yourself.' Dawn and Destiny led Ben to the surface.

There was an odd stomach churning moment where the gravity realigned as they passed from the lower level of the planetoid to the upper. In the lower level the pseudo-grav system held them to the floor with head towards the core, whereas on the upper level flooring their heads were towards the sky.

The dark sky seemed empty compared to the not-so-dark skies of Earth.

'The stars here seem much fainter.'

'That's because on Earth you look through the stars out towards galaxies.' Destiny explained. 'Here you are just looking at galaxies.'

'Why have you brought me here?'

'There are a number of reasons, Ben.' Dawn answered, leading the way back inside. 'First off because *that* is how it happened.'

'Right.' Ben didn't feel any the wiser.

'Coming here has saved your life, but there is a cost. Everything has consequences.'

'What cost?'

'There are a number of things you are required do before you return.'

'These...*experiences* will help you to understand things differently,' Destiny added.

'This is What-If,' Dawn introduced the core of The Apple. 'It is the planetoid's reality drive.'

'Reality drive?'

'Yes Ben,' Destiny explained, 'there are six dimensions of travel. Up and down, left and right, forwards and backwards make up the first three dimensions. Time is the fourth dimension with past and future, but when time-travel was first trialled by the ancients some theories were proven correct whilst others were disproven. For every event point there is a divide in realities. There are an infinite number of universes, the multiverse, where any eventuality imaginable is played out. Many are exactly the same until the moment a critical event differentiates them.'

'This sounds like science fiction to me.'

'I'm sure it does, Ben, but it's fact. When we send you back in time, you will do as was done. If you do not then you would switch to an alternative reality, leaving your home reality behind.' Destiny pointed above their heads at the mass of glowing tubes, 'What-If is the only 5D drive able to navigate the realities. It keeps timelines intact by using time-slaves to ensure events happen when they happen.'

'Where are these slaves?'

'You're looking at them.'

'You two? Can't you escape?'

'No. We can only do what is to be done. Resistance is futile. Desire for anything other than complete compliance is pointless. Acceptance of one's lot is the only way to maintain sufficient well-being.'

'And what about the sixth dimension?'

'6D remains only theory as no such drive has been developed to document proof of travel across the sixth dimension. This is because the sixth dimension is proposed to contain universes which exist with one or more laws of physics different to our home reality within the sixth dimension. It is expected that 6D travel would at best be a very risky endeavour.

'Okay. I'm glad we cleared that up. So how does *this* core work?'

'We do not understand the ancient technology behind it,' Dawn lifted her left hand to touch a tube, holding her right hand out palm up, 'but we interact with it through contact with the tubing. We could speak our musings or wishes of *what if* this or *what if* that, but in truth the drive simply reads our thoughts.'

A package appeared in the air and dropped into Dawn's hand. It was wrapped in paper and tied with string. It looked heavy. She handed it to Ben. 'This is for Adam.'

'Is it a Flintstone?'

'Yes.'

'Right well I suppose I better be getting back. Time is getting on.'

'Time is of no consequence here, Ben.' Destiny remarked with a hint of amusement.

'No consequence to you maybe, but I have a son who needs picking up from school.'

'You could stay here years and still get back in time for Robbie.'

'Okay, so The Apple is like a Tardis then, only here you two have got this thing that grants wishes. What if I touch the tubing and wish away my cognitive issues?'

'You will try but find you cannot, because the remedy for your brain damage is already under development. You will have it further along you're time-line.'

'But I'd rather be healed now. What if I stop the accident from happening?'

'In other reality lines that is what happened. In some of them you are happy, in others you are dead.'

'Dead?'

'Yes.'

'So what does my home reality future have in store for me?'

'I don't think you want to know, Ben,' warned Dawn.

'Yes I do, just enough so that I know when it happens that this hasn't just been a hallucination. Because right now that's what it feels like.'

'Okay, well MI5 are going to be looking for you.'

'MI5? Why?'

'You will be going to prison.'

'Why?'

'Because of what you do.'

'What if I don't do it?'

'But you do.'

Ben tried to lift his free hand towards the tubing, to change his future, to heal himself immediately. His arm seemed frozen. He tried lifting the hand with the package with the same success. He tried to outsmart the drive by moving his free arm to his chest and his arm complied. He moved his hand up to his face but as he tried to quickly lift his hand above his head his arm froze again.

'Okay, I don't know how this drive knows my every move and controls my muscles but I get the picture.'

'It knows because everything from the big bang to the end of the multiverse has already happened and happens the way it happens,' insisted Destiny.

'So is it always controlling our bodies to ensure we follow our time-lines? Or does it only run *corrective* interference?'

'Interference is certainly one way of looking at the experience of one's expectations being frustrated. We call it *meta-interference* since What-If will interfere with any attempt to interfere with a time-line.'

'Is that interference driven by good or evil intent?'

'It is hard to say. It seems rather random.'

'So what if instead of selfishly seeking to heal myself I wish a good deed for someone else, just to prove that I've made it work?'

'It would only work if that is what happens.'

'So what you are saying is that I would think I had suggested a change but really I would only have imagined what happens in the future.'

'Yes.'

'But I would want to wish for something highly unlikely and unexpected, to prove it was my doing and not something that was bound to happen anyway.'

'Whatever the event you imagine, it will only happen if that is what happens, as I said. All your intent for something extraordinary will achieve is to change your own perception or belief of control.'

'Sounds like bullshit to me, but here goes.' Ben lifted his free hand and this time touched a section of tubing.

Nothing happened immediately but he smiled to himself, looking forward to admiring the evidence of his intention when he returned.

'If you are finished Ben, we should deliver that package for Adam,' said Dawn, pointing behind Ben.

Ben turned to see another hole opening up in the air, like a door. Neither Dawn nor Destiny had appeared to activate the portal.

'It is time.' Dawn gestured that Ben should go first and he walked through onto Adam's drive and called out 'Adam!'

'Stop, Ben.' Dawn followed him onto the gravel. 'You and Adam are working.'

'Oh...Well I'll leave this for him in the garage.'

'You throw it through the window.'

'Why would I do that when I can just put it inside?' He turned to look at the windows. The pane he knew to be broken wasn't, yet.

'That's right Ben...It was *you*.'

'Fuck, no.' Without further thought Ben threw the package and it broke through the glass, exactly as it had.

'Good.' Dawn clapped as if Ben had chosen to comply, even though they both knew he had not. 'Now something for Meg.'

'Meg?'

'Yes. Follow me.' Dawn led Ben down the drive, past where the portal had been and onto the lane where she turned right.

Ben was intrigued and followed.

As they walked Ben had an inspired idea. 'Is the random serial killer Adam is looking for actually *Time*? These women die in the manner they do, when they do, where they do, because that is *their* death? If that is the answer, then that is pretty disappointing.'

'Yes, yes and no. That certainly is the manner of their death, or they would not be dead. As a conclusion, that in itself would certainly be disappointing. There is however a murderer, who *will* kill again.'

'Why can't you say who it is? Is it Destiny?'

'Destiny? Ha. I wouldn't put it past him…or me for that matter…but no.'

'Can't you give me a clue, or is the *meta-interference* just too strong?'

'Like someone who has watched a mystery before it seems pretty obvious to me, even though all the cards are not yet on the table.'

'We are relying on the police to determine the connections and patterns, to work out the motivation and means. Can't you give us something extra?'

'In time.'

'How about now?'

'Here we go.' Dawn stopped and turned right into the undergrowth of some woods.

'Shouldn't we stick to a footpath?'

'No.'

Through the trees they went. Nothing seemed familiar to Ben, yet Dawn knew he had been here once before, before his accident.

Dawn brought them to a bramble thicket behind a big rhododendron bush. 'Look in there.'

'In the brambles? What am I looking for? Brer Rabbit?'

Dawn said nothing so Ben turned his attentions to the brambles. He pulled creepers this way and that, trying to avoid their snagging sharp thorns. Then he noticed some deadwood in there, caught up in what looked like string. In fact the closer he leaned in it looked very much like some camo netting he had once lost. He reached for his phone to help cast more light. There was something under the netting.

'Meg's car!'

Dawn had offered no help in retrieving Meg's lost car, beyond telling Ben that he would need to bring a new battery when he and Adam came to extract it. Ben was beginning to understand Dawn had no choice.

Dawn also had no choice about what task she had Ben do next.

A while later, with that traumatising task complete, Ben had been returned, to stand feeling numb and helpless by the low pile of plasterboard inside the *Eco Beech* visitor centre.

He became aware of car doors closing outside and an engine start. He found himself striding out of the centre just in time to see the BMW with Max, Mic and him inside speeding away from the yard.

For a moment he stood quite still, considering that for a while there was once again two of him on Earth. He wondered whether there was any limit to how many of him could be present at any one time.

Slowly he moved out into the middle of the yard. Nothing was going to feel the same again. He had been given a mind altering experience. As he walked he had the distinct feeling that he was no more than a passenger, no longer fooled into believing he was controlling his body, maybe not even his own thoughts. Everything was as it would be.

Ben stopped and looked around at the building site. Nothing had changed. He spotted Cameron in the Bobcat finishing off the trench now that Adam was away with the police.

Ben waited a little longer for something to happen, for that thing he had wished for. He tried considering that maybe none of this was real.

'Shit. I forgot to say *when*.'

27

The return journey from Bishop Auckland was as fast as it had been getting there. They had been some considerable time at Café Noir. Eventually Adam mentioned he really had to get back to take Ben to his kid's school.

As Henley drove with the blues and twos going again, DI Carmichael used this time for a group debrief.

What had been found at the café had stirred up something of a hornets nest. It wasn't so much because they were operating on Durham turf, and the locals had had to be informed, but because of the circumstances of the deaths.

Cotes had been duty-bound to report the cause of death as possible neurotoxin. MI5 had then got involved. The whole situation was now being directed by Cobra emergency control.

The statements that Henley had taken had all corroborated one another. A couple had seen the young woman, identified as Miss Geri Evens, empty a sachet of sweetener into her coffee. Cotes said that the remains of the sachet would have been one of the things going off to pathology. However, Harriet Wallace, the woman who turned up from MI5 just before they left the scene, had taken all this evidence off Cotes. She had claimed that if this was a neurotoxin then it was a possible threat to national security. If it wasn't, the evidence would be returned in good time.

DI Carmichael sighed at the messiness of it all. Much of this case now looked like it would get him thrown off the force if he reported it honestly. The video evidence on his phone would be called a hoax.

'So what we know to date is: The killer has access to possible specialist chemicals, or at least some new designer drug.

'They continue to target women.

'Their link to Adam here is via message verses on Flintstones sent by Dawn Summers.

'Summers would most likely have access to such chemicals going by the technology we have witnessed her use.

'She claims not to be the killer, yet refuses to tell us who the killer is, for reasons unknown. My gut feeling is that she is lying.'

'Why though?'

'Isn't it obvious Adam? Because she *can*.'

'It seems to me we need to know a lot more about these victims.'

'I agree. I'm going to get a finer detail search run on these women. As yet we don't know whether they knew one another, whether they were all part of a group.'

'Don't you think such a group would have reported that their members were being knocked off if that were the case?'

'Not if it were a secret group doing something that needed to be kept under the radar.'

'That sounds a bit fanciful to me.'

'Does it? With the rise in vigilantism due to national cutbacks to the police, there are all sorts of clandestine groups forming these days.'

'Really? Sounds like conspiracy theory to me.'

'And that is less believable than a woman who can walk through a hole in the air?'

'I see your point.'

'So I will have background checks run on the victims and I'll go over the coroner's reports again, see if I can spot any pattern that's been overlooked.'

Adam was dropped off at the construction site gates and as he reached the yard he found Ben already standing by the van. He noticed the bruising to his face. 'What happened to you?'

'It's been a long day, Adam. I'm not the man I thought I was.'

'What have you done?'

'I can't talk about it.' Ben sounded depressed, not his usual self at all.

'Okay well let's get you to Robbie.'

Whatever was troubling Ben he wasn't opening up on the drive to North Shields. Adam was so concerned about Ben's monosyllabic responses to his questions that he decided to wait for Ben to get Robbie then drove them both home.

Ben said no more than 'Thanks' when Adam dropped them off.

'I'll pick you up on Monday.'

'Sure.' Ben closed the van door and turned his back on Adam.

Adam made sure they both went inside. He wondered about waiting around for Meg but put the van into gear and pulled away.

Robbie followed Ben into the house and on into the kitchen. 'I'm hungry Dad.'

'Y'mum'll be home soon.'

'I want a MacDonald's.'

Ben realised that he felt like one too. 'That's not going to happen.' He took a beer from the fridge and went out into the back yard and sat on the bench.

Robbie followed him out and sat next to him. Ben anticipated a second request for food. He felt bad, but maybe the truth was he was supposed to.

'Did this one fight back, Dad?'

'What?'

'This woman. Didn't she want saving?'

'What are you talking about?'

'Your face.'

'What's wrong with my face?' Ben hadn't thought to look in a mirror. He was too dazed by his new order of existence.

'It's all bruised.'

'Oh, that…Just some trouble at work.'

'Was it the manager? Did your brain damage make him angry?'

'No. It was…other workers. Some people can't help looking for trouble…till they find it.'

'Why not?'

'Because that's what happens.'

Robbie heard a sound in the house and went inside. Ben took another swig of beer and stared at the shed without seeing it.

Meg came out and stepped in his line of sightlessness.

'Ben! What's happened now?'

'I…had a bad day.'

'Were you in a fight?'

'Ha.' There was a hint of irony to his laugh. 'Don't let the beating on the outside fool you, luv. It's the inside that's beaten.'

'What?...What are you talking about?'

Ben didn't want to explain. Maybe he couldn't explain. Maybe this was one of those critical events. He couldn't tell his wife that he had been abducted by aliens to deep space. He couldn't even tell her he was suffering from delusions about aliens. She would worry for the safety their kids and tell him to leave. If he shared his new experience of *time*, at best she would declare it as fatalistic, at worst she would understand and then she would feel beaten too.

'Well?...I'm waiting.'

'Robbie is hungry.'

'I'm not standing for this anymore, Ben. Get your stuff and get out. You are scaring me…and the kids. I can't cope with it anymore, d'you hear?'

'Loud and clear.' Ben emptied the can in one and got up.

Meg felt bad. Tears began to stream down her cheeks, but she had to do this for the kids. Hopefully this was the kick Ben needed to get act together.

Ben went upstairs to gather his kit. It took him a while to fill his Bergen because he wasn't sure what some of his kit was.

Finally he clumped down stairs.

Meg caught him in the hallway. 'Where are you going?'

'You told me to get out.' There was doubt in his voice. Was that another delusion? His loving wife throwing him out on the street?

'Where will you go to?'

'Wherever my legs take me.'

'Right. Are you going to say goodbye to Robbie and Beth?'

He thought about it but found himself saying 'I'll be back,' like Arnold Schwarzenegger.

28

Adam looked through the hallway window as Toyah sat killing herself in the car.

'It's a dream.' He told himself, but he didn't wake up.

'It's not real.' But it looked real.

'It's *my* imagination.' He opened the front door and strode over to the car.

'Toyah!'

She turned and looked at him.

'You're smothering yourself!' He tried the car door but it was locked.

She seemed to become more conscious of her actions and began to panic, clawing at her face.

'Open the door!'

She couldn't get a grip on the polythene. She started to scream.

'Open the door! Open the door!!'

She clicked the lock.

Adam yanked the door open, grabbed the keys from the ignition and pierced the cling-film over her mouth. She gasped air in deep gulps.

Adam got fingers into the hole and tore it wider. He was saving Toyah. She was going to be okay.

'What's happening, Adam?'

'You're going to be okay.'

'What have you done to me?'

'I didn't do this. You did it to yourself.'

'Bollocks! I drove over here to see you and you lost your mind!'

'No. No! Someone killed you. I need to know who.'

'Adam, you've gone completely insane!' She grabbed her keys back off him, pushed him off and closed the door. Pulling the remains of the polythene from her head angrily, she started the car.

'Wait!' Adam had to have more time with her. He had lots of questions.

Toyah turned the car round and pulled away.

'Toyah!!' He ran after the car.

She sped up, pulling out onto the lane without looking, watching him in her rear-view mirror.

The Mercedes was hit by an oncoming truck. It was the one from the Tyne Bridge accident.

'NO!!' Adam screamed as he woke.

He was going to need another session with Candice.

Adam phoned Candice mid-morning on the Saturday. She sounded pleased to hear from him.

'Come round for lunch, if you like.'

'No, no I couldn't.'

'We can just talk, over some soup and bread rolls. All home-made this morning.'

'Well I don't know if I could turn down an offer like that.'

'We can just chat and you can decide whether you want to give the hypnosis another try.'

'Okay, I'll head across shortly.'

'Great. See you in a bit.'

As Adam headed towards Newcastle he started to wonder. If he decided not to do the hypnosis, then what was in it for Candice? Was she just confident he would give it another go, which to his mind was the whole point of calling her in the first place, or was it something else? Did she make lunch for all her clients? She'd already made the food though, but did she share it with her other clients? Was she actually more interested in him?

He arrived just before twelve, a little earlier than expected. He had anticipated the traffic being worse.

Candice welcomed him in, leading him into the kitchen. 'We can eat at the breakfast bar, or would you prefer I set the table in the dining room?'

'Oh here is fine. You've gone to enough trouble already.'

'Don't be silly. I love cooking.'

'Here is fine, really.'

'Okay then.' As she got the dishes ready she asked 'What made you decide to come back?'

'The continuing nightmares I guess. Only this last one I found I wasn't just a helpless spectator. I was able to take some control.'

'Oh that is a good sign, Adam.'

'Is it.'

'Yes. That is lucid dreaming, when you realise you are in a dream and begin to direct it without waking up. It can allow you to explore what's going on in your subconscious.'

'Right.'

'So what happened? Can you talk about it? Or would you prefer to leave it till later?'

'I saved Toyah.'

'Did you?'

'Yes. I wanted to find out who killed her. Only she blamed me.'

'So you still feel you are to blame.'

'I guess.'

'You mustn't blame yourself. Throw those negative thoughts away. You are a good person.' Candice placed a butter dish on the breakfast bar then put a small basket of rolls next to it. 'So how did the nightmare end?'

'Toyah still died. Her car was hit by a truck in the lane.'

'That could be the brain telling you to accept her death was fate. If it hadn't been by suffocation it would have been some other means. It was her time.'

'You don't really believe a person can have a set time, do you?'

'I think I do, yes. We don't often know when it will be, so we should make the best we can from every day.'

'That's a very positive attitude.'

'Well I don't want to look back with too many regrets.'

'Do you mind me asking how old you are? You seem quite grown-up for a student.'

'I'm a mature student. I came to university later than most, though there are students of all ages across the faculties.'

'So what were you before you started university?'

'I was an outward-bounds instructor actually, working with disadvantaged kids.'

'Oh. What made you give that up?'

'It was a rewarding experience, I was able to help a great many children gain confidence and move on from the situations fate had dealt them. But I kept feeling there was more I could do. In my spare time I took an interest in alternative therapies. That's when I decided to do a Psychology degree. What about you?'

'Oh I was never very academic. I've been an odd job man and in the building and renovation trade since leaving school. Initially I worked with a partner down in the South West. However, when my father died I inherited his property and ended up living in the North East.'

'I guess you prefer it here.'

'Yes. It's a lovely part of the country.'

Candice poured the soup out. 'So, these Flintstones you have been receiving…You got them down there as well as up here, which means it must involve someone who followed you.'

'Yes.'

'Someone you know. But you moved on your own, right?'

'Yes. But I know now who has been behind the Flintstones. Dawn Summers.'

'The woman you saw picnicking across from your barge?'

'Yes. She has been following me.'

'And others, surely.'

'Possibly.'

'No, certainly. Or else she would have been too young when you were a child.'

'You'd think.'

'Do you believe in immortality?'

'I'm not saying that. There may be other explanations.'

'Like what?'

'I don't think I can say at this point. I fear it would make my mental health sound even worse. I would sound delusional, even though I have witnesses.'

'Witnesses to what?'

'I think Dawn can travel in time.'

'Ha ha…Oh, you are being serious…sorry.'

With the awkward moment behind them Adam and Candice finished lunch. After half an hour of idle chit-chat to let the meal settle they retired to the lounge.

Adam now reclined on the couch, quite relaxed, and under hypnosis.

In his mind Adam was back in the kitchen, knowing what must be going on in the Mercedes outside, feeling guilty that he was still messing on with the cooking.

'Stay calm Adam. Remember none of this is your doing. You are just running through it all again to check for anything you missed, like watching it on video.'

'The food is ready but Toyah has not come in. I'm going to the front door, opening it. Toyah is sitting in the driver's seat, motionless. I dash to the car.'

'Pause there, Adam. Can you stay away from the car?'

'Why?'

'I want you to look around. Can you see anything out of place? Anyone there who you didn't see before?'

'Okay I'm trying to look. Oh but I can't seem to turn my head, or my eyes.'

'Don't panic. Some people feel locked by the memory. Try using your peripheral vision.'

'I don't see anything unusual.'

'Okay continue with the memory. Go to Toyah.'

Adam recounts how he tried to rescue Toyah by going for a rock. As he is picking the rock up he thought he heard something. He paused, but again he could not turn his head to look. He moved on. A little later, on the gravel with Toyah he heard something again but still saw nothing in his field of vision and could not make himself turn to look.

'What does it sound like, Adam?'

'Sort of a growl, like stifled anger.'

'Okay. Remember how you took control of your dream? I want you to feel in control again and get up off the gravel.'

Adam struggled, becoming distressed. He couldn't do it.

'Just relax Adam. I want you to stop watching that memory. We have made some good progress again but it is time for you to come back out. Just relax. Think about your breathing. Deep breaths now, deep calming breaths.'

Shortly Adam was blinking his eyes open and smiling. 'I think we got somewhere this time. Didn't we?'

'A little further Adam, yes. Do you remember where we got to?'

'No, sorry, nothing, but I'm feeling good.'

'We were trying to find out whom or what was making the noise you heard when you were trying to save Toyah.'

'And?'

'You couldn't move to go look.'

'You think it's important to keep trying?'

'I think it may be a part of what's causing the PTSD.'

'Will it resolve with further sessions?'

'It may do. There *is* something else we could try but you need to think it over before deciding what you want to do.'

'What's that then?'

'In the South American rainforest some Shaman use a psychoactive plant extract to induce an out of body experience. Some people who have taken it have reported feeling like they become their animal spirit looking down on their human form. I have used this with some of my clients who have then gone into their hypnotic trace and had a more enlightening experience.'

'But surely that is just a hallucination heightening their imagination.'

'Possibly. But if it opens the door to resolution of the PTSD is that not what you want?'

'I guess so.'

'So you will think it over?'

'No. I'll try it now.'

'It's too soon. You have only just come out of a trance. You need to rest a while.'

'But I feel fine, really…Okay let's go out for some fresh air and then give it a go when we come back.'

Adam drove Candice north to the Northumberlandia landscape artwork. It turned out that neither of them had been there before.

Sitting down on a bench having walked around some of the paths, Adam opened up a little more. 'I think being with you is helping me too. Don't take this the wrong way, but I think it is helping me move on from the grieving. Maybe in another life, had we met, we could have been something more. It will be good when you sort my PTSD out. I have every confidence in you. But I'll be sorry to say good bye. You are a good person Candice.'

'Thank you.'

'Right. I really am ready for that out of body trip now.'

Adam was sent to the bathroom to take the extract. He had been warned that it had a bitter taste and people often threw up trying to swallow it. Nevertheless, Adam got it down and it stayed down. He was sure he had tasted worse.

After five minutes his stomach still felt settled but he was reporting feeling light-headed. Candice led him back to the couch in the lounge.

He went under very easily in this state and soon he was back in his kitchen.

'My vision is blurring.'

'It usually clears.'

'I feel like I'm steaming. But the steam is me, leaving my body. I'm floating to the ceiling.'

'Try to control your movement, Adam.'

'Okay I'm coming down off the ceiling now. Floating next to myself, like a ghost. Bizarre. Now my body is going to the hallway and I'm floating after it. I can't see out of the window because I'm in the way.'

'Wait till you return to the kitchen.'

'Okay my body has gone back but I can't see much different. Toyah has put her arms down.'

'Can you open the door?'

'I cannot hold the handle. My hand passes through.'

'So can you pass through the door, like a ghost?'

'Yes, yes I can. I'm drifting into the air. There's someone hiding behind a bush. NO!!'

'Do you recognise them?'

'Yes!...Yes…'

29

Ben didn't know where he was going. He just let his legs do the walking. His thigh still ached from the hammer injury so he walked with a limp but he kept going, stopping only once in a while for some water.

By last light he was somewhere North West of Newcastle. He slept on a ledge under a bridge over a river where he filtered some more water for drinking.

It felt good to be out on his own, though he had no idea where he was. He had all weekend before he needed to call Adam, phone signal coverage permitting. Maybe he could take the Monday off and just keep going.

When Ben woke early in the morning he lay there for some time listening to the birdsong over the babble of the water. He began to wonder whether he had accepted Meg's demand to get out too quickly, as an excuse to run. But Ben now knew he could not run away from his time-line. So even lying there under the bridge was not his choice but just what happened. He felt trapped. Death was the only way out. He felt depressed but not suicidal. His SAS training drove him ever onward.

Breaking camp he breakfasted on one of the fruit and nut bars he had bought from a corner shop. Not wanting to make a mistake he had asked the shop assistant for the supplies he needed. He didn't care about the odd look it got him. He was used to such looks now, though the half closed black eye would have added to his odd appearance no doubt.

Ben found himself taking some public footpaths. He couldn't read the finger-post signs, but that didn't matter. It was good to be out. Ben told himself he was having a mini-break. It had been a long time since he and Meg had been able to afford a proper holiday. He wanted to make that right, some day.

After mid-day, walking along a metalled lane, he had the feeling he should recognise where he was. A bit further on he saw a house up ahead and when he reached the driveway he realised he had managed to walk to Adam's. That couldn't have happened by chance. Either he subconsciously knew the way, or it was just what happened.

Adam's van was there but his car was gone. Maybe he had gone shopping. Ben hoped Adam wouldn't mind returning the favour and putting *him* up for a while.

He tried the garage door. It wasn't locked. Ben went inside and removed his pack. He had an idea. Searching the tool racks and draws relying on his sense of touch more than vision he found a small saw, some secateurs and a pair of thick gardening gloves.

Donning his Bergen and closing the garage door behind him Ben walked down the drive and turned right. He was going to check whether his time with Dawn had been a hallucination. If it turned out to be real then the retrieval of Meg's car might just restore his wife's confidence in him.

Adam had had to stay at Candice's for some time drinking lots of water to flush the drug out of his system before driving home. He laughed a lot at first, feeling very light headed but that was not to last.

When Candice had thought Adam ready to listen she had told him in detail what he had described seeing under hypnosis.

It was almost dark when Adam pulled up outside his house but it was light enough to see Ben standing by the garage.

Ben looked pleased to see Adam return.

Adam strode up to him and punched him hard in his good eye. 'It was *YOU*!!'

Ben was surprised by the attack but did not fight back. 'What?'

Adam thumped him again, this time in the chest, knocking Ben back against the garage door.

'It was *you* in the bushes, watching Toyah die.'

'Dawn told you then.'

'Dawn? No, it was Candice.'

'Who the hell is Candice?'

'My therapist. A hypnotherapist. I had a session with her again today. She said I saw you behind the bushes there,' he jabbed a thumb over his right shoulder. 'Said I described you having a bruised face. But what I don't understand is you didn't have a bruised face when Toyah died.'

'I'm sorry Adam, Dawn made me do it.'

'She made you kill Toyah?!'

208

'No, no. On Friday, when you went off with the police, she made me watch Toyah die.'

'Whatever for?'

'She said someone had to watch and it wasn't you. I'm so sorry. It was dreadful. I couldn't move.'

'What the SAS guy couldn't come out of hiding behind the bush and save his mate's girlfriend?!'

'No. I couldn't move a muscle. It made me so angry. I wanted to change the what happened but the meta-interference wouldn't allow it.'

'Meta-interference? What are you talking about?'

'Dawn…She took me to The Apple and introduced me to her partner Destiny. They explained it all to me. Then made me do stuff to *help* me understand that what they were telling me was the truth.'

'It sounds like you are delusional, Ben. What are you doing here? Did Dawn send you to do something else?'

'Not exactly. Oh by the way, that Flintstone that was thrown through your garage window. That was me too. I couldn't stop myself.'

'You need help.'

'I know. Dawn showed me where Meg's lost car is. It's in the woods just down the lane. I've been clearing a bramble thicket from it. It needs a new battery and a good clean, but maybe it will help me win Meg back.'

'Win her back?'

'Yes. She's thrown me out.'

'I'm not surprised.'

'Can I stay at yours?'

Adam couldn't believe he was going to let this man, who watched Toyah die without lifting a finger, stay with him.

30

When Adam woke up and made it down to the kitchen he saw the remains of what looked like some of his crunchy nut in a bowl in the sink.

Ben was out on the back lawn doing press-ups.

Adam got himself a glass of water, put some bacon on the grill and went outside.

'Did you sleep okay, Ben?'

'Not really.'

'Me neither.'

As Ben stopped and got to his feet to face Adam he looked like a puffy eyed panda, with his two black eyes.

'When you said Dawn made you do stuff on Friday, she was at Café Noir with me.'

'It doesn't surprise me. I've been in two places at the same time myself now. That's time travel for you I guess.'

'You seem to be quite accepting of the idea.'

'After what was done to me, that's the least of my worries. It seems I'll be doing time for something I've yet to do.'

'Did Dawn tell you that? She told me she will be killing me soon. Carmichael tried to detain her but she vanished.'

'Well I hope she doesn't make me do her dirty work, though that could be why I go to prison. Shit!'

'Maybe you should leave.'

'To be honest Adam, if it's going to happen there's nothing either of us can do about it. Let's try and think positive. I do not want to kill you. I even forgive you for hitting me. I could do with your help sorting out Meg's car.'

With the bonnet of the Peugeot up, they both looked at the state of the engine.

'Looks like you did a good job of clearing the vegetation out, Ben, but I think I should deal with this bit. Do you want to clean the interior?'

'Okay.'

While Adam removed the battery and checked out the levels of the oil and the water, Ben started to deal with the damp inside. He opened all of the doors and gave the windows a wipe down.

All the tyres were soft but one was actually flat and after the length of time it had been down it was going to be permanently distorted. Ben opened the boot, took out the spare tyre but came to a halt trying to figure out the jack.

'Sorry, Adam. I can't figure out how to put this jack together.'

Adam peered around the bonnet, heaving the battery out onto the wing as he did so. 'That's the foot pump.'

'Oh.'

'I'll sort it in a sec.'

'Thanks.'

'This battery hasn't dried out you know. You did try starting the car, didn't you?'

'Yes. Yesterday. Dawn was right.'

'Well you may not need a new one. I have a trickle charger in the garage we could try first.'

'Great.'

'I'll just sort the jack for you and take the battery down. Do you think you can change the wheel okay?'

'Sure.'

A little later, halfway down the lane, Adam's phone rang. Reaching into his pocket he read the caller's name and thumbed the answer icon.

'Hi Candice. I was thinking I might call you later.'

'Is everything okay?'

'Possibly.'

'Do you think yesterday's session might have helped?'

'Maybe.'

'When I arrived home I found Ben waiting for me. After what you told me about him watching Toyah die, I hit him.'

'No!'

'Yes. A couple of times.'

'But Ben, that's not how this works. These sessions are to help the subconscious to resolve the trauma. That psychoactive substance I gave you wasn't a magic potion. All you were seeing was what your imagination wanted you to see.'

'Adam admitted that it was him though.'

'What? After you hit him enough, you mean.'

'Ha no. It would take a lot more than I could give him to make him say something he didn't want to. No, he told me what happened. He's really down about it. I'm trying to get his mind off it by keeping him occupied fixing his wife's car.'

'Right.'

There was a pause as Candice thought through what Adam had just said, and Adam tried to decide whether to tell Candice what he knew he had to.

'Look Candice I want to try something different. Can you come to mine for tea and I'll explain?'

'Okay, if you think it will help.'

'I need you to bring some more of that plant extract.'

'Oh I don't know that I should.'

'I'll pay for what I've used.'

'It's not that. You only had some yesterday, there may still be traces in your system.'

'Let's give this a try, please.'

'All right then.'

'Thank you.' Adam gave Candice his address and hung up. A plan was coming together. He felt more positive now.

He strode down the path and into the garage. Putting the battery on a bench he searched the shelving for the trickle charger.

He came across a spare battery he had forgotten about. He pulled that onto the bench and looked for his ammeter. Testing the battery he decided there might be enough charge to it to turn Ben's engine over. He tested Ben's battery. Dead.

He returned to his search for the charger and finding it he set up Ben's battery to charge.

Taking his old battery Adam headed back out, but on the drive he had a premonition. He returned to the garage, picked a mallet off the wall rack, replaced it and took down a club hammer.

'That ought to do it.'

Fifteen minutes later he was back at the car. Ben was pumping up the last tyre.

'Look what I found. See if we can get her started with this.'

'I knew you'd come through, Adam.'

Minutes later, battery connected, Adam sat in the driver's seat and turned the key. The car tried to turn over, sounding exhausted. Ben watched on, not looking hopeful. Adam tried again and this time the engine came to life.

'Yes!' Ben cheered.

'Close the doors.'

As Adam closed the driver door, Ben closed the passenger door behind, and went to the boot. He chucked the foot pump inside to join the jack and flat, then closing the boot he shut the other rear passenger door and jumped in the front.

Ben winced and pulled the club hammer out from under him. 'What's this for?'

'Insurance.'

Frowning, Ben closed the door and Adam released the hand brake, selected reverse gear and went nowhere. He selected first gear and stayed put.

'The brake blocks have seized.'

'Bollocks!...Clever.' Ben lifted the hammer with understanding now.

Adam nodded, switching the engine off. 'I'll get the jack back out.'

Adam and Ben managed to get Meg's car back to Adam's and give it a good wash down. It was nowhere near as good as new, with patches of rust needing attention, but it was getting there.

'Thanks for this mate. Meg should be pleased.'

'I have a favour to ask.'

'Oh?'

'I've invited Candice round for dinner.'

'Have you?' Ben was surprised. 'Oh I get it. You want me to make myself scarce. Maybe retire to the barge, or is that where you are taking her?'

'No, no, nothing like that. I want you to join us for dinner.'

'Really?'

'I'm going to ask her to give me another session, only this time I want you present. She might not be up for it but I want to ask.'

'Whatever for?'

'When she does this hypnosis thing I don't remember anything afterwards. She has to tell me what I've described, like she told me about you being behind the bushes.'

'So…you don't trust her?'

'Maybe she isn't telling me everything. You know, protecting me. Concerned that she may worsen my trauma.'

'Right.'

'So are you up for it?'

'Sure, if she is.'

Candice was surprised to find that Ben was going to be joining them for dinner. Not what she was expecting. Neither was what was to come later.

Adam introduced the two of them. Ben thought Candice something of a stunner but kept that to himself.

'You look just how I imagined from Adam's description Ben, except you have two black eyes instead of one.'

'Yeah well Adam thought I'd look less dangerous with two black eyes.'

'How's that?'

'Everyone adores a panda.'

'Ha…ha ha.' Candice wasn't sure how to take Ben.

Over dinner there was idle chit chat with some humour, sharing background stories. This included telling Candice some of the pranks from their disbanded Admissions group, which left Candice less sure about Adam and Ben.

After the meal Adam began to explain to Candice what he had in mind.

'When we do the hypnosis with the out of body drug, I would like Ben to be present.'

'That's not how I do things, Adam.'

'But would it really be a problem?'

'Well as long as you can relax and Ben doesn't distract or interfere in any way.' She turned to Ben. 'Are you okay with observing your friend?'

'Sure. It could be interesting.'

'Right then,' Adam smiled. That was the first hurdle over. 'So before I explain what I want you to help me try, Candice, I need to tell you something about last night's nightmare.

'The incident replayed as I remembered it until I was on the gravel with Toyah. This time Ben came out of the bushes. He was trying to tell me something. I couldn't hear what he was saying, because of the sound of the blood rushing in my ears. I read his lips. He was repeating one word at me. *Rewind.* Then I woke up, and for once I wasn't screaming, I was thinking.

'Remember how you told me to think about the hypnosis experience as a video that can be paused, fast forwarded or rewound. Well I want to take that drug and attempt to rewind Toyah's arrival, following her car back to her place to see what happened to her.'

'Oh no Adam. You don't understand how this works. You can only stretch into your own memories, not someone else's.'

'But this would be an out of body experience, right?'

'Yes, but pure imagination.'

'But that's what you said about Ben being behind the bushes when I told you I had hit him. But his presence turned out to be true.'

'That must have been coincidence Adam, or maybe your subconscious recognised the sound you heard as Ben.'

'Well? Do you think you could be open-minded enough to help me try, Candice, please?'

'Okay, okay, but if I feel you are heading into something more traumatic, I'm pulling you out.'

'Fine.'

Adam drifted through his front door as Toyah wound the layers of cling-film round her face. He entered the car, trying to stay calm and focussed. He positioned his invisible cloud-self in the passenger seat.

'I'm in the car. She's torn off the roll and put it down. She's smoothing the plastic down, behaving like some robot.'

'Pause, Adam. Pause.'

The scene stopped. Adam turned to his left and could see Ben with one black eye the other side of the bushes. The look in Ben's eyes was a miserable helplessness.

'Start to rewind, but stay in that car, Adam.'

The movement was slow at first. In fact it looked like it was going forward again for a moment as Adam looked back at Toyah and she was smoothing the polythene. Then the roll was picked up, the plastic film reconnected and started coming off. Round and round till the final piece came away from her neck.

Adam felt sick. The bitter taste of the plant extract was in his mouth, but he continued to describe what he saw.

Toyah put the roll down and started the car. This was the moment of truth. She reversed out of the drive onto the lane, not looking where she was going.

Adam didn't know whether he felt car sick or excited. It seemed to be working.

The car drove slowly down the lane, Toyah watching where they had been, while Adam watched where they were going through the back window. It was not a comfortable experience.

'It's too slow, Candice. I don't know how long I can do this for.'

'Okay try fast rewind.'

Everything sped up to a blur. Even at speed Toyah looked devoid of emotion. Adam kept looking around. He half expected the car to suddenly stop and someone get Toyah out of the car undress her unwrap the plastic, dress her and then undrug her, or something that would explain the madness in reverse.

'I think I'm going to throw up.'

'I didn't think the dinner was that bad mate.'

'Shh.' Candice warned Ben.

'We've arrived at Candice's.'

'Okay Adam, slow the rewind.'

Toyah left the car, locking it and walked backwards into the house, closing the door in front of her. Adam passed through after her. She went upstairs to her room and Adam followed.

There was no one else up there, no one else to blame.

Toyah got undressed. Glistening with cling-film she stopped to make her call to Adam, to unsay that she was on her way with something mind-blowing to show him.

Adam watched as she picked up the roll of cling-film that she had brought out of the car and it reattached itself. Then she stood in front of her mirror unwinding it all, arms, legs, and torso till all that she had left on were her panties.

'Now she's going to the bathroom to unshower.'

'That's it Adam. I think you have seen enough.'

Adam watched her in the shower. Even though the water was coming up onto her from the drain, at this point she was more like her normal self, enjoying the experience.

31

Candice had stayed with Adam through the night. After he had been brought out of the hypnosis he had started being sick.

Ben helped with the cleaning up, the best he could. However, even after Adam's dinner had all been returned he went on to vomit the water back that Candice was giving him.

Bit by bit Adam was able to keep more down but Candice realised it was going to take longer to flush Adam's system this time. To make the situation more frustrating Adam managed to find it all highly amusing.

'I told you I didn't think it was a good idea to take that plant extract again so soon.'

'No worries. Look on the bright side. I'm feeling better by the minute *and* I got to see Toyah strip one last time, *apparently*. Ha ha ha.'

Candice looked at her watch. 'I'm going to have to head off in a couple of hours. I have Uni and none of us have had any sleep. I only have a supervision meeting to attend but I think you two should call in sick. At least *you* have been, Adam.'

'Oh no no. Can't do that. Cameron has made it quite clear we are *way* behind schedule.'

'Well at least let Ben drive you in.'

'Ha ha ha. Good one.'

'You are up to driving aren't you, Ben? You are able to see out of those eyes aren't you?'

222

'Oh I can see fine enough. I just don't have a driving license anymore.'

'Oh.'

'I have a head injury which affects object recognition, among other things.'

'Really?'

'Why do you think he was trying to cut that steak with a spoon?'

'Now you come to mention it that probably explains why I saw him cleaning up vomit with a saucepan and jumper.'

'Ha ha ha!'

Adam was laughing a little less when he reached *Eco Beech*.

Ben had used the journey to power nap, ignoring Adam who was muttering to himself and laughing at his own jokes.

'Ha ha ha!' Adam couldn't believe his eyes. '*Now* I'm hallucinating. Ha ha. *Fantastic*!'

Ben opened his eyes to see that the drive into the yard was now a drive into a tarmacked car park, with all the white parking bays marked out.

As Adam brought the van round they saw the site manager's porta-cabin up on the back of a flat-bed truck. Round to their left was the visitor centre. It looked all finished.

'Fuck me...! Someone *has* been busy over the weekend. Ha ha ha!'

Ben just smiled to himself. Here was his proof that *What-If* worked.

They got out of the van and walked in to the centre. Not only was the floor tiled, walls painted, and exhibits up, but it had a reception with guide books and a till. Across the way was a café and bookshop. All that was missing were staff. The only other people around were similarly confused construction workers.

Wandering outside and looking across the site the plants and trees still needed tending. They hadn't had any weekend miracle grow.

Ben followed Adam to the porta-cabin, smirking behind Adam's back, wondering when he should tell him this was all his doing. He decided to leave Adam thinking he was hallucinating just a little longer.

The door of the manager's office was open and there was a stack of crates at the side of the flat-bed as makeshift stairs to get in.

Cameron was at his desk, head in his hands.

'Don't worry Cameron. I reckon everything will be back to normal by lunchtime.' Adam tried to explain. 'I just need to keep drinking water and I'll be good to go. I've just not had any sleep. *We've* just not had any sleep.'

A dazed Cameron looked up slowly, like he had also lost the plot. 'What happened to *you* Ben?'

'Max and Mic didn't accept my apology over the BMW. So I guess this was payback.'

'Except for this eye,' Adam pointed. 'That was me.'

'What's the matter with you people? I should never have involved Frank in this project. Not that it matters now. It all appears to have been finished. *How* I don't know.'

'Gorilla construction, maybe,' offered Ben with a smirk.

'Gorilla construction? Did *Earth's Calling* get in another firm?'

'No, as in gorilla gardening. People who just come in and do stuff when you're not looking. Construction site SOS...Maybe it'll be on TV.'

'There's a thought.' Cameron turned to his computer and started clicking the mouse. 'What the fuck is going on?!'

'What?'

'The site's CCTV system has lost all of its recordings since Friday.' The phone rang. 'Eco Beech, Site Manager...Say again...Right...I know how you feel...No need to apologise. These things happen, *apparently*...I know. It's a mad world...Let me know when you have stock back in.' Cameron hung up and sighed.

'What was that?' Ben asked.

'That's the second call this morning from a supplier for materials that we needed. They appear to have had their goods stolen over the weekend by someone who has then made the online stock system and accounts balance.'

'Weird.'

'You can say that again.'

'So what do you want us to get on with this morning?'

'Nothing, Adam. It's all been done.'

'Well what about the landscaping?'

'There's a company contracted for that, long term. You'll have to see if Frank's got another job for you. Sorry but you're all done here.'

When Adam rang Frank, he had already heard the news from Cameron. However, he sounded in good spirits and suggested Adam and Ben come around to his place to talk things over. He gave directions and the two of them headed over straight away.

'Whatever happened to you Ben?' Frank wanted to know on seeing the state of him, at his door. 'Come on in.'

'To be honest it was something of a disagreement with Max and Mic.'

'I see. Mic did mention that you were going like a bat out of hell with the work, making the other guys look bad.'

'Oh it wasn't that. It was because I scratched his beamer.'

'Oh dear. So where are they now?'

'I thought they might be here.'

Frank turned one way and the other, arms outstretched, 'Not here.'

'Well when I regained consciousness in the visitor centre after their beating they were gone.

'Well no matter. They were a couple of loose cannons anyway. Ex-Spesnatz you know.'

'What's Spesnatz?' Ben feigned ignorance.

'Russian special nationals. The Russkies version of the SAS.'

'Wow. Really. Maybe they were called back.'

'Mmm…Maybe. Anyway enough of that. So the job is complete.'

'Yes.'

'Way ahead of time.'

'It looks that way.' Ben wasn't about to own up to why.

'So it looks like *Earth Calling* got in some other contractors, who did a remarkable job in just two days. You wouldn't happen to know anything about that, would you, Adam.'

'No. Ha, you should have seen it. It was like one of those DIY SOS shows. They must have had hundreds of people there over the weekend to accomplish all that.'

'Yes, no doubt. And I'm given to understand there is oddly no security recording of any of it.'

'It would appear so…So Ben and I were wondering if you had anything else for us?'

'As a matter of fact I do.'

'Great.'

'You'll find this a bit more challenging though.'

'Oh we don't mind a challenge.'

'Good. Glad to hear it. Before we get down to business though, let's celebrate this completion. Come through to the conservatory.' As Frank led them through the kitchen he got a bottle of champagne out of the fridge and took some glasses off the worktop.

In the conservatory he handed each of them a glass then opened the back door onto the garden. He unwound the wire round the foil and when it popped the cork flew over the back fence into the field beyond.

He poured the champagne into each flute.

'You not having one?' asked Adam.

'To be frank, I can't stand the stuff.'

'Ha.'

'Do you mind if I have a cigar instead?'

'It's your house, your rules.'

'Quite so.' He lit the cigar and took a couple of puffs, then with a beaming smile made a toast. 'To an uncertain future.'

'Uncertain?'

'Well of course, Adam. If everything in our future were certain, it would be nothing short of hell, wouldn't it?'

'He's got a point, Adam.'

Adam joined Ben in taking a swig.

'So how long have you lived out here, Frank?'

'Ten, fifteen years. I've had quite a bit of work done in that time. Would you like to see my man-cave?'

'Sure.'

Bending down, Frank lifted the edge of the rug. As it came up it brought with it a counterweighted trap door, revealing a stair case.

'Neat.'

'I like to call this my whine cellar.'

'A wine cellar as well?' Adam finished off his glass. 'You're something of a party animal then?'

'You could say that.' Frank led them down, switching the lights on as he went.

To the right of the stairs was a bar area. Further to the right was a wall of glass bricks about chest height, beyond this was a small theatre.

'Wow, Frank.' Adam was impressed. 'One helluva home cinema you've got down here. You must be able to seat what thirty, forty people.'

'Yes. Another nice little earner.'

Adam noticed something on top of the wall which almost sobered him up. 'How long have you had this, Frank?'

'I've never seen it before. What is it?'

'It's a Flintstone. It's mine.'

'Don't be silly Adam. How can it be yours? It's on my property.'

'Yes, see, it has a verse on it.' Adam was a bit dizzy as he turned.

'I'm not sure you should have had that champagne mate, on top of everything else.' Ben warned.

'On top of what?' Frank enquired.

'Oh err, he's um been on medication…for stress.'

Adam tried to focus on the verse. The words were starting to blur.

Your time is running short
Surely you've not forgotten,
Now Ben must make a jump
Taking to the air from Shotton.

'We've got to go Ben.' Adam's legs gave way and he crumpled to the floor. Ben went to him, feeling a bit light-headed himself. That champagne was strong. He felt for a pulse at Adam's neck. It was weak.

'I think you may need to call for an ambulance, Frank.'

'Oh don't be so silly. You know that's a waste of time these days. Let me deal with this.' Frank took out his mobile and speed-dialled. 'Monica, it's Frank, can you let the *Audience* know we will be having ourselves a *Party* tonight.'

Ben struggled to get to his feet, trying to make sense of what he had just heard Frank say. 'You…you put something in the champagne.'

'Oh how very astute of you Ben. Considering your cognitive difficulties, it's a wonder you can work out anything of what is going on around you from one minute to the next.'

'You bas…'

32

Ben was first to come round. Once again his training cut in. He remained limp, eyes closed, listening, getting a sense of his situation.

He was tied down in a sitting position. The only sound he could hear was breathing. He opened his eyes slightly. Adam was alive, that was a positive, but he was also tied to a chair, facing Ben.

There was no one else around. They were in the cellar, at the front of the theatre. The floor was like a wet room, with a drain between the two seats.

'Shit.' Ben hoped it wasn't really a drain, just a pattern, but considering their situation it looked likely it would be.

He tested his bonds. He was held fast with cable ties to the metal chair. He looked around for options. He wasn't sure what he was looking at.

'Fuck!'

There was a sound from the stairs. Ben turned to see Frank coming down. 'Nice of you to come back.'

'What do you want Frank? I told you I don't know where Max and Mic are.'

'And I told you I wasn't interested in them.'

'What then?'

'It's nothing personal. I'm just a business man. I have my fingers in a lot of pies. Some of those pies involve legitimate businesses like construction. Others involve productions for the Dark Net. Hi-end films for a rather wealthy audience. Nevertheless, some of the audience prefer to view performances first hand.'

'What are you talking about?'

'I have a side-line in torcher-porn and snuff movies.'

'Oh get real.'

'Oh it does get *very* real, I assure you, Ben.'

'What's going on?' Adam was stirring.

'Welcome back Adam. I was just explaining to Ben here that there is a lot of money to be made out of torture for a paying audience.'

'Torture?!' Adam seemed to notice his bindings for the first time and began to struggle.

'Don't waste your energy. You are going to need it all for this evening.'

'But we work for you.' Adam complained naively.

'Well your contract with me runs out this evening. I lost money on that *Eco Beech* job.'

'That's not our fault.'

'Nevertheless, you are an easy and hopefully entertaining way to recoup my losses, probably even make a little more. We'll have to see. I normally work with performers a great deal younger than you two.'

'Performers?'

'Okay, victims, if you must be melodramatic about what's in store for you.'

'You are a sick man, Frank.'

By the time the guests were turning up, neither Ben nor Adam were any closer to getting loose. They were appalled at the number of people who looked like respectable citizens, filing in like church-goers, to watch with relish. These must be people in positions of responsibility and power. The fact that they were here, showing their faces, meant that neither Ben nor Adam were expected to survive.

'What do you think you are doing here?!' Adam yelled. We are not a couple of actors you know.'

This got a couple of laughs from the bar.

Adam guessed if this had been a play the actors might say such a thing as part of their pre-performance script.

'Adam. Adam!' Ben tried to get Adam to focus.

'What?'

'You know we get out of this, don't you?'

'Do I? How?'

'Dawn said I go to prison and didn't you say *she's* the one who kills you?'

'Well maybe she was lying, so we wouldn't see *this* coming. Or maybe Dawn is going to turn up and do the deed.'

'What kill you and let me go? What would be the sense in that?'

'What's the sense in any of *this*?' Adam struggled with his restraints again.

The last of the guests came in and took their seats. They were quite a mixed group. In among the well to do were some stereotypical hard-faced villains, all watching on with expectation.

Finally Frank came down to the wet-room stage, tracked by the cameraman and camerawoman to either side of the stage front.

Frank pulled a trolley on casters after him, bringing it to a halt behind Adam and Ben. He ran through the selection of surgical instruments as if to educate his victims, intending only to increase their fear and disgust.

'Don't worry gentlemen, everything is clean. Some of our audience pay extra to consume certain parts of the human anatomy, and its extracts. Like Adrenochrome.'

'What the fuck is Adrenochrome?'

'Well I wouldn't expect you to know, Ben. It helps give users their youthfulness back, until they stop taking it of course.'

'So when did you stop taking it Frank?'

'Still got a sense of humour? That's good. I hope you can keep it up while I enjoy your slow dismemberment. I'll start with small things like fingers and toes and work up to those more essential organs.'

'You are insane.'

'It has been said. But I pride myself on my skill. If you pass out then I will start on Adam and vice versa. It always works best to have two or even three performers on the go.'

Frank picked up the surgical cutters and stepped round to the side of Ben.

Ben was sure it was going to be now or never. Frank was going to release one of his arms and he had to make his first strike count.

'Oh that's right, pick on the disabled person.' Adam fought for time.

Frank shifted round to Adam's side with the cutters, to Ben's frustration. Adam wasn't going to be able to get them out of this.

'It's fine Adam. I can take it.'

'Don't Frank! He's only saying that because he has brain damage.'

'Oh do stop trying to appeal to a caring side. I am a child trafficker and paedophile. I was *born* without morals. If you saw some of my award winning films you'd understand what you have got caught up in. There is no way out of this money making machine.'

'Fucking arsehole.'

'Start with me Frank,' Ben tried again. 'After all, it was me who arranged those other contractors.'

'Oh. And how did *you* manage that?'

'Shan't say.'

'We'll see about that.' Frank stepped back beside Ben and with a nod of his head two assistants stepped out of the shadows into the floodlit centre-stage.

One bent down and grabbed Ben's left wrist, cutting the binding free with his right hand.

With speed, aggression and surprise Ben whipped his arm round in front of him, using his elbow to help twist he wrist free.

Pulled slightly off balance, the first assistant lost his grip. Ben's left hand lashed out, striking the man's throat. He buckled forward, raising both hands to his neck. On their way up Ben removed the blade from the assistant's hand. Then he opened up the man's femoral artery with a downward stroke then cut loose the binding on his right wrist.

Ben was just leaning forward to cut the bonds round his ankles when the second assistant recovered his wits. He struck Ben a blow between his shoulder blades, stunning him. A second blow from the assistant's baton gave Ben a dead-arm and he dropped the blade.

Wasting no time with the first assistant's pleas for aid, the second assistant secured Ben's right arm back behind him, then he took hold of the left hand.

Ben clenched his fist as tight as he could, but the assistant began to force loose his little finger, to present to Frank.

'Good.' The audience watched on with amusement.

'Don't worry Ben. I won't be cutting your fingers off one at a time. There's really no rush, as I take pains to explain to all the children. We'll do this one knuckle at a time so you can get used to the hopelessness.'

'Sick fuck!' He struggled against the assistant but the blow had badly weakened his arm.

'I'll pay you to let us go!' Adam blurted desperately. This brought much laughter from the audience. 'Oh I know…I can tell you something valuable.'

'Can you indeed?'

'There's someone called Dawn. She's going to destroy you all if you don't let us go.'

'Dawn who?'

'Dawn Summers.'

'Never heard of her. Is she your *secretary*?'

The audience laughed at Frank's taunt.

'No. Just a *very* dangerous woman.'

'Oooo…A *dangerous* woman. Really Adam, I think you've been watching too much *Killing Eve*.'

Frank closed the cutters and removed the end of Ben's little finger. Ben gave a grizzled yelp between his teeth, to a moan of pleasure from the audience.

Frank threw the fingertip into the audience and some members sought to catch it.

'That wasn't so bad was it Ben. You're still conscious.' Frank brought the cutter to the second knuckle.

'Stop it!' cried Adam.

With an audible crunch the next section was gone too.

The pain was intense. Ben winced, fighting it the best he could. He knew from training that the only way to take an opportunity for escape was to try and keep calm and positive or else he could lose control.

The assistant on the floor had fallen silent, continuing to bleed-out.

Another crunch of the cutters and Ben's little finger was all gone. His hand throbbed with pain.

Frank turned to the audience. 'Other little finger, or toe? Show of hands. Finger? Toe?...Toe it is.'

The assistant secured Ben's bleeding left hand behind his back. Then cut the binding on Ben's left leg. Holding it securely to prevent Ben kicking out, he proceeded to remove the shoe and sock from a sweating foot.

Blinking back the pain, Ben was the only person to notice the dark figure, wearing what might have been a gas mask, coming down the stairs at the back. On the other hand it might just have been a latecomer in fancy dress.

However, in one hand they held a dripping blade. In the other hand they held a hissing canister. This they threw down to the front of the theatre, over the heads of the audience, before raising their Heckler & Koch MP7, fitted with a suppressor.

Before Ben passed out he remembered mumbling 'Tad late, but I think the cavalry's just arrived.'

33

Adam was the first to come round this time, but Ben wasn't far behind, as Adam kept yelling 'Oh my God! Oh my God!'

Ben opened his eyes to see their torture had ended. Adam had fallen from his chair into a mess of blood. At first Ben thought it was the assistant's blood, but there was far too much of it for one person. It was coming from the full length of the audience seating.

'What the *fuck*?!' Standing up Ben realised he had also been unbound.

Looking across the seating, every audience member, the men and the women, were slumped in their seats, their throats slit.

Behind Ben were the bodies of Frank and his second assistant, throats similarly gaping wide.

The blood was no longer pumping so the attack had not just happened.

'Dawn saved us, Ben.'

'I don't think all this blood is Dawn's thing.'

'Who then?'

'I don't know…Hello!...Hello!!'

There was no response. Whoever had done this was gone. Ben was thankful that they had unbound them before leaving.

Ben remembered the figure in the NBC suit. If this had been an official police raid then Ben and Adam would have been removed to hospital and no doubt questioned later. This

239

smacked of the increasing accounts of vigilantism in response to continuing cuts to police funding.

The police would certainly be all over this place at some point. Ben's instinct was to remove all evidence of them being there, but he was bound to miss something in all this gore, like a piece of finger.

Ben looked at his aching hand. The wound had stopped bleeding as fast, but still needed treatment. He sat back down and tried to put his sock back on with one hand.

'Adam, can you give us a hand.'

'Oh, sure.'

Sock and shoe sorted, Ben then led Adam up the side of the room, stepping over the dead camerawoman. They looked along the rows of seating at all of the dead in their finery.

'What goes around comes around, you evil fucks!' Adam cursed them. 'But you know Ben, I reckon whoever did this will have pissed off the police. Killing them all will have hampered further investigation, won't it?'

'Somehow, Adam, I rather think whoever organised this little massacre will get to those connected to this business a whole lot quicker than the police would. *And* they won't be letting any of the fuckers buy back their lives with information or intimidation.'

Before they reached the stairs, Adam grabbed the Flintstone and the thought struck him. Dawn had known they would be there, but had let Ben lose his finger. What sort of person was she?

Upstairs they found two more dead, with throats slit.

'Who does this sort of thing, Ben?'

'Don't know mate, but I owe them one, big time.'

In the kitchen Adam looked for a first aid box for Ben but soon gave up and handed him a clean tea towel from a draw.

Then they went outside to the van, only to find it wasn't where Adam left it. 'I don't believe it. Someone has stolen my van, with all the tools in!'

'No mate, they would have got rid of it. Frank would have had it removed. It's probably a burned out wreck in a quarry somewhere now.'

'Shit!'

In its place was a Ferrari.

'It seems to me that a settlement needs to be made for damages, Adam.'

'What do you have in mind?

Ben walked across the drive to the garage door and felt for a lock handle in the middle of the double width door.

'I think this is the lock, Ben.' Adam pointed at a panel on the wall to the house side of the garage. It had no keypad.

Ben felt it. 'Okay. I'll be back in a minute.'

Adam waited outside in the dark. He could hear some sheep in the distance and could see some light from a neighbour's place, but all was still.

Ben returned, lifted his hand to the lock and the garage door began to open.

'How did you manage to find the key so quick?'

'Well you know Frank had it on him all the time.' Ben dropped Frank's thumb on the gravel.

As the garage door came up, it revealed a Lamborghini, a Tesla and a Porsche 4x4 with blacked out windows.

'Well if I'm seeing what I think I'm seeing,' said Ben, 'none of these are going to be inconspicuous. So what do *you* fancy, Adam?'

'Well obviously the sports car, but I guess it wouldn't cope well with some of the potholes on my lane. I don't have a charging point for the Tesla, so I reckon I'll just have to take the 4x4.'

'I guess so.' With the security system on the door, Ben half expected to find the car's door unlocked. It wasn't.

The two of them went back into the house of horror to look for the keys. After a few minutes they reached Frank's office. It was a mess.

Whoever had raided his place knew exactly what they were there for. His safe was open and empty. Files seemed to have been removed from cabinets. His desktop computer was torn apart and its hard disk removed. Even the security system which was still showing views of the house and cellar was now diskless.

'Here we go.' Adam located the Porsche keys in the desk draw. 'There's also this.'

'A Glock 9mm.' Ben said as he took it off Adam to have a feel. He then felt inside the draw and pulled out two spare clips for it.

'What are you doing?'

'I'm taking it with us.'

'Whatever for?'

'Insurance. I don't know if you've noticed but things are kinda turning to rat shit around us.'

'Okay, well as long as *you* know what you're shooting at, considering your object recognition problem.'

'Good point. Maybe *that's* why I go to jail.'

Adam sat with Ben in the Newcastle RVI A&E waiting room, turning the Flintstone over in his hands.

'I can't stop thinking about all those bodies. I'm probably going to need more treatment for that from Candice.'

'Oh you'll love that.'

'What's that supposed to mean?'

'Come on…Even I wouldn't throw her out of bed, and I'm still married.'

'Hey, I'm still grieving Toyah's loss.'

'Yeah, sorry…You should try thinking of something else. Just like me, trying not to think about this flaming torch which used to be my fully functioning left hand.'

'Okay, sorry. Thanks for putting things into perspective.' Adam stopped turning the Flintstone over and over and read the verse again to himself, then got out his phone.

Seconds later he was clearly onto something. 'Look Ben, there's this sky-diving centre south of Durham.'

'So?'

'You do know you are going to have to do a parachute jump as soon as I can get you a time-slot booked.'

Ben was in no mood for this. 'Will you listen to yourself, Adam? Are you seriously asking a guy with a cognitive disability, two black eyes and a busted hand in a hospital waiting room to go jump out of an airplane? On the off-chance he might actually save a woman this time?'

'Well when you say it like that it does sound kind of stupid, but hey, it's written in stone.'

'Fuck off.'

'Maybe you don't have to jump. If you get onto their refresher course you might work out who the woman is before you even get in the plane. You know, sound them out.'

'Forget it. Anyway, for health and safety reasons they'd never let me jump with this.' He raised his flaming torch.

'You could wear a glove over it, so no one would know.'

'Do you know the first thing about parachuting?'

'Well no. That's why you are the named jumper I guess.' Adam said, tapping the verse.

'Yeah, well, I only have your word on that.'

'So we'll ask someone else to read it…Excuse me.' Adam tapped on the shoulder of a woman in front. 'My friend and I haven't brought out glasses, would you mind reading the verse on this stone.'

Passing the Flintstone over to the reluctant woman it was surprisingly heavy. The stone slipped from her grip and landed on the very ingrowing toenail she was there waiting to have looked at. People jumped with her agonised cry.

'Sorry, I should have warned you.'

'You damn fool!'

'Here, I'll read it,' said the irritated old man with glasses next to her.

When he read it out, and handed it back over, Ben gave a resigned sigh. 'Even if the glove fools the staff, I'll have to pack my own chute, watched by a Rigger. If he or she notices any odd behaviour I'll be out of there.'

'Yeah but I'm confident you'll do a good job. I bet you can still sort out kit like that blindfolded.'

'With my problem I might as well be blindfolded.'

Carmichael was getting a taste of how uncomfortable it was to be sitting on the other side of an interview table. MI5's Cynthia Cartwright, up from London, was asking some hard questions. At her side making notes, was Harriet Wallace who Carmichael had already met before leaving Café Noir.

'If I answer your questions truthfully I believe I will be thrown off the Force.'

'Detective Inspector, if you *don't* answer my questions truthfully I *know* you will be thrown off the Force.

'Right.' Carmichael sighed. 'But just to be clear, I mean it, if the word gets out I *will* lose all credibility and with it my job. My two colleagues have already agreed to keep the incident off the records. We could all lose our jobs. Everything will get covered up anyway, right?'

'Look upon it as being for the good of your country. We are dealing with a very dangerous neurotoxin which behaves like a narcotic. It has been confirmed as unlisted on any security service database. We need to know its origin and if this was a test then what is the intended target?'

'I don't know anything about the toxin.'

'The lab techies at Porton Down have given it a serial number. But since that doesn't exactly roll off the tongue, they are calling it *Rapture*. Inspired by the customer statements which your WPC Henley had taken. We will be interviewing her after Cotes. So, as the person in charge of the investigation, *what* were you doing there?'

'We had reason to believe a female's life was in danger.'

'Because you had received a tip-off about *Rapture*?'

'Not exactly…We had no idea what form the threat to life would take, this time.'

'This time?'

'Yes there have been a series of deaths, all by different means.'

'Such as?'

'Asphyxiation, drowning, road accident, now poisoning.'

'And they are all connected because?'

'We are still looking into the connections. However, a man called Adam Underwood receives Flintstones with the tip-offs etched into them as cryptic verses.'

'Arr yes Underwood. Wallace went to his address but he was out. She ran a registration check on the two vehicles that were there and found a Peugeot that had been reported missing quite some time ago.'

'I don't know anything about that.'

'Yet that *is* on your patch.'

'Well I rarely get involved with vehicle crime.'

'It sounds like this Underwood could well be more Underworld; involved in this deeper than you think.'

'I know he's involved but I've met him a number of times and he seems quite sincere about wanting to stop getting the Flintstones. He has even involved his partner Ben McGregor in...'

'McGregor? The missing car was registered to a Meg McGregor.'

'Right.'

'So they might both have history of being involved in petty crime.'

'Well McGregor did admit that they had been involved in a number of pranks.'

'*Rapture* is no prank, DI Carmichael. We have two people dead and no idea what is coming next. So who gives Underwood these tip-off stones?'

'Dawn Summers. Underwood and I attempted to interview her at Café Noir.'

'Attempted? What was the problem?'

'I found her somewhat *evasive*, yet she was very relaxed and confident. She said she would tell us what she could but she wouldn't tell us who was responsible for the killings.'

'Wouldn't or couldn't?'

'Oh she admitted to knowing but couldn't bring herself to say.'

'Well surely you detained her for obstruction?'

'That's the thing.'

'What thing?'

'This is where all credibility is lost. Imagine you are watching a detective programme or reading a thriller and this *thing* happens. You would go "Oh for God's sake that's ridiculous! Where's the simple gun shot or stabbing we're all used to?!" then you'd switch over or off, or you'd throw the book in the bin.'

'Well? I'm waiting?...We're not going anywhere until the truth comes out.'

'Can I ask that this is kept *off the record*?'

'Other than Wallace's notes there's only us in the room and there's no recording of the interview. This is as good as *off the record* as it's going to get.'

Carmichael groaned and put his head in his hands. It had been easier being on the level with Cotes and Hanley on the drive back, with Underwood there to vouch for him.

'Maybe you should ask Underwood first. He was right there with me.'

'I'm asking *you*. As I said, we have not yet been able to locate Underwood.'

'Okay, well don't say I didn't warn you. I didn't believe McGregor when he described what he had seen Miss Summers do…Okay, so Underwood and I had been questioning Summers in the manageress's office. Summers was on the chair, Underwood and I were standing to one side. Before we had finished with her she said she had to go and stood up. There appeared a strange shadow on the wall

248

behind her as if a light was suddenly coming from our side of the room. She stepped towards us, and was gone.'

'Gone? What do you mean gone?'

'Talking it through on the way back to *Eco Beech* where Underwood had been working, he had described it as a temporary portal that takes Dawn back to The Apple.'

'And how does she operate this *portal*?'

'It was as if it was done for her.'

'Well, I think this *thing* is easily explained.'

'Really? Do the government already have such portal technology?'

'Don't be a bigger fool than you are Carmichael. You'll be telling me you believe the Queen is a clone, the Earth is flat, and no one ever landed on the moon, next.

'Listen. The explanation is perfectly simple. You and Underwood must have been hallucinating. Summers must have dosed you both with something. Did Miss Summers make contact with you at all?'

'No, in fact she made a bit of a thing about not being touched.'

'Okay. Did she use any hairspray or scent?'

'No, although now you mention it she did smell quite attractive, to me anyway.'

'In what way *attractive*?'

'Well you know like pleasant. Like you'd want to spend more time with her and get to know her better.'

'Like pheromones maybe?'

'I don't know what *they* smell like.'

'They are a sexual attractant.'

249

'Well I suppose. She was certainly a very pretty woman.'

'Well we are going to have to bring Miss Summers in for questioning ASAP.' Cartwright said turning to Wallace.

'Good luck with that.' Carmichael chuckled. 'We have no contact address other than The Apple, which isn't listed on Google, unless it really is just a pub. You best ask Underwood and McGregor who have had more contact with her.'

'Well we have people looking for them now. Hopefully she has not killed them already.'

'Well now you mention it, she did tell Underwood she was going to kill him, just before she vanished into thin air.'

'You mean before you allowed her to exit the office, while you and Underwood hallucinated. Summers has to be the source of this neurotoxin, and therefore the killer you are seeking.'

34

By the time Adam and Ben were heading back to the house it was starting to get light. On the way back they began trying to second guess what would happen once the police did visit Frank Chesney's. Adam thought it might be an idea to park in the layby near the bridge and then walk along the riverbank to the barge. From the back of Adam's place he could observe any visitors.

Adam and Ben were concerned the police might think the massacre was their doing, considering the weirdness they were already involved in. The bottom line was that with another woman to try and save they hadn't got time to get caught up in another line of enquiry till after Ben jumped.

There was no sign of movement at the house as they both observed from the undergrowth.

'The house might be under surveillance.'

'I doubt it, Adam. They will just be after some answers. They won't have enough cause to warrant the budget for that level of activity. Mind you, if they don't find us here, they'll drop by Meg's.'

'She'll just tell them she threw you out.'

'Yeah, which could raise further concerns and they may try and track us by our phones.'

'Really?'

'Sure. That's a quick cheap way to get results. In fact, I think you should give me your phone.'

'What you going to do?'

'I'm going to put them through your door.'

'No. *I'll* put them inside. You might put them in the bin.'

'Hey, I'm not that bad.'

Adam agreed with Ben that they ought to get a few hours sleep and then discuss what to do next. However, sleep was not doing Adam much good.

The cavalry weren't coming this time, the surgical cutter bit through Ben's little toe and he cried out.

'You shouldn't have watched,' said Toyah, holding the cutters.

'He couldn't help it, Toyah.' Adam pleaded.

'He *should* have saved me!' Toyah cut through the next toe and the audience clapped again.

'It wasn't his fault, Toyah! He…' A hand came over Adam's mouth to shut him up.

Adam woke up to find it was Ben's right hand covering his mouth. 'We've got company, mate.'

Adam listened, gathering his thoughts. He nodded, then in a similar hushed voice said, 'You hide in the loo. I'll go see who it is. If I get taken, it's important that you still make that jump.'

'If you say so.' Ben headed forward as Adam went aft.

Coming up on deck Adam saw two women. He recognised one of them.

'Mr Underwood?'

'Yes?'

'I am Cynthia Cartwright. I believe you have already met Harriet Wallace. We are from MI5.'

'Urr yes.'

'Is Sergeant McGregor aboard?'

'Sergeant McGregor?'

'Ben, Adam, your colleague?'

'Oh, urr…Why?'

'Is he or isn't he?'

Adam thought about asking for a warrant or whatever you were supposed to do in these situations but sighed. 'Yeah…Would you like a coffee? I'm afraid I don't have any milk.'

'That won't be necessary. I'm hoping this won't take too long.' Cynthia stepped aboard followed by Harriet.

'I think he's just in the loo, Cynthia. He'll be right out.' Adam said in a slightly raised voice as he hurriedly folded the two bunks away to make sofas for the four of them.

'Quaint hidey-hole you have here. Who'd expect to find a canal-boat in a stream at the bottom of a garden?'

'Well I have to admit, I am a little surprised that *you* found us so soon.'

'It wasn't difficult.'

'Satellite tracking?' Ben hazarded a guess as he joined them.

'No. Much cheaper and easier than that. When Harriet was told you were not at the house and that your work van was gone, we had *Eco Beech* checked out.'

'Oh. How did you know we were working there?' Adam was impressed by their intelligence.

'DI Carmichael told us.'

'Right, of course.'

'However, a rather confused Mr Atherton told us you had finished there.'

'Oh, Cameron the site manager.'

'Yes. He put us onto Frank Chesney.'

'Oh dear.'

'Yes, *oh dear* indeed Mr Underwood. You do seem to mix in some pretty dark circles, don't you. Neurotoxins *and* mass murder.'

'Hey, that wasn't us.' Ben defended.

'So anyway…we find Mr Chesney's Porsche is parked near your house, with recently trampled undergrowth along the riverbank, and here we are.'

'So what now?' Ben didn't want to be involved with *Five*, and another step closer to prison.

'It is imperative that we get hold of Dawn Summers.'

'You know Dawn?' Ben wouldn't mind betting that a number of people knew Dawn, or at least had experienced the consequences of her actions.

'DI Carmichael told us all about Dawn.'

'*Everything*?' Adam wasn't convinced.

'Yes. We know that Miss Summers is using some form of hallucinogenic substance to convince people that she can…*teleport*.'

'But…'

'We also believe that she was responsible for testing that neurotoxin at Café Noir.'

'No, no. She was just there to watch.'

'Like I said, *testing* it.'

'No. She's helping us catch the killer.'

'You both seem quite gullible guys. So let *me* convince you… Dawn admitted she knows the killer, but won't tell you. Carmichael also told me that Dawn mentioned she will be responsible for your death, Adam. Dawn must be stopped.'

'Good luck with that one.' Ben scoffed.

'She has told you she works out of The Apple. We've had various places by that name under surveillance and nobody fitting her description has shown up yet, but it's only a question of time.'

'*Time*, yeah that's a good one.'

'Why is that amusing McGregor?'

'Well, Dawn took me to The Apple through one of her portals which bend space and time. The Apple is in deep space. I saw it for myself. The stars were all much further away.'

'Oh dear…What you saw McGregor, was a hallucination. You *must* accept that.'

'Well it felt pretty real to me.'

'Of course it would. People who can design a substance like *Rapture* can design all sorts of drugs.'

'Rapture?'

'Yes, it's the name that has been given to the Café Noir toxin.'

'Right.'

'We need to know more about what we are dealing with before there is another attack. So how do we find Miss Summers quicker than simply waiting around for her?'

255

'You could try calling her,' suggested Ben with a smirk.

'You have a phone number?' Cynthia sounded incredulous that this had escaped her attention.

'No. I mean you could go up on Deck and call out her name. Maybe do it three times, like for Beetlejuice. It seems to me she is listening all the time. She certainly seems to know more than seems credible.'

'Please don't waste my time McGregor.'

'I suggest that we get on and save the next woman,' Adam put in. 'Dawn is more likely to put in an appearance then. No guarantees of course.'

'Next woman? So you know of another attack?'

'Attack is a bit strong. This one appears to be death by falling.'

'Falling? After being drugged?'

'Now you mention it that could be the link. All these women might have been drugged. And if it is some new toxin it might not have been picked up by police forensics.'

'Yes.' Ben agreed. 'Adam is insisting I do a parachute jump to identify and save this next victim so that we can finally take a step closer to the killer.'

'Well McGregor you don't need to worry about that. We can take over from here. So which sky diving school are we looking at?'

'It's one near Shotton.' Adam explained, 'But if you replace Ben with anyone else it won't be the right time.'

'What are you talking about?'

'The Flintstone…'

'Arr yes the *Flintstone*.'

'The verse on it clearly states Ben and Shotton. Until Ben does a jump from Shotton the time won't be right.'

'Ludicrous. How would anyone know ahead of time when Ben would be jumping?'

'Dawn does. It's literally written in stone.'

'Nonsense. There has to be an explanation for this.'

'We are telling you but you are not listening.'

'So you are telling me that whenever Ben gets to do his jump is the right time?'

'Yes.'

'You know, if I let you organise that jump, the booking could be weeks away. If you let me pull some strings, it could be just days.'

'Great. So you go play puppet mistress, Cynthia, and we'll wait to hear from you.'

'Thanks mate,' Ben sounded anything but grateful. 'I rather liked the prospect of weeks left to live.'

'It's me she kills not you.'

'You whose death she causes.' Cynthia reminded.

35

Meg looked at Ben's face and then his bandaged hand. 'You look a mess Ben. Don't think for one minute I'm letting you see the kids, looking like that. And what have you done to your hand?'

'The boss got a bit over enthusiastic.'

'Adam?'

'No, not Adam, Frank. But all that's behind us.'

'So what are you up to now?'

'Well right now, I have a surprise for you.'

'I'm not really in the mood for surprises Ben. I'm tired, and seeing you is surprise enough.'

'Look I just want to make it up to you.' Ben pressed a button on his phone and waited.

'Well?'

'Any second.'

'This better not be some prank involving Adam.'

'Well it does involve Adam but it's not a prank. It's more like making amends for an old mistake.'

They heard the car coming down the street, then it was pulling up outside.

'Ben. My car! You found it!' Meg's face broke into an astonished smile. 'That's going to make life so much easier. Thank you. Where did you find it?'

'Dawn showed me where it was.'

'Dawn?' Meg's voice went cold again.

'Look, now that I'm here can't I at least talk to Robbie and Beth?'

'No. I already told you. I'm tired and you're a mess.'

Ben cursed himself for mentioning Dawn. 'But we were hoping for a lift back to Adam's.'

Adam walked up and handed Meg her keys. 'We've had to do quite a bit of work on her, but she's good to go now.'

'Thanks Adam,' Meg took the keys. 'Now if you boy's will excuse me I have kids to bath.'

As she turned and went inside, closing the door. Adam and Ben felt quite taken aback.

'I didn't expect that reaction Ben. You must have *really* pissed her off.'

'Oh she's just tired…Sorry Adam, I know you've paid for all the repairs, but can you cover a taxi?'

'Looks like I'll have to,' Adam shook his head in disbelief then had an idea. 'What d'you say we pop into town for a few beers first, like in the old days?'

'*Now* things are looking up.'

The hand grabbing Ben's right wrist at the bar of the Bacchus stopped him in his tracks with the pint in hand.

'It's no wonder you've got two black eyes son. Pinching other people's drinks.'

Ben tried to control his natural responses. 'What do you mean? This is *my* Guinness!'

'Look again son. On what *fucking* planet does a Strongbow Dark Fruit look like a Guinness?'

Adam had just been handed his pint of Tetleys then Ben had turned back to get his own pint and must have got confused. It was packed at the bar and Adam had thought Ben stood a better chance of getting the drinks in, so had handed him a twenty. Now Adam was trying to prevent a brawl breaking out. 'Sorry. My mate's had a long day.'

Seeing that there was two of them now, the cider man, with a firm hand on his left shoulder, calmed down and let go of Ben's wrist. 'No problem I guess.'

Ben picked up his Guinness correctly, and took a sup. 'Cheers.'

Joining Adam the two of them moved out of the crowd.

It was then that they noticed a familiar face across the room, looking surprised, sitting at a table with a friend.

'Adam!' Candice waved at them to come over.

Seconds later they had squeezed round the table.

'Adam and Ben, this is my friend Karen.'

'Hi.'

'Adam and Ben are a great laugh Karen. They've known each other for years. They used to pull pranks on people with a couple of other guys, didn't you?'

'We did.' Adam admitted then quickly added 'But not anymore.'

'They were telling me some of their *Admissions* the other night when I went round Adam's for dinner. Tell Karen the one about the bus joyride.'

'Oh she won't want to hear that.' Adam attempted to play it down.

'Oh yes she will,' grinned Candice.

'I'm a bus driver,' Karen explained, waiting expectantly.

'I see,' Adam felt even more reluctant to tell the anecdote now. 'Why don't you tell it this time, Ben?'

'Well let's see, the story involves a GP who was going through something of a mid-life crisis. He was one of our Admissions team but he had not been doing so well with his pranks, then as you'll see he overstretched himself on this one.

'Medic had plenty of time to calculate and plan his prank, but it remained extremely risky. He needed a bus, preferably a single decker and the smaller the better, as a lower volume of air inside the vehicle would make the prank easier to pull off.

'He had considered a minibus, but he needed sufficient passengers on an evening run, so it needed to be a reasonably well-used service.

'After choosing some potential routes and then checking the maps to confirm the most promising, he decided on the Eldon bus station's 604 to Prudhoe.

'A cylinder of nitrous oxide, a.k.a. laughing gas, was easier to purloin than a bus. Using his white GP overall and stethoscope as a disguise, he had wandered around the RVI until he got the opportunity to steal a cylinder.

'He employed a number of other disguises as he travelled on the 604 a number of times between eight and eleven at night to get a feel for the route and the behaviour and routines of the drivers. He had noted how the drivers always took the moneybox with them to the office or the toilet.

'The preferred modus operandi for Medic's plan was to overpower the driver and gas him unconscious in the toilets. Medic would then don the driver's uniform and leave him locked in a cubical.

'His contingency plan was to board the bus as a passenger and then overcome the driver using the main gas canister. This was obviously more dangerous, especially if the bus was in motion when the driver lost control. Medic wasn't intending to hurt anybody.

'He waited for the last 604 of the night, wearing yet another disguise, an anorak with the hood up. He had already locked a large shoulder bag and a bundle of large flat-packed cardboard boxes in one of the toilet cubicles. The 604 turned up late, but as planned the driver removed the moneybox and headed for the toilets. Medic followed him in.

'The plan went like clockwork, leaving the driver bound and gagged, sitting on the toilet leaning to one side, wearing the anorak. The uniform was a bit tight on Medic, but it would do. It would have to.

'He returned to the bus with the moneybox, his shoulder bag and the large flat cardboard bundle, hoping he would make it without being stopped by a genuine bus company employee.

'Opening the door to the driver seat, he slid the moneybox back into position, sat down and closed the door. He had noted every detail he could about bus driving, beyond actual experience.

'The passengers came on and he issued tickets, having a little problem with some of the change but no one suspected a thing.

'Once underway, he had problems with the semi-automatic gears and the steering didn't handle quiet how he had imagined. He kept thinking about the size of the bus so that he wouldn't hit anything. He knew the proportions to the inch, as he had needed to calculate the interior volume in order to work out how much laughing gas he would require. But knowing the exact bus dimensions didn't make it any easier to drive.

'His racing heartbeat slowed and the driving seemed to get easier as he went along. The couple of stiff whiskeys he'd had beforehand seemed to help, he thought.

'He had wrestled with his conscience over having the whiskey, but if the plan went wrong, having had a couple of drinks was hardly going to matter in the grand scheme of things.

'He coped with the passengers he took on, giving out tickets but avoiding eye contact as before, sensing that a number of them were cross with him for being late. One man at Central Station told him so and Medic mumbled an apology, which seemed to satisfy the man enough to turn him to his seat.

'At the traffic lights round the corner from the Centre for Life, Medic reached into the shoulder bag side pocket then pushed two nasal plugs into his nose. Next, he took out his home made gas filter. He was really pleased with this, having made it look like a cigarette. He started breathing though the filter and out the side of his mouth as practised. Finally, he opened the valve on the gas cylinder and began to discharge the anaesthetic.

'At the same traffic lights he had planned to change the '604' sign to 'Not in Service', but the red turned to green quickly for once.

'He pulled away, turning right first, shortly followed by a tighter left turn onto the Redheugh Bridge. A car in the oncoming lane swerved and blared its horn as he was well out of lane.

'Some of the passengers laughed, and the humour spread with the gas, but the annoyed man from Central Station got up for a word.

'"Please sit down sir." Medic warned out of the side of his mouth as he spotted him in the mirror. The fake cigarette flapped about and he almost lost it from his lips.

'"This ticket is wrong."

'"What?"

'"You gave me the wrong ticket."

'"Sit down sir."

'"I said Ryton. This says Blaydon!"

'"It doesn't matter sir."

'"Yes it does. I paid to go to Ryton."

'"So go! The ticket's just a meaningless piece of paper!" Medic glanced at him.

'"Just like your fucking driving license. Watch out!"

'Medic returned his attention just in time to avoid going into the crash barrier.

'"And you shouldn't be smoking!"

"'I'm not. It's a vape." Medic wished the man would drop.

'The bus continued in the left lane, not pulling out to the westbound.

"'Where are you going now?" The man asked, desperately holding onto a pole, as two passengers tumbled out of their seats and just lay in the aisle.

'The gas was supposed to have everyone under by now, trust fate to give Medic this gas-resistant annoying little twat.

'Medic decided to ignore the man and hope to God he collapsed soon. Keeping in the left lane he came off the bridge to the roundabout and did a full loop to return to the bridge.

'Everyone seemed to tumble to the left of the bus and this made the man begin to laugh.

"'I asked you where you were going?"

"'I forgot my sandwiches." Medic was too busy trying to stay in control of the bus to multitask any more.

"'Sandwiches?"

'Medic had had enough. With the middle of the bridge just ahead, and no traffic behind him, he slammed on the brakes. The man lost his grip, striking the top of his head on the windscreen before slumping to the deck.

'Flicking on the hazard lights and reaching for the shoulder bag with the now empty gas canister, Medic tried to swing open the side gate but it was jammed.

'Looking down to the floor he noticed what looked like a rugby scrum of bodies with the twat on top. He had to clamber up and over to get out of the driving seat, and he swore as he scraped his shin on the moneybox in the process.

'This bridge was as good a place to start as any. He opened the doors, threw the empty cylinder over the bridge, and quickly dragged the twat plus one other passenger from the bus.

'Taking two of the large cardboard rectangles, he quickly made up two cardboard boxes with practised efficiency. He put one body in each, checked for a pulse, and abandoned them.

'Back in the bus, he quickly closed the door, pulled the other two passengers up the aisle away from the side gate, made the signage change, switched off the hazard lights and continued across the bridge.

'Blackett Street had been the next intended drop, but too many people were milling around, so he was forced to keep going.

'It was quieter at the next drops though and two more passengers went behind the library building, complete with card shelters, and another across the road from the Hancock Museum.

'The old lady and the drunk he put across from the RVI, one at the edge of Leazes Park on a bench, and one in a doorway near the stadium.

'With the bus emptied, Medic returned to the south side of the Tyne, and turning the signage back to '604' he continued along its route, as fast as he could.

'He skipped all the stops, waving at the wannabe passengers who were fuming over

266

his lateness. Leaving them dumbfounded or shouting obscenities in his wake, with no alternative service to catch at that hour.

'Medic avoided Prudhoe town centre, he reckoned that there might be police there waiting by then. He drove down through the trading estate disobeying its ridiculously low speed limit and tested whether that speed-camera actually worked.

'At the final roundabout he slowed only enough as to not turn the bus over. Then he headed for the level crossing and the very narrow bridge beyond with his foot to the floor.

However, looking ahead he saw that the stop lights were on and watched the barriers close. A freight train was coming, but Medic didn't remove his foot and the bus kept accelerating.

'This was the final part of the plan. He wanted a perfect ending to what he considered to be a perfect prank. Members of the general public, who had probably never bought a single copy of Big Issue, would soon feel what it was like to wake up disorientated like one of the homeless they ignore; Cold but alive, waking to find themselves in their cardboard homes.

'The police by now in pursuit, as was described on Crimewatch, also noticed the barriers come down ahead and were confident they had the driver trapped. That was until they noted the lack of deceleration. There wasn't time for them to warn anyone about what was to happen next.

'The bus smashed through the barriers just ahead of the freight train. The police could hear the train-driver's delayed reaction with the horn over their own siren, but could do nothing more than wait for it to pass on through. When the train was gone, they were met with the sight of the bus wedged firmly into the bridge with the rear emergency door open.

'Medic had gotten down to the cycle path below, stumbling grazing his knees, but pushed himself onward. He couldn't stop of course. The prank was pretty much in the bag.

'Later he stopped in the woods, regained his breath, swapped the uniform for a tracksuit, and then made his way on to Wylam where he had left his car in readiness.

'The police were left with very little to go on, which was why it had been given airtime on Crimewatch as well as the news. But the near comical reconstruction on television carried no sense of the homelessness theme Medic had very much intended.'

'I remember hearing something about that,' said Karen, 'Yes, I think the bus driver who was left in the toilet ended up quitting. It was terrible. And you guys thought that was funny?'

'Well, a little, back then. Medic was getting desperate to impress, and to be honest Admissions was close to finished by then,' Adam explained.

'Only because you wrecked it,' said Ben.

'What did you do, Adam?' Karen seemed eager to hear more.

'Oh no. We can leave that for another time.'

'He only went and hospitalised Medic, Leeroy and I.'

'That's was not the plan though,' Adam went on the defensive.'

'You say that.' Ben was starting to enjoy riling him once again over this, which was making Karen and especially Candice laugh along.

'This guy,' Adam pointed at Ben, 'This guy hospitalised *himself*. Ended up with a plate in his head.'

'Oh that's right. Pick on the invalid.'

'Oh dear.' Karen wasn't sure she wanted to hear more now. These guys sounded a bit too *Jack-Ass* reckless. 'So where did you and Candice meet?'

'Oh…Urr…In a car park actually.' Adam tried not to sound evasive. 'We…just hit it off, I guess.'

Candice could see what Adam was doing and tried to help out. 'Adam is trying to find a murderer.'

'What? Are you police?' Karen looked at Ben and Adam in disbelief.

'No. They are in construction, but Adam is keen to find out who killed a number of women in the region.'

'Why aren't the police handling that?'

'Well they are,' Adam tried to explain without saying too much. 'But I keep getting sent the tip-offs as to who is next.'

'But surely you just tell the police.'

'It's not that simple. There is only ever a vague reference to time and place, no names given.'

'That's fucked up.'

'I know right.'

'Like you are being toyed with…abused even.'

'Yes, absolutely,' Adam turned to Candice, 'I do feel abused.'

'But you'll get to the bottom of it. So have you had any more Flintstones?'

'Flintstones?' Karen looked lost.

'Yes, that's how I refer to the clues, Karen. It seems the next threat to life involves a parachute jump.'

'No way!' Karen couldn't believe it, another coincidence. 'I do sky-diving.'

'Do you? Ben has to go and see if he can sus out who is the next target and hopefully rescue them. He was a paratrooper.'

'Where are you going from?'

'He'll be going from somewhere near Shotton.'

'Unbelievable. That's where I jump from, the Blue-Skies sky-diving school. When are you going?'

'We don't know yet. The arrangements are being made by…the police.'

'Wow. Well if it is the day I'm there maybe I can help you sus out the killer *and* their victim.'

'That would be great, but we are not sure the killer will be there. They try to make the deaths look like misadventure.'

36

True to her word, before leaving for London, Cynthia had pulled some strings and got Ben onto the very next class at Blue-Skies.

That Saturday morning Ben was driven there by Harriet, who then got disguised as a cleaner as agreed with the school. Blue-Skies were not happy to learn that there may be an attempt on a client's life, neither were they keen on losing business, so they were thankful for the show of support.

Blue-Skies staff had been primed about Harriet and Ben, but not about the method of attack, since no one was quite sure. Blue-Skies provided the details of those expected to attend. For Harriet and particularly Ben's sake *Five* had done a background check on each client. However, Harriet was more than a little disturbed to find out that Ben could not read. She had to read the material to him in the car when they arrived.

Part of Harriet's mission was to determine whether there was any source of neurotoxin already planted in the school. She had been given some kit by the techies at Porton Down, but it wasn't fool-proof. It meant going around with gloves on, which was why Harriet was dressed as a cleaner.

Since the previous attacks had all involved single targets it was not expected to be a hit on everyone there though that couldn't be ruled out. So the water fountain was tested along with the tea and coffee kit.

There had been some discussion as to whether an employee was involved. However, if there was inside involvement the attack would likely now have been called off. Unless they were so confident that the MI5 presence was of no concern.

Ben was the first of the clients to arrive. He was there early so that he could work with the Rigger and Coordinator, Andy Metcalf, to check all the kit in the hangar was in good order.

'Why are you feeling everything, Ben?'

Ben didn't want to admit to his cognitive difficulties, nor his lost finger. 'Harriet and I are wearing special blue-tooth nanotechnology gloves that can detect substances and hidden material failures.'

'Really? That's amazing.'

'Yeah. You don't know the half of what goes on these days.'

'Like what?'

'You wouldn't believe me if I told you and if you did I'd have to kill you.'

'Yeah, right. So if you don't mind me asking, how did you get those black eyes?'

'Spot of bother with a couple of Russians.'

'I thought the cold war was over.'

'Sure but they still have chips on their shoulders.'

The kit check also involved examining the aircraft which was in the hangar too. The pilot was there doing her own checks. Ben said hello but she was clearly preoccupied.

When Ben got back to the classroom two people had already arrived. There was Peter from Darlington, who came across as a rather cocky attention-seeking guy to Ben, and Angela from Crook who seemed to hang off every word from Peter. Ben guessed they were an item, or soon would be. Nevertheless, neither of them seemed at all suicidal or otherwise unhinged.

'What happened to you, mate?' asked Peter.

'I got mistaken for a celebrity from a reality show.'

'Really? Which one?' asked Angela.

'I don't know. I've been hit that hard they all look the same to me now.'

Next to arrive was Dave from Gateshead. Ben tried to strike up a conversation with him but Dave didn't seem to have much to say for himself. Ben wasn't sure, not knowing Dave beyond this meeting, but he might be feeling a bit down. The deaths had all involved women but did that really mean that the next victim would also be a woman?

An ironic thought occurred to Ben. What if he was checking everyone out and all the time *he* was the next to have an *accident*. But then he'd have to live through it to be going to prison, he reasoned, unless, of course, Dawn *was* lying. His gut still told him she wasn't.

Next to arrive was Kevin from Haltwhistle. The clients were certainly keen enough to travel some distance. Kevin was chatty to say the least, asking Ben more questions than Ben was comfortable answering.

'How did you get those black eyes, Ben?'

'Would you believe I fell down stairs holding a door knob?' Ben knew that best cover stories involved keeping lies simple and not giving away too much.

Ben was thankful when Mary arrived so that he could excuse himself from Kevin and go talk to her. Mary seemed quite nervous. She was wringing her hands. However, this was by no means her first jump going by the background check.

'Hi. I'm Ben.'

'Right.' Mary was clearly reluctant to talk.

'I'm just here for a refresher.'

'Right.'

'I used to be in the paras years ago. I'm thinking about getting back into sky-diving.'

'Right.'

'I didn't catch your name.'

'Mary Lewis.'

'You seem a bit uptight Mary. Is everything okay?'

'Oh I'm always a bit nervous before a jump. It's nothing.'

'Where are you from?'

'Seaham.'

'I'm from North Shields.'

'Right.'

'I have…'

'I'm just going to go make myself a hot chocolate.'

'Okay…'

Ben noticed the last client arrive. Knowing the list he was not as surprised as she was on seeing *him*.

'Ben! So we *are* on the same jump.' Karen beamed a smile, then in more of a conspiratorial voice as she strode up to him, 'Have you had time to suss out who the target or killer are?'

Ben was concerned that Karen was too excited by this situation. He didn't want her to blow his cover with an inadvertent comment.

'I have a strong hunch about the victim, but if you are going to help keep an eye on her you need to be really subtle about it.'

'Is it her?' Karen said pointing at Angela who didn't notice because she was too caught up in fawning over Peter.

'Don't point, Karen. This is serious. Use your peripheral vision, so you don't stare straight at anyone. I believe it is Mary Lewis, over by the coffee machine.'

'Oh her. She's an odd one alright. Always nervous, until she does her first jump, then as high as a kite after that. You literally have to pull her off the hangar ceiling,' she laughed, pushing hair behind her ear as if to hear better.

'Well today we need to keep an extra close eye on *her* then, without arousing suspicions. But at the same time watch out for anything else odd around here.'

'Okay.'

'I'm glad you are here Karen. The fact that you know a number of these people could help make my job a bit easier.'

'Glad to help out.'

'Fancy a coffee before things kick off?'

'Sure.'

Ben let Karen go first with the machine and remembered what buttons she pressed for her drink.

'Oh I thought you wanted a coffee, Ben. You've gone for a Bovril like me.'

'Urr, yeah, I changed my mind when I saw what you were having.'

'Bovril always reminds me of that old Billy Connolly sketch.' Karen giggled.

'Oh yeah. *Hey you. Get me some Bovril.*' Ben put on a Glaswegian accent like his late father had and chuckled. He was enjoying himself and wondered whether he shouldn't get back into some sky-diving after all.

'Ben.'

'Yes?'

'That cleaner over there is a bit odd. I've never seen her before. She's paying more attention to us than what she's cleaning. Maybe *she's* the killer!'

'Shhh. She's with me. That's Harriet.'

'Oh.' Karen's excitement drained away to disappointment.

Andy, as Coordinator, called start of session, and ran through the order of the day. After kit check and chute packing they would be making two jumps before lunch. The weather for the afternoon could turn unsettled so they would have to see what the conditions permitted in terms of further jumps.

When the class went through to the hangar they all stood with Andy as the Rigger. They all watched as each person in turn packed their chutes, using the same method of folding which ensured a snag-free canopy deployment.

Only Ben's packing process differed somewhat because he was feeling everything.

'Come on mate.' Peter urged. 'We haven't got all day. We're usually up by now.'

'He's almost done,' said Andy.

'Trust us to get a new guy who's a tad OCD.'

'Oh shut up, Pete.' Karen went on the defensive.

'Don't you tell my Pete to shut up Kaz,' snapped Angela.

'There I'm done.' Ben got up shouldering his pack.

'Right follow me.' Andy got onto the plane and saw everyone into their positions.

With the door closed the engine started and they taxied for the runway.

A bit later Pete shouted over the engines, 'If I'd known we needed a bus ride, I'd have joined a club closer to the airstrip!'

Only Angela laughed. Most of them had heard his gags all before.

At the end of the runway the engines changed their tone and they were off. All the time Ben kept checking up on everyone's expressions and behaviour, the best he could considering his difficulties. It was even more problematic now that they all had helmets and goggles on. Tone of voice was easier for him to judge.

Still nothing unusual stood out. Even when the side door was opened and everyone was blasted with the air, there was a shared buzz of excitement. Only Mary remained nervous.

When it came to the jump Ben was to be last out, but Mary hesitated, suggesting Ben go first, but he insisted and she went without further delay. Ben was immediately on her tail, leaving Andy and the pilot behind.

Watching Mary in particular but everyone else too, as they dropped in freefall, there was still nothing odd happening.

In the event that someone didn't open their chute at the agreed altitude an air pressure and speed trigger, the AAD, would automatically release their canopy. So, even if someone lost consciousness the fail-safe should bring them safely to the ground. That was of course dependent upon not coming down somewhere dangerous, like power lines or busy road.

Ben knew that the next stage of threat would be when the chutes were deployed. One by one in quick succession the canopies opened perfectly, Ben's last of all. Everyone used their square canopies to get in as close as possible to the field marker.

When Ben touched down he hit the X dead centre, but was only certain of the target because that was where everyone else was headed.

He was relieved that everyone was still alive, but that only meant that someone was still in danger. Maybe this was the wrong day, because MI5 had become involved, like involving the police had made Adam late getting to Café Noir.

Anyway, Ben had enjoyed his jump and was looking forward to the next. He wouldn't object to having to come again another day, since *Five* were now picking up the tab. Ben was determined to make the most of his day out.

A truck took them all back to the hangar. There they were each observed checking their chutes and rigging for signs of damage, then repacking their kit.

That done, they got back onto the plane. Mary seemed to have had a personality transplant. She showed none of the previous hand-wringing nervousness. Now she was slapping her thighs with excitement and whooped when the plane finally lifted off the runway.

Ben wasn't fooled. Mary was still a concern, possibly even more so now.

Reaching altitude, with Andy and the pilot taking into consideration possible changes to the wind conditions for the Drop Zone, the door was opened again.

On Andy's signal everyone went out one after another cleanly, without any hesitation, Ben last again.

However, this time Ben noticed Karen pull her chute early. She shot up past him as he dropped by. Ben knew that could only mean she had a problem.

He tried looking up, and turned over almost going into a tumble before holding a stable backwards fall position. He made out what he guessed was the plane first. It was continuing on its way. Then he noticed there was something wrong with Karen's canopy. It was losing control and folding. Then he thought he saw something hurtle past him. Karen's canopy above was collapsing because she was no longer in the harness. She was below him now, without a pack.

Turning back over, Ben couldn't see Karen. Wasting no time he went into a dive, bringing his arms and legs in as he scanned for Karen. He had to save her.

Ben plummeted below the other sky-divers, searching and searching desperately. It was like scanning a shifting lawn for an ant.

Then he spotted what he hoped was Karen up ahead and not just a crow further below. He zeroed in on her, calling her name, knowing she wouldn't hear against the roar of the wind.

Getting closer he could see she must be conscious. She was controlling her fall. There was no sense of alarm in her posture. She didn't look back or around. She didn't know Ben was there, yet as he came almost within reach she shifted forwards and to the right.

He tried to catch up with her, but again as he got close she shifted position, this time to the left. Ben managed to come level with her and tried to look at her face. She seemed oblivious. He went to grab her outstretched wrist, but it was his bad hand and he lost his grip. She still appeared not to notice his presence.

Quickly Ben shifted position to come round behind Karen. The turbulence in her wake made it difficult but he came close enough to grab for the belt on her jump suit.

He managed to get a firm grip on her that he wasn't going to let go of. He just had to bring her in close, couple her to him with a carabiner then support her with his left arm and legs before deploying his canopy.

As they passed the lower altitude limit, going much too fast, the AAD deployed Ben's chute, before he had the carabiner connected. The force of his deceleration ripped Karen from him.

Ben considered jettisoning his canopy and going after Karen, but he knew it was already too late. The auxiliary chute would deploy instantly.

Ben watched to the very last moment of impact and his heart ached with frustration as it had while watching Toyah die.

By the time Ben got to Karen's body Harriet and others already had the situation under control. Karen would be going straight to forensics. They had to know whether she had been in contact with a neurotoxin or any hallucinogenic substance.

Ben watched as Karen's crumpled and bloodied form was zipped into a body bag, and knew what would come next. While everything would be gone over with a fine-toothed comb, everyone on the jump would be interviewed about the incident. Ben would be no exception.

37

Harriet conducted the interview at a government office in Newcastle, off St. James Boulevard. Even though Ben was helping with enquiries, the interview was still carried out on a formal basis, with video recordings made. There was only Ben and Harriet in the room.

'Wouldn't it have been helpful to have Adam at this too?'

'We don't need any distractions. I just want to get the facts first, then we can get Adam involved, if need be.'

'Well we could have saved time if you'd let me talk in the car.'

'I need to be able to make notes as we go. It helps me form ideas and raise questions later.'

'Even though you're recording my account?'

Harriet sighed, 'So McGregor, in your own words what do you *believe* happened?'

'Karen just seemed to lose it and took off her pack mid-jump.'

'Please start from the beginning when we both arrived.'

'Really?'

'Yes. Context could be key.'

'Okay then.' Ben sat back and thought for a moment. 'We entered the Blue-Skies offices. While you went to get changed, I got talking with Andy. We went and checked the kit out. We both agreed it was fine.

'The clients were coming in so I talked to them. Most seemed fine. Dave seemed a bit down, oh and Mary seemed pretty nervous. I was concerned about her, enough to warn Karen who I already told you in the car I knew from a few days ago.'

'As the friend of Adam's friend Candice.'

'Yes. So I asked Karen to help keep an eye on Mary. She was okay with that, but not very subtle.'

'How d'you mean?'

'A bit too excited. Amateur first-timer, you know. So we went up and everything was done by the book. Everyone came down safely.

'At that point I was starting to doubt that this was the time it was going to happen. I was thinking that maybe Adam should have booked it in, as he would have if Cynthia hadn't helped.

'Anyway, we all came back to the hangar. We checked and packed the kit then went back up.

'Nothing was out of the ordinary. Mary was over her nerves but Karen and I kept an eye on her as she still seemed the most likely person to flip.

'Each time we jumped I was last in line, as agreed, to have best eyes-on.

'This second time, however, as I'm going down, Karen, who is beyond Mary, pulls her ripcord early.'

'You saw her pull it?'

'Well no. It happened so fast I was surprised. She went up past me. I turned to look. Karen's canopy was folding. Then she dropped right past me…Without her pack.'

'Do you think she had been confused and had meant only to jettison her primary chute?'

'She would have had to be very confused for that. Different fastenings, and if it was a mistake you would have thought she would have been screaming as she dropped past me.'

'Well sure, so there was nothing?'

'Nothing. But she wasn't unconscious and tumbling. She was in a controlled descent. I tried to catch her up. She didn't acknowledge that I was there and yet, as I drew closer, she made some evasive moves.'

'Yes, that's what it looked like to me as well. I was watching from the ground through binoculars. You managed to grab her right?'

'Yes. Twice. I lost grip with my busted hand first time and…'

'Busted hand?'

'Yes I didn't tell you but Frank Chesney chopped my little finger off piece by piece at his house of horror.'

'Dear God! Why didn't you say anything?'

'Adam and I couldn't afford to let you or Cynthia veto the jump.'

'You are some friend, Ben.'

He shrugged. 'So anyway, second time I had Karen in my right hand by her jumpsuit belt. That's when she was torn from me by the AAD.'

'AAD?'

'The Automatic Activation Device for canopy deployment. Goes off when you pass the lower limit too fast. A safety measure.'

'I see. I thought you had opened your parachute when you thought you had a good grip of her. So you didn't make a mistake then, it was just very bad timing.'

Ben sighed and shook his head. 'It was just how it was meant to be. All of this. From the moment we arrived, through to the moment Karen went into remote control to her death.'

'Very clever, Ben.' Dawn made Harriet jump out of her skin.

'Where the *hell* did *you* come from?!' demanded Harriet.

Dawn ignored her. '*Remote control*. You could be onto something there, Ben,' Dawn mocked as if also struggling with the mystery.

'Well you *would* know, Dawn.' Ben wasn't taken in.

'This is Dawn?!' Harriet drew her sidearm from her shoulder holster. 'On the floor! Now!!'

Dawn looked at the gun then at the floor, lifting one foot then the other. 'I already appear to be *on the floor*, Harriet.'

'Don't be a smart-arse. Who are you working for?'

'Time, I guess.'

'The publishing house?'

'Now who's being a smart-arse?'

'We have been looking for you Miss Summers. What has brought you to this government building?'

'You are going to shoot me.' It was a statement not a question.

'No I'm not. Just answer my questions.' Harriet decided to calm herself. She holstered her weapon to prove Dawn wrong. She went to the corner of the room and brought another chair to the desk next to Ben. 'Please sit. I need answers and I need them now.'

Dawn sat, and waited.

Harriet was a bit flustered. She still didn't know how Dawn could have got into the room unheard. She thought about Cynthia's theory of a hallucinogenic, but wouldn't that mean that Ben gave it to her? Come to think of it, he would also have been the prime person to give it to Karen. But Ben wasn't at Café Noir when Rapture was first used. Maybe there were a number of killers involved.

'In your own time,' Dawn prompted.

'Are there a number of killers involved in this?'

'Yes.'

'Are Ben and Adam involved?'

'Yes.'

'Hey, I didn't kill anyone…recently.'

'No. Adam and Ben are not killing these women.'

'But you are, aren't you, Dawn.'

'Not *these* women no.'

'What do you mean, not *these* women?'

'I do kill and some of them are women.'

Ben turned to Dawn. 'It was you who swooped in and killed Frank Chesney and guests, wasn't it. Thanks for that, Dawn. But you might have been a bit quicker off the mark.' Ben raised his still gloved left hand.

'That wasn't me, Ben.'

'So was that Destiny then?'

'No.'

'Who then?'

'Not for me to say, but you two will meet again…one day.'

'Hey, don't hijack my interview, Ben.' Harriet knew she might not have time to waste. She had to focus on getting the origin of the neurotoxin and any future plans out of Dawn. 'Who is Destiny?'

'He is my partner, from The Apple.'

'Where is that?'

'Deep space.'

'So let me get this straight, The Apple is a company and Deep Space is what? The building it is in, with other companies?'

'Oh no. The only company I keep is Destiny. When I say *deep space* I mean *beyond your galaxy.*'

Harriet sighed. 'And is that where you keep the neurotoxin?'

'Rapture?'

'Yes. I *knew* it was you!'

'No. We don't keep anything there.'

'Oh, so you manufacture it there and now it has all been distributed?'

'No, Rapture is not our product.'

'So whose is it?'

'I won't be able to tell you that.'

'Do you know where it will be used next?'

'Yes.'

'You must tell us.'

'I cannot.'

'Is it soon?'

'I believe it is very soon, in fact any minute now.'

'Where?' Harriet believed a life was now in her hands. 'Tell me!'

'I cannot.'

In desperation Harriet stood up and drew her side arm again.

'Hey hey! Not cool Harriet.' Ben assumed Harriet had drawn her weapon and attempted to defuse the developing situation.

'Tell me, Dawn. Or I will put a bullet in you,' she warned pointing at Dawn's chest.

'You will. The clock is ticking.'

'Are you nuts Dawn, don't wind her up.' Ben stood up and turned to Harriet. 'She means it.'

'That's right I mean it.' Harriet was starting to breathe faster.

'No, I mean Dawn means it. If she says she can't say, it will be the meta-interference. Dawn, show her.'

'The next victim of what you call Rapture is…' Dawn's mouth froze.

'Say it!!'

Dawn looked like she had switched off. She just sat there in mid attempt to finish.

'Right then, I'm going to count to three...One…Two…Three.' Harriet couldn't believe she was caught up in such a situation. She felt helplessly committed now. She felt her finger tightening on the trigger, as if it had a mind of its own, so she started to lower her weapon but then she felt it recoil.

'As I said you would,' Dawn seemed to come back to life with no sense of distress, 'You have shot me.'

As Dawn stood up Harriet saw the fabric of Dawn's skirt had a hole in it. But then the material mended itself. Dawn hitched up her hem to reveal the bullet hole in her thigh.

Placing a hand under the hole no blood came out, only the round, the hole quickly healing up after it.

'Yours I believe, Agent Wallace.' Dawn dropped the impact distorted round onto the interview table. Even Ben could not believe his eyes.

Dawn sat back down as if it had all been an easily forgivable rooky mistake. 'Where were we?'

'I urr…This meta-interference…Is that what is causing you to obstruct our investigation?'

'Yes.'

'If you cannot help us, then why do you come?'

'Because that is what happened.'

'I don't buy that. Everything happens for a reason.'

'Like your grandmother dying of sepsis after she had just recovered from cancer?'

'How do you know about that?'

'I have access to all that is known, via What-If.'

'What's that, a computer?'

'I don't think so. It was constructed before my time and it will not tell of its origin or design. It is the core of The Apple.'

'The Apple's core? So what am I supposed to believe, that you are an android or something?'

'I'm a Time-Slave. With Destiny we do our bit to make certain significant events happen in the multiverse.'

'Like what? What's next on your to-do list, Dawn?'

'Destiny and I have to go and pin down Juliz Starshooter.'

'Who's she? A pawn star you've been contracted to kill?'

'No the task takes place on an asteroid. Starshooter is a Captain in the OSS.'

'Well you can't mean the Office of Strategic Services.'

'No…Ochoba Space Spetsnaz.'

'Space Spetsnaz?' Ben laughed.

'A different time-line to yours and Harriet's, Ben.'

'And then I suppose you'll be dropping by to help out Dr Who.' Harriet made no attempt to hide her cynicism.

'The Doctor doesn't need my help, yet.'

Harriet rolled her eyes. 'The Doctor is a *fictional* character, Dawn.'

'In *your* reality, yes. But everything you can imagine is happening out there, somewhere.'

'So what task comes after dealing with Juliz?'

'I have to load some critical information onto a quantum computer belonging to the UN, to ensure that Imogen Powers and her crew are attacked over the Sonoran Desert.'

'We're getting nowhere with this. I have to get to the source of the Rapture before that victim dies. Can you at least tell me where to look?'

'It won't do you any good. That victim I mentioned is now dead, but there are others following. They are also on another planet.'

'Wait…Another planet? So you are saying the origin of Rapture is extra-terrestrial?'

290

'Yes.'

'That has to be a lie. I don't believe in any of that alien mumbo jumbo.'

'Whether you believe in it or not doesn't make it any less true.'

'But the SETI project has found nothing tangible in all the years it has been running.'

'There's a reason for that.'

'What? Meta-interference?'

'No, A cover up. It seems that those who control your governments feared a loss of power if people knew, and panicked.'

'You are just spouting conspiracy theory.'

'I don't have time to waste on such things, since I already know the truth for each time-line *and* have a busy schedule.' Dawn got up.

'Stop. I haven't finished.' Harriet needed a way to get something useful out of Dawn. She ran to the door to bar the way.

Dawn smiled at Harriet's naiveté, gave a wave and stepped through a hole in the air.

'There she goes…' Ben sang the first line of the Sixpence None The Richer hit, smiling at Harriet's discomfort.

38

Harriet used the time in the car, taking Ben back to Adam's, to report in to Cynthia.

'...So Ben was unable to save this victim, but luckily had had previous conversations with her. So like with Toyah, we have a better profile of this victim, if that actually helps and these aren't just all random incidents.

'So then I debriefed Ben. He confirmed what seems to be coming out of some of the other statements. These victims appear to enter a state of almost remote control as cause of death.'

'That will be the effect of the neurotoxin, Harriet.'

'I tried to get confirmation of that. But it's too early for the toxicology report. However, Dawn came to the debriefing.'

'Dawn Summers?'

'Yes. I tried to apprehend her but after some questioning she left.'

'Left?'

'Through one of those portals.'

'Harriet, you must have been hallucinating.'

'No I wasn't Cynthia.'

'Ben or someone must have given you something.'

'I wondered that too. But I don't believe that now. Apparently this Rapture neurotoxin we have not seen before...It's extra-terrestrial.'

'*Harriet*, you are still under the influence of the toxin.'

'No, Cynthia. I have it all on video.'

'I seriously doubt that…You're not driving in that *state* are you?'

Harriet rolled her eyes. 'Say again?'

'You aren't driving are you? I can hear traffic.'

'You are breaking up.' Harriet hung up. 'I guess she had to be there, hey Ben?'

'Cynthia seems a bit narrow minded, or overly focussed. Probably feels safer that way. Not sure she would have seen things any different if or when she does meet Dawn though. It does kinda give a bit of a shake-up to your perception of what's real, doesn't it. If you'd told me a few weeks ago what we would be experiencing *I'd* have thought you were on something rather than onto something.'

'I know what you mean. I'm wondering whether I should check to see if there are any other cases like this happening elsewhere.'

When Harriet eventually pulled up outside Adam's, he was clearly out. Adam's car wasn't there and Frank's car had been impounded. Ben had a key to get into Adam's house anyway.

He opened the car door awkwardly with his right hand.

'Ben…I appreciate what you did for us today. It can't have been easy, the condition you're in.'

'Well, you just soldier on to the best of your abilities.'

'What are you going to do now?'

'I was planning on raiding Adam's fridge for a few beers. Want to join me?'

'Another time maybe.'

'Do you think *Five* will continue with this then?'

'Probably keep an eye on it yes and there's also the question of who went on that killing spree at Frank Chesney's.'

'Isn't that a police matter?'

'Sure. But there's a growing concern at *Five* about the increase in organised vigilantism. There's a fine line between the definition of vigilantism and terrorism.'

'Right.'

'And seeing how you handled yourself today, I wouldn't mind betting we meet again before too long.'

Adam was at Candice's, consoling her after breaking the bad news about her friend Karen after Ben had called him.

Candice kept breaking down in tears. 'I still can't believe it, Adam.'

'Me neither. But it's just like what happened with Toyah. They had no reason to kill themselves.'

'But how does that happen? Fine one minute suicidal the next? God it could happen to any of us!'

'Don't think like that. Look, I'm thinking of getting away for a few days. I don't have any work on at the moment. Why don't you come along too? Just as friends of course.'

'Well I suppose I could. I doubt I'll be able to concentrate on my studies. Where had you in mind going to?'

'Well Toyah once said Skye was really picturesque. Maybe we could make it a camping trip, seeing as you're an outwards bound type of girl.'

'Ha, yeah, I'd like that, Adam.'

'I think I have an old tent somewhere.'

'I have a two person bubble tent, we could use that. I also have a ton of maps. I'm sure I have a couple covering Skye.' Candice seemed to cheer up a little with something else to think about.

An hour or so later, Adam's car was packed with Candice's camping gear and they headed off to Adam's.

Adam and Candice took Ben shopping to get in a week's supplies.

'I get why you both want to get away from all of this shite. But don't you think Dawn can get to you wherever you go?'

'The killings all appear to be happening in the north east though. So if we can leave the police and MI5 behind, even for a bit, it has to help, doesn't it.'

'We won't be gone more than a few days, Ben,' Candice sounded tired out. 'I'll have to be getting back to my studies then. I just can't focus at the moment with the shock of it all.'

'Well maybe you both need a guide.' Ben was concerned they might not be in the right state of mind to be going into the wilderness. 'I know Skye like the back of my hand. Used to go there with the lads to do the Black Cullins ridge and stuff.'

'Thanks for the offer Ben but I think Adam and I will stick to something safer.'

'Suit yourselves. Three's a crowd anyway I guess.'

'No, it's not like that,' Adam insisted.

'So what do I do if someone calls for you? Mobile reception is still not good up there.'

'Tell them they'll have to wait. The way I'm feeling right now, Dawn can damned well sort it. All of this failure to save people is an *abuse*!'

'I must admit, what with Dawn saying that Rapture is extra-terrestrial, and with her *having* to cause good *and* bad events, I'm thinking this all has to be her and or Destiny. I mean who else is alien round here?'

'But you know, Ben. If it has been Dawn and Destiny all this time, then they've been lying to us all along.'

'But that is exactly what abusers do,' said Candice.

Adam nodded.

'Oh yeah,' Ben remembered something else. 'Did I mention that Harriet shot Dawn?'

'What?'

'Yeah, in the leg, to stop her leaving I guess, to try and get the truth out of her. Dawn even predicted she would shoot her. In fact Harriet put her sidearm away at first to try and prove her wrong, I think.'

'So what happened?'

'Well Dawn definitely isn't human. She's like T2 or one of the X-Men. The wound didn't bleed. It just expelled the round, which Dawn dropped on the interview table. Then her wound healed up. She didn't even seem to register any pain.'

'So do you think this *Dawn* really is an alien then?' Candice was having trouble believing Ben. 'Could she not be from the future?'

'She is. She told us she was. But I really don't think she's the next evolutionary step for mankind, if that's what you mean.'

'It would be kind of cool though, wouldn't it, not having a worry about getting injured.'

'There's more to it than that, Candice. When she took me to The Apple to see What-If, their reality-drive, she explained to me they are Time-Slaves.'

'Wait a minute Ben, you're losing me. You're telling me you were abducted by aliens now?'

'I guess so, but the important thing is that once you realise that there is only one future for you as there was only one past, you're only one step away from becoming a Time-Slave.'

'And what would *they* be then?'

'Beings who have access to all knowledge past and future, and know everything *they* do for eternity.'

'God…You'd feel like a machine or something.' Candice looked out of the window at the people all around as they arrived at the superstore, 'and nobody knows any of this is going on.'

39

Ben relaxed at the back of the *Obsession* listening to the birds singing, to the backing of tumbling water. He was just taking another swig of beer when his phone started playing the theme to *Ghost in the Shell* and vibrating in his pocket.

'It's me.' The female said before Ben could ask.

'Sorry, I can't read the caller ID. Me who?'

'Harriet, sorry.'

'Oh hi. I'm just having another beer. Free to join me *now*?'

'Fraid not. Still busy. I can't seem to get hold of Adam.'

'Not surprised. He and Candice went up to Skye for a few days break.'

'Skye?'

'Yeah, that's right. They're camping along the Northern escarpment that runs past the Quiraing and the Old Man of Storr. There's probably no reception. I did warn them.'

'Right.'

'Has something come up?'

'Nothing that can't wait. We did a check like you suggested. Nationally and internationally. There are no similar recorded incidents of deaths linked to the appearance of Flintstones, or even just a rise in strange deaths of women.'

'Well I guess that's something.'

'Yeah…If I hear anything else, I'll be in touch. Oh and Ben?'

'Yes?'

'Don't sit on your ass all day drinking.'

'Why not? There's not much else to do round here.'

'You never know, I might…need you.'

'I'm still spoken for.'

'Not like that.'

The first night, Adam and Candice had stayed at a B&B with a wonky floor, in Crianlarich because it was getting late. They made an early start the next day.

Parking at Uig with the intention of eventually getting the bus back across from Portree, they camped on the clifftops each night.

They had headed north from Uig on that first day, then after lunch, passing the triangulation point headed in a more easterly direction. They manage to make camp in the last of the light pitching above the Quiraing.

This was the first time they had slept together, having taken separate rooms at the B&B. This is where Candice got first-hand experience of Adam's nightmares.

Adam's phone was ringing. He managed to get it out of his pack before it went to voicemail.

'Hello?'

'Adam, thank God. Come back.'

'Who is this?'

'What do you mean, *who is this*? It's me, Toyah.'

'Toyah?'

'I know you are with *her*. Come back to me!'

'What? No. You're dead, Toyah…'

'Is that what *she* has you believing, with those drugs and hypnosis of *hers*?'

'No, I found you dead. I couldn't save you…'

'Do you *love* her, Adam?'

'What? No. We are just friends. She is helping me get over my PTSD.'

'If you don't leave her right *now*, I'm going to…'

The reception seemed to break up. It sounded like crackling and rustling. 'I can't hear you. You're going to what?'

Adam heard the whisper of cling-film coming off its roll. '…Kill myself.'

'This isn't funny…Don't.'

'It's going on.'

'Stop.'

Adam listened to the polythene winding on.

'I can't breathe,' the voice mumbled.

'Stop it! I believe you! Stop! I'll come home!'

Then there was only the sound of Toyah's desperate smothered cries.

'Toyah! Toyah!!' Adam screamed into the darkness, sitting up in his sleeping bag, feeing the cool damp tent wall brush across the right side of his forehead.

'It's okay Adam!' Candice urged, though sounding frightened herself, trying to gather her thoughts. 'Adam, it's just a bad dream…Adam.'

Adam was panting. 'Fuck, but those dreams seem so real. I thought I'd be getting over them by now, but they just keep incorporating new material. It's like my imagination is punishing me.'

'You have to stop feeling that you are to blame, Adam. None of it was your fault. I've told you that.'

'Try telling my subconscious.'

'I have been, during the hypnosis. It's not a quick process…Just lie back down.'

Adam did as he was told but didn't get to sleep for ages, until the pitter-patter of a passing rain shower soothed him on his way.

The next day there was no discussion of the disturbed sleep as they made their way south to make camp early on Beinn Edra.

'It is so quiet here, Adam.'

'It *was*,' he responded with a smirk.

'But seriously, if you just listen, it's almost like being deaf.'

'Yeah. I can hear the blood in my ears.'

'I can't hear any birds or sheep even.'

'No. The road is only a few miles away but I don't see any traffic on it.'

As they ate their evening meal, watching the sun drop closer to the horizon they caught sight of a white-tailed fish eagle over the sea.

'I'm so glad you suggested this, Adam. It's beautiful here.'

Adam's mind thought *like you Candice* but he chased the notion away.

That night, tucked up in their sleeping bags, Adam had trouble falling asleep but Candice didn't. She began to snore. It wasn't an irritating noise, it was almost soothing. It reminded Adam to think about his breathing and eventually his eyelids grew heavy and he was off.

He woke to silence. Candice had stopped snoring. He waited for her to start again but she didn't, and as he waited he strained his ears. He couldn't hear any breathing at all.

Adam turned his head. In the very faint light he tried to look at the profile of Candice's face. From that angle she almost looked like Toyah. Was this a sign that he would never be able to forget Toyah, or a sign that he might be able to move on, with Candice.

There was still no sound. Adam slowly got an arm outside of his sleeping bag and felt the tent's inner wall pockets for his phone.

Switching its screen-light on, he looked at Candice's blissfully sleeping face, only it wasn't, it was Toyah's plastic wrapped dead face.

'Toyah!!' Adam woke up for real, screaming as he bolted upright once more, with Candice quick to follow.

'Adam! It's okay. It's okay.' But Candice was beginning to wonder if she was talking out of her arse.

The next morning both of them woke feeling unrefreshed and more than a little irritable so did not say much over breakfast.

From Beinn Edra they continued south along the clifftops to the triangulation point on The Storr, above the famous Old Man of Storr. Even before they arrived they could see the line of tourists making use of every hour of light to walk up to the spires of rock from the road and then back.

'We really have had a good run of weather, Adam,' Candice remarked over the evening meal.

'Yes. I think we have been very lucky. The west coast is notorious for its rain.'

'True. We are well over half way to Portree now. Fingers crossed the weather holds.'

Adam took a photo of Candice sitting there holding her cup of coco. He had taken a number of shots along the way. He thought it a shame that the signal was so poor, he would have liked to send the photos on to Ben. He hoped Ben wasn't going stir crazy on his own.

That afternoon, bottle in hand, Ben had been crossing the lawn back to the house when he was seized by an idea. What Adam really needed, to break up the monotony of all that grass was a pond.

Placing his beer on an almost level section of rockery Ben went to the shed and came back with a spade.

The turf came up so much easier than would be imagined. Especially when he tried using the spade the right way up. In fact the soil below was relatively easy to dig out too, and soon there was a large mound building to one side.

Then the soil seemed to bottom out. Looking closely Ben could see there was black plastic sheeting, the type that is laid down under gravel to stop weeds growing through. But what was it doing there and at that depth?

Ben cleared more soil away from it until he found an edge. He started pulling. This didn't come away quite so easy. Its removal would involve a bit more digging. Ben started to get frustrated.

Standing straight, hands behind back he questioned himself. 'Why did I start this?'

Ben looked back at his half bottle of beer on the rockery stone. He couldn't be bothered to climb out of the hole, so returned to his digging.

Eventually, with a mighty pull, Ben got a large section of sheeting over to one side.

There in the soil beneath was a raised section. Ben took the spade and dragged it across. The soil shifted aside, to reveal what looked like old clothing.

'What the fuck? How long has that been there? Didn't Adam's dad own the place before Adam had it? Is this Adam's mother?'

Quickly Ben dropped to his knees using his hands to scrape the soil away. Realising that he had revealed the chest by the feel of the ribs, Ben worked his way upwards to the head.

Ben's fingers became such a blur. He seemed oblivious to his injured left hand.

Then enough of the face was uncovered to recognise the corpse.

Ben shot to his feet with alarm and confusion. 'You have *got* to be pissing me!'

It was Adam.

40

Adam screamed into the dark but this time it sounded more confused than heartbroken.

At his side Candice didn't even bother to sit up to console him, just groaned and pulled the sleeping bag up over her ears.

'It wasn't Toyah this time...It was me.'

'Mmm...'

'I was dead. Ben dug me up in the back garden. What do you think that means?'

'As your counsellor I'd say it definitely means you should lie back down and get some sleep.'

In the morning Adam was desperate to talk about his latest nightmare, but Candice was clearly enjoying the view, so he decided that it might be best to say nothing.

There was only one more night left on Skye. The planned pitch was to be on the hill just north of Portree, to ensure that they would be in town in time to get an early bus to Uig and the car. The only question mark over that was whether the good weather was going to hold much longer. It already appeared to be on the verge of breaking.

Even as they finished breakfast and broke camp, the wind was picking up.

'I think the weather is turning, Adam.'

'I think you're right.'

'Let me check the map again.' Candice took the map from her pack while Adam fastened her tent to his pack.

Looking from the map to the landscape and the fast changing conditions, Candice advised a change of route.

'I suggest we drop down from here, cross the A855 and get to the cliffs the other side of Loch Leathan. The wind should not be as strong lower down.'

'Sounds sensible to me.'

'We'll see how close we can get to Torvaig, here,' she pointed at the map again. 'We'll look for a sheltered pitch somewhere near there.'

'Right.'

By the time they crossed the A855 it was already raining.

The wind picked up further and even lower down the rain was being driven hard, slowing progress. It was times like this that the beauty of the Scottish landscape was lost to its elements and walking became a chore.

By lunchtime they were nowhere near where they intended to be. They both huddled in the lea of the wind provided by a large outcrop of rock, eating from their dwindling food supply.

'I know it's not ending well, and I've not been the best of company in the evenings, but thanks for coming on this trip with me, Candice.'

'No problem. It's been good to get away. I managed to forget about Karen for a few moments here and there. I don't know what drove her to die that way, but she didn't deserve that.'

'No.'

'I'm done and getting cold sitting here. Are you ready to make a move?'

'Yep.'

Through the afternoon they continued walking south along the clifftops, still at a sensible distance from the edge, stopping a couple of times for water.

Even when the rain became softer and the wind dropped, the cloud was still low.

Along the way they passed a large peat bog, the sphagnum moss was a near luminous green, even under such a grey sky.

A little further on, they came across a sheltered area of flat ground. Following a short discussion they agreed that they were both quite tired, so pitched the tent early. It would mean getting up at first light in the morning to make good time to Portree, but it did feel like the sensible thing to do.

Once they both had the tent up and their bedding sorted they ate their last supper.

A little later, in a gap between drizzle showers, Candice went out among the boulders for her bathroom break.

Adam went out too, but simply walked nearer the cliff to take a leak. However, he noticed that the wind was coming towards him from the angry sea below. Not wanting to spend the night soaked in urine he moved away to find a more sheltered location. By the time he returned to the tent, Candice was already back and tucked up in her sleeping bag.

Adam wasn't far behind in settling down. Securing the flysheet and removing his boots before zipping up the door flap of the inner, he was soon wriggling his way into his bag.

It had been a tough day but in some way it had made for an interesting change to the days before. He seemed to feel more relaxed in his exhaustion, and was soon asleep.

Ben was sitting at the back of *Obsession* watching a vixen in the undergrowth beyond the opposite bank. He contemplated going to get Adam's binoculars from inside, but felt sure that if he moved she would be gone. The fox seemed not to have noticed him yet, his position was upwind.

She was on the hunt, checking out the brambles for fruits and possible rodents. Suddenly she stopped, lifted her head, her ears pricked, she turned her head and then she was off.

It was clear to Ben that something had spooked her. He looked along the bank for a clue but instead made out the sound of beating rotors coming his way.

'Bloody aircraft.'

The helicopter came closer getting louder and louder. Soon it sounded like it was dropping lower than normal for a standard flight path.

Then Ben's phone started playing *Ghost in the Shell* again. He hoped it was Meg.

'Hello?!' he called over the sound of the helicopter, which now seemed to be circling over the canopy. 'Harry who?! You'll have to speak up! Some idiot's right above me in a chopper!'

'I said, get your shit together Sergeant, I'll brief you in the air. It's Harriet!'

The black AW-109C landed in the field next to Adam's house. Ben was up through the woods, clearing the barbed wire fence and running low under the downwash in what felt like seconds.

The door closed after him and they were in the air even before Ben secured himself.

Harriet, like the troopers aboard, was dressed in an NBC suit, with masks, head gear, their weapons stowed to the side. She handed Ben his flight helmet and mouthed 'Just put this on for now!'

With the helmet on he could now hear everyone and speak without shouting.

'You can put your kit on later, Ben. For now let me start by introducing the Territorial SAS team then I'll brief you.'

'Thanks.'

After running through the names, Harriet got down to the details. 'Cotes emailed me a report late this afternoon. I got here as quick as I could. The report covers all the possible links between the female victims, from the surely not relevant to the bloody important.'

'Let's hear it then.' Ben was getting impatient. He hadn't had anything close to this level of excitement in days.

'All the women were between twenty-five and thirty-seven years old. They all showed a higher than normal ppm of micro-plastics.'

'Micro-plastics?'

'Yes, they are getting into our foods and…'

'I know what they are. I just wondered why these women have a higher level than normal.'

'Poor diet maybe, I don't know. Also, they were all wearing the same type of bladder-leak underwear, not that that can be relevant. However, what certainly has to be relevant is that all the victims except Karen Thompson had suffered from one form of mental health issue or another.'

'Maybe their issues caused weak bladders.'

'Possibly. Anyway, these women had all gone for at least one session of mental health counselling at the same Newcastle facility, which connects to the person who is now our key suspect. The friend of Karen and Adam; Candice Sefton.'

'Shit! I see. So we are heading for Skye?'

'Yes, but it's going to take us longer than I'd hoped, with the weather closing in. The pilot says we'll be in for a bit of terrain hugging to avoid the cloud base once we skirt past Glasgow airport's airspace.'

'I just hope we're in time.'

41

Adam started mumbling with anxiety which woke Candice. This time instead of sitting it out, she unzipped her sleeping bag down the side and lifted out a drinks bottle with what might have looked like apple juice had there been sufficient light.

Removing the top she propped herself up on one elbow, looking for the dip in Adam's sleeping bag around his groin. Listening to his increasingly disturbed mutterings, she waited for her moment.

Less than a minute before Adam made his predictable scream, Candice poured what she had prepared earlier onto the dip in the bag. The warm fluid was still draining through as Candice returned the top to the bottle, the bottle to the bag, zipped back up and lay down again.

'Toyah!!' Adam bolted upright, but for a change to the scheduled program he went on to add, 'Oh no, that *was* a bad one, I think I've wet myself.'

'What? Oh you haven't.'

With an exploratory hand he confirmed. 'Yes. Sorry.'

'Well you can't lie there like that till morning. You'll have to change.'

'Right yes. I have one spare pair of boxers left in my kit.'

'Forget them. I have something better.' She sat up rummaged through her bag then handed him something.

'What are these?' They felt like boxers made out of a stretchy material with a padded panel.

'They are just bladder-leak underwear.'

'I'm not wearing something like that. I'll be fine with my boxers.'

'Well you weren't with the ones you've got on, now were you. I'd think again if I were you. Your nightmares are clearly getting worse since you've now deteriorated to bed-wetting.'

'Shit. I thought I was going to be getting better.'

'Look, just get them on and we can work out what to do next to sort this mess out.'

The AgustaWestland was tearing along the valleys, close to its top speed at 190mph. The pilot was flying by visual flight rules, VFR, wearing night vision goggles. These gave him a wider and clearer view of the terrain ahead than could be achieved in the dark with the helicopter's flood lights.

If the cloud dropped much further, things could get tricky. There would be no turning back however. The pilot understood this mission was extremely important. In the case of worsening conditions he would have to switch to instrument flight rules, IFR, or as he liked to joke this meant *I Follow Roads*.

Before the helicopter began its terrain hugging, Ben got changed into his NBC suit. He knew that it was purely a precaution, in case *Rapture* was used against them by Candice in an attempt to escape capture.

Harriet was convinced that Candice would explain all in a way that Dawn had been unable to. They needed her alive. That didn't equate to uninjured though, just immobilised. The TA SAS were all armed with supressed MP7s.

There was no weapon for Ben. Harriet hoped that she wouldn't need to explain why. Ben certainly hadn't raised the question when he got kitted up.

He sat next to Harriet, with his flight helmet back on, arms folded, waiting patiently for any updates from the co-pilot.

Adam looked around with his head torch. The beam highlighted the fact that it was starting to rain again. The tent was nowhere to be seen, but Candice was there with him. They both appeared to be walking with purpose.

'I think there must be a house up ahead, Candice.'

'I can't see one.'

'Look, there's a lawn.'

'Where?'

'That flat grass up ahead.'

'Oh yeah, I see it, with a rosebush.'

As they got closer, Adam was seized by the need to apologise once again, 'You know that I'm really sorry that I have been waking you with my nightmares, every night. I'll make it up to you.' Adam strode on for the bush to pick Candice a rose.

'Oh, I appear to be sinking in the lawn.' Adam sounded almost drunk.

'You *are* sinking into the lawn.' Candice laughed.

Adam made no attempt to get back, stretching out for the rose bush. He sank further in.

Candice laughed at the stupidity. 'What are you doing, Adam?'

'I'm going to pick you a rose.'

'But I don't see any roses now.'

'There. I have one.' Adam tried to head back but the lawn was swallowing him.

'I can't see it.'

'Here.' Adam lifted his arm higher, lighting his hand with the head torch.

'I don't see it.' But what she did see was something big, lowering itself out of the cloud behind where Adam was sinking.

This object appeared to be ghost-like, as if it was a hologram. There was movement inside it as it came to rest on the ground beyond the bush, which looked more like marsh grass now.

Figures came out, through the hull of this large craft. The first one out looked like a Gorilla with the head of a Doberman. That figure was followed by two thinner figures, grey with large dark almond eyes.

Candice nodded towards them, '*They* have come for me.'

Still holding his imaginary rose high, Adam attempted to twist around to see, and sank further into the peat bog. It was up to his nostrils. While he felt a little confused he did not feel any anxiety. This wasn't like any of his usual nightmares. It was all just nonsense.

Adam could see the three figures coming across the heather from what looked like a giant sunflower seed. Next, a roaring could be heard approaching from behind. Adam made the mistake of turning to look, but he didn't see the flood lights that came up over the cliff, because his eyes sank below the bog.

Ben, Harriet, and the SAS team had ditched their flight helmets. They now wore their hooded gas masks and battle helmets equipped with night vision. The doors were opened in readiness. They were just waiting for the pilot to bring them in low enough.

The team disembarked from both sides of the AW-109C onto the rough ground, trying to get their bearings. Even as they cleared the downwash of the rotors they had difficulty accepting what they were seeing before them.

Candice was standing at the edge of a peat bog. In the bog was an extended forearm looking like it was gripping something. No sign of a head.

Ben forged on towards Candice, rushing across the heather, but felt like his object recognition problem had suddenly got a lot worse. He could see that Candice was standing still but nothing else was registering. Where was Adam? Ben knew in his gut that Adam was in trouble somewhere, but what could he do? The situation seemed to be turning into a dream sequence.

What looked like green and pink curtains of the aurora borealis streamed down from the base of the cloud. Then tubes of light came down over the two Poolormanocks and the Nuzinamam and they stopped walking.

Another ghost-ship hull, even larger, came out of the cloud directly above. A series of white beams of light followed and what looked like six large armoured gorillas with canine helmets glided down to the ground. From there they advanced on the three alien figures.

The troopers didn't know what to do. There were no clear aggressors. So they followed Harriet as she made to capture Candice.

Ben's focus was to try and find his partner. 'Adam?!'

There was no reply. Ben reached the edge of the bog and there, too far out to reach, he thought he saw Adam's hand sticking out of the peat, but maybe it was just a branch.

Suddenly, whatever it was, vanished below. The surface of the peat sank down as if the bog had gulped, and a ripple spread out to the edge.

The Nuzinamam and the Poolormanocks were escorted away by the armoured figures, white beams lifting them into the large translucent hull. Then the green and pink curtains suddenly switched off and both ghost-ships lifted back into the clouds.

'Harriet!' Ben roared down his throat mic, 'I think Adam may have gone down in the bog!'

Two of the troopers raced back to the chopper to look for something to reach into the bog with.

'Oh my God! What is happening?!' Candice was suddenly looking around alarmed. 'What is going on?!'

Harriet reached her first and barked through her mask. 'Where is Adam?!'

'I…I don't know an Adam!'

'What have you done with him?!'

'I haven't a clue who you're talking about!'

'What were those things?!' Harriet pointed above them.

'What things? Who are you?!'

'It's Agent Harriet Wallace, Candice!'

'Who?'

'You haven't forgotten your name too, have you Candice?'

'No. I know my name. I just don't recognise you, with that mask on.'

Troopers arrived at Ben's side with telescopic poles, with loops on the end used for water extractions. Ben guided them towards where he had thought he had seen a hand. They began to probe but there seemed to be nothing there.

In all probability Adam had sunk deeper than they could reach. Ben knew it was a waste of time now. Even if they had managed to catch an arm with a loop, they were more likely to tear the arm free with the force of the bog's suction, than to raise the whole body.

Ben had experience of trying to get his legs free of a peat bog. The suction force was incredible. The only way to retrieve Adam's body now would be to drain the bog and dig the body out. He was gone.

Candice was becoming hysterical. Just the sight of the black clad troopers with guns was more than enough for Candice, who had no idea where she was or how she got there.

What concerned Harriet the most, in terms of getting to the bottom of this unexplained event, was that it actually sounded like Candice was being honest in her confusion.

'Do you know where your tent is, Candice?'

'No…I don't remember coming here.'

'You walked here.'

'I'm telling you I don't remember *anything*.'

'It is important that we find the tent quickly and any evidence.'

'Evidence of what?'

'Evidence that you killed Adam Underwood, Karen Thompson and a number of others including Adam's girlfriend Toyah Pembroke.'

'No! I never killed anybody! I don't even know a those people!'

'You were treating Toyah for mental health issues.'

'Was I? When? I'm an outward bound instructor.'

'It was some weeks ago.'

'No. That's not possible. I would have remembered, wouldn't I?'

Everyone was staring at Candice trying to decide whether this was an act when a light came from the left, casting a long shadow of a female form out over the surface of the peat bog.

'Maybe I can help.'

'Dawn,' Ben greeted.

The troopers turned, raising their weapons.

'Don't waste your rounds on her lads,' Harriet advised.

'You won't get anything useful out of her. The Nuzinamams have removed all evidence of their manipulation since her first abduction.'

'What?'

'Yes, with their nanotechnology it's as easy as wiping security camera footage. When you interview Candice she will tell you she is a twenty year old outward bound instructor. When she finally understands that she had lost a big chunk of her life, it will hit her pretty hard.'

'I'm right here!' Candice didn't appreciate being talked about as if she were not there. 'Who is this woman?'

Harriet turned to the troopers. 'Take Candice to the chopper. Check her for neurotoxin.'

'You won't find any on her,' Dawn offered. 'The Nuzinamams were the ones with access to Rapture.'

'The ones who have got away?'

'Yes that's right, the youth with the two Poolormanocks that you just saw being arrested for interfering with a protected planet and its species.'

'You could have given us better warning, Dawn.'

'I think you know I couldn't.'

'So, what are you saying? This is *case closed* now, for lack of evidence?'

'If you like.'

'No I don't *bloody* like!' Harriet said, pulling off her helmet, mask and hood. 'You tell me, *right now* what all of *this* has been about! And

319

don't give me anymore of your meta-interference bullshit!'

'The young Nuzinamam, was one of a number, supported by their Poolormanock servants, who have been killing humans, to pass the time.'

'To pass the time?!'

'Yes, for them, it was over a period of a couple of their days, but using their time and space vehicle they made a number of visits over quite a number of Earth years.'

'But why? Why torment and kill these women?'

'You have to understand that to these advanced beings you humans are no more than critters. Like a bunch of your youngsters playing in a rock pool and deciding to pull the legs off crabs, or feed shrimps to anemones.'

'That's…That's totally unacceptable!'

'Which is why they were arrested.'

'What will happen to them?'

'They will face disciplinary procedures but remember a human life does not equate to a Nuzinamam, or even a Poolormanock, in their eyes. You are a young and backward species. Critters like I said.'

'But *you* are of human form.'

'I used to be human yes, till I was taken on something of a journey. Now I do what I do.'

'And you…let this happen.'

'I had no choice.'

'What about Adam?' Ben asked.

'I did tell him that he was not long for this world. He is gone now, as I must go.'

'Where?'

'I have a baby to switch.'

'What?'

'Surely you have heard of changelings. Destiny and I switch babies from time to time to cause significant future events.'

'That's just wicked.' Harriet was getting to like Dawn even less.

'I suppose, and yet it feels no worse to me than the planting of Adam's Flintstones.'

'What about Candice?'

'Shit happens, but that was not my doing.'

'How has it been possible to manipulate a person's actions and memories so absolutely?'

'That is down to the nanotechnology penetrating muscular tissues and the nervous system, in short turning the victims into remote control toys. Those humans were little more than avatars for the Nuzinamams own actions and experiences, amusing themselves with not-so-virtual reality.

'The tech was delivered via skin contact with what looked like bladder-leak underwear. You people will have picked up the tech as high levels of micro-plastics.

'No doubt you thought little of this since humans and other animals are getting higher levels of micro-plastics through the misuse of polymers.

'Candice, was only different in that the Nuzinamams used her as a go-between to reduce the risk of getting found out. Which was why it took until now for them to be caught red-handed.'

'Why did they come for Candice?'

'They were worried that they would get caught if they continued much longer, so were intending to abduct her, have a last bit of fun, flush the tech out of her system, then see what she tasted like.'

'So, she was lucky we all arrived when we did then…What am I going to put in my report?'

'Well Harriet, I don't need to tell you how your career would pan out if you decided to report sightings of aliens. Alien abductions and mind-control are still very much frowned upon, am I not correct? So any account of the Nuzinamams and their Poolormanocks, or the nanotechnology bladder-leak underwear would be considered the stuff of third rate TV, don't you think.'

'Hells bells!'

'And on those notes, I say must good bye.'

'Wait!'

Dawn didn't. She turned and stepped through her hole in the air.

Ben looked to Harriet, searching for something constructive to say. 'I haven't a clue what to make of all this. If it were at all possible for human science I'd like something to help *me* forget about this misadventure.'

'Maybe that *can* be arranged, Ben,' Harriet offered.

The team headed back to the AW-109C, to go and track down Candice's tent.

42

Adam was confused. Maybe this was just another nightmare. By the ache in his backside he felt like he had fallen down hard. He also seemed to be suffering some degree of memory loss, since he couldn't remember where he had just been.

The deep blue sky was getting lighter. He looked at the pile of soaking wet peat that he was sitting in.

His clothes and the peat smelled of bad eggs. What's more, as he stood up he noticed he was wearing some strange pants that he didn't recognise.

None of his immediate proximity fit with what he remembered of Skye. He stood on very tropical beach. He slowly walked down the beach to the sea. The sand was cool under his bare feet, but the water was cooler. He went further in and rinsed himself off, hoping to make sense of this soon. He had a vague recollection of wetting his bedding it the tent. Maybe that's what this water really was.

The sun was about to come up, but its light was pulsing oddly from the horizon. As Adam sat watching he noticed the sun rise but then go down again. It did this again and again, each time rising a little higher. Eventually he realised that what he was looking at were two suns rotating around one another at speed as the planet he was on turned to face them. If this was a dream, it must be what Candice called lucid, since he wasn't waking up.

There was a splash nearby, like a big fish. Adam willed Toyah to appear. However, this was not like any dream Adam had had before. The head which surfaced beside him was Dawn's.

'Hello Adam.'

'Am I…Dead?'

'Not yet.'

'Is this a dream?'

'This, Adam, is a fork in realities.'

'What do you mean?'

'You appear to have a choice to make, but in truth you do both and this time-line divides so that you take both paths.'

'Both? So what are those paths?'

'In both time-lines you put the past behind you. In one you remain human and live a number of decades on this planet, traveling around its tropical islands, having adventures in *Obsession*.' Dawn gestured down the coast a little way.

Moored next to what looked like a rather stealthy cruiser was Adam's barge.

'*Obsession* is a canal boat. It wasn't built for the sea.'

'You'd have to take special care then wouldn't you…The other path sees you become like me.'

'A Time-Slave? I don't think I'd ever be willing to agree to that.'

'No. I'm referring to becoming a metamorph.'

'A what?'

'A shape-shifter.' In the growing light, Dawn became Harriet, became WPC Hanley, became Toyah then became Adam.'

'What on Earth?'

'*Not* on Earth. You can never return, but as a metamorph you *could* live for forever, as long as nothing destroys you of course.'

'This is too freaky. How is this possible?'

'I only have to touch your skin and the transformation will begin.'

'I mean how can you do that shape shifting?'

'I'll teach you. It's all about moving your colony around.'

'Colony?'

'Yes. We metamorphs are colonies of cellular organisms, sharing thoughts, abilities, and opportunities.'

'Oh I don't know about this. Neither option feels right.'

'In the reality where you become a metamorph you travel around in a craft called *Obsession II*. Visiting worlds and people and sorting out problems you come across along the way. That's it moored next to your barge.'

'Surely there has to be another option, where I go back to Earth and continue to work with Ben and…'

'You have nothing to go back for, much more to look forward to. There's no one who will really miss you there anyway, is there.'

'Oh thanks for that.'

'Ben and Meg will think of you from time to time, for sure, but your future lies elsewhere.'

'What about the life I had? What was the point of the Flintstones?'

'The Flintstones served to prepare you for the seriousness of the tasks you will take on as a metamorph.'

'And those nightmares I've been having?'

'Nightmares are a gift.'

'A *gift*?!'

'Nightmares help you deal with what is *yet to come*.'

Dawn offered her hand.

Meg answered the door, hoping it wasn't Ben. She still wasn't ready to deal with him. Life had become a little easier in his absence, once she had got sorted with her new routine.

'Mrs McGregor?'

'Yes?'

'I'm Harriet Wallace and this is Detective Inspector Carmichael.'

'Oh hi.' Meg smiled at Carmichael thinking he looked familiar but then her smile turned to a frown. 'Is this to do with Ben?'

'I'm afraid so.'

'Damn it! What's he gone and done now?'

'Can we come in?' asked Carmichael.

'Oh of course, would you like a cup of tea?'

'No thanks.' Harriet shook her head. 'This shouldn't take long.'

'It just didn't seem proper to be saying it out on the street,' Carmichael added.

'God, Ben's not dead is he?'

'No, no. Far from it. Do you know what Ben was mixed up in, Meg?' Harriet enquired.

'You mean getting injured chasing women with Adam?'

'Well that's part of it I guess. I have to tell you that Ben was recently involved in another incident, where Adam Underwood disappeared and is now feared dead.'

'Oh my God, no. What happened?'

'I'm afraid we cannot give you any details, but suffice to say Ben has taken it badly.'

'Can I see him?' Meg didn't sound like she really wanted to.

'No, I'm sorry Mrs McGregor. I doubt that will be possible for some time. I will see that you get some…*support*.'

'Support?'

'Ben has been, shall we say, *sectioned*.'

**Other titles by
Kevin H. Hilton**

Breakfast's in Bed

Possession

Afterlife

Singularity

Northern Darks

Dark Net

The Newsagent

Printed in Great Britain
by Amazon